3 0132 021

CW00924889

N

sh d

FIGHTING FOR THE DEAD

Recent Titles by Nick Oldham from Severn House

BACKLASH
SUBSTANTIAL THREAT
DEAD HEAT
BIG CITY JACKS
PSYCHO ALLEY
CRITICAL THREAT
CRUNCH TIME
THE NOTHING JOB
SEIZURE
HIDDEN WITNESS
FACING JUSTICE
INSTINCT
FIGHTING FOR THE DEAD

FIGHTING FOR THE DEAD

A Detective Superintendent Henry Christie Novel

Nick Oldham

severn House

This first world edition published 2012
in Great Britain and in the USA by
SEVERN HOUSE PUBLISHERS LTD of
9–15 High Street, Sutton, Surrey, England, SM1 1DF.

British Library Cataloguing in Publication Data

Oldham, Nick, 1956-
  Fighting for the dead.
  1. Christie, Henry (Fictitious character)–Fiction.
  2. Detective and mystery stories.
  I. Title
  823.9'2-dc23

ISBN-13: 978-0-7278-8213-4 (cased)

All Severn House titles are printed on acid-free paper.

Severn House Publishers support The Forest Stewardship Council [FSC],
the leading international forest certification organisation. All our titles that
are printed on Greenpeace-approved FSC-certified paper carry the FSC logo.

Typeset by Palimpsest Book Production Ltd.,
Falkirk, Stirlingshire, Scotland.
Printed and bound in Great Britain by
MPG Books Ltd., Bodmin, Cornwall.

To Belinda

ONE

'Hope you're not the squeamish sort.' The white-coated, pasty-faced mortuary technician grinned crookedly at Detective Superintendent Henry Christie who, in turn, blinked, kept a stone face and said curtly, 'Just open the drawer, please.'

'Okey-doke,' the technician said brightly.

The two men were inside Lancaster Public Mortuary, the squat, single-storey detached building within the grounds of Royal Lancaster Infirmary. They were standing in front of the bank of brushed-steel doors that opened into the vast refrigerated unit in which the dead were stored at an optimum temperature so that they could be kept for as long as necessary.

There were two rows of square doors and behind each was a sliding metal tray on runners on which might, or might not, be a corpse. The little card slot on each door gave the game away. A card inserted with a name scribbled on it meant the space was occupied. No card meant a vacancy.

Each row consisted of ten doors and all but one had a card in the slot. Nineteen bodies: almost a full house.

From experience, Henry knew this was pretty usual. He had once been in this mortuary during a very severe winter when the place was overflowing with cadavers. Mainly bodies of old people, hit by the freezing weather, and many had been doubled up, laid on top of each other on the sliding trays. Gruesome, slightly weird, but necessary under the circumstances.

Most of the bodies that came through here were from the hospital wards, awaiting onward transportation to an undertaker. People who had died tragically, certainly, but the causes of the deaths already known and therefore, usually, no requirement for a post-mortem.

But this was also a public mortuary. A place where bodies of people who had met sudden, untimely, unexplained, violent or accidental deaths were brought, kept, then examined to determine the cause. If there were no further complications and the local coroner was satisfied, they would then be released back to their families.

It was also a place to which murder victims were brought.

Henry Christie knew that of the nineteen bodies in the mortuary at that moment, two had been murdered.

One held no interest for him. A female, the victim of a domestic murder, who had already been subjected to a post-mortem. The offender had been arrested, charged and remanded in custody and the dead woman was due to be collected by the family's undertaker later that day.

Henry knew this because he was a senior investigating officer – SIO – on Lancashire Constabulary's Force Major Investigation Team, or FMIT, and had overseen the investigation into the woman's murder. Now all that remained for him to do was steer the case through the courts and do his best to get a life sentence for the bastard of a boyfriend who'd stabbed her forty-eight times because she hadn't made his tea for him. Henry was finished with her body and she would soon be making space for the next one.

It was the second murder victim that was of interest to Henry.

'You sure about this?' the technician said.

Henry pursed his lips with irritation, decided to say nothing, just nodded.

'OK then, but masks and gloves first, please. Health and safety, you know,' he said patronizingly.

Henry fitted the surgical mask over his nose and mouth and eased his hands into the latex gloves with a 'snap'.

The body was behind the door on the lower far right of the unit. Henry guessed it had been moved over time. When bodies were brought into the mortuary, they were usually slotted into spaces near the double doors. If they stayed for any length of time, which was fairly unusual, they tended to get shuffled down the line, away from the door. Most bodies came and went quite quickly.

But this one had been here for over five months.

Henry glanced at the name card in the slot, which read: *'F/male. No ID. Murder Vic.'*

The technician, mask and gloves fitted, gripped the handle of the door and swung it open, then pulled out the tray with the body on it to about two feet. It was at a level with Henry's thighs. As is the case with all bodies stored post-mortem, it was wrapped in an off-white flimsy muslin shroud from head to toe, rather like an Egyptian mummy.

'I need to see the whole body, please. Unwrapped.' Henry sensed a certain hesitation from the mortuary technician. 'And yes, I'm certain I do. And I'm not squeamish.'

'Okey-doke.'

The technician wheeled a gurney from the side of the room, adjusted the height with a pneumatic foot pump that made little farting noises and slid it into place an inch underneath the tray. He then smoothly pulled out the tray on its hard rubber runners, onto the gurney in a well-practised move. He closed the fridge unit door, but not before Henry got a quick glance inside and saw the rest of the bodies lying on their respective trays, all the way down the unit. Eighteen people, all there for different reasons – but also the same one: they shared death in common.

The gurney was steered across the tiled floor and into the post-mortem examination room.

A steel slab occupied the centre of this room. On it lay the body of an old man, dissected from gullet to groin, his body prised open, ribcage missing, all organs removed, his body cavity like a hollow cave. The top of his skull had also been sawn off and the brain removed.

The pathologist and his assistant who were carrying out this examination, their backs to Henry, were working at a stainless-steel sink and draining board. Henry saw a sliced-up heart and a mass of body organs slopped gruesomely into a pile on the board, all having been dissected and examined. Blood ran into the sink.

The pathologist was holding up the dead man's brain in the palm of his left hand, reminiscent, Henry thought, of a gore-fest version of *Hamlet*. The pathologist was slicing the brain with a razor-sharp knife.

Henry looked away, focusing on his body of interest.

The technician carefully unwrapped the shroud, revealing the corpse. Henry watched, his features still set hard behind the face mask, thinking how difficult it was to do a catch-up on what was essentially a cold case. Much better to be in at the death, he thought humourlessly. Almost six months down the line was no time to be picking up a murder investigation.

The body was that of a teenage girl, estimated age seventeen to nineteen.

Henry cringed. It felt like he had only just wound up an investigation into the nasty murder of a teenage girl and now here he was, looking into another. It was this kind of thing that could tip an unstable SIO over the edge. Good job Henry was sound in mind and body . . . 'I wish,' he thought, and concentrated on the task in hand.

Five months in the chiller had given the girl a frosty sheen, but in no way could it disguise what had happened to her.

Beaten, strangled . . . horrifically. Henry knew the details, had them in the file, and looking at her simply confirmed what he'd already read. But he had to look, see the flesh, get a true feel for the murder. Looking at photos in a file told him nothing, gave him no sense or feeling of the crime.

The purple mark made by the ligature to half-strangle her was still deeply indented in her neck. It was believed a man's neck tie had done this. On her cheek there was also the pattern of the sole of one of the shoes that had stamped on her face, which could possibly be useful if a suspect was ever identified.

The injuries around her head and shoulders, chest and lower stomach, where she had been kicked, stamped on and punched, could still be seen in spite of the terrible scars left by the postmortem itself.

Her head was an appalling, distorted mess, having been jumped on repeatedly by someone wearing heavy shoes. The dislodgement of her lower jaw, broken in many places and with terrific force, her facial features smashed beyond recognition, did not stop Henry from realizing this had once been a very pretty girl.

His eyes took in all these things. His imagination worked to recreate her last moments of life. He did not like what it saw.

Then he took hold of her left arm, cold like a twig in winter, and turned it gently outwards, to inspect the many needle marks on the inside of her elbow. An addict.

And probably a prostitute, the original investigation had concluded.

That meant an individual who took risks, put herself in possibly dangerous situations and maybe, Henry had heard whispered, got what was coming to her.

His nostrils dilated as he thought, 'Screw that.' No one deserves a death like this.

The technician stood back as Henry stepped around the gurney, taking in all aspects of the body. As he stood at her feet and looked up across the body, he saw that, with the jaw having been broken so badly, the girl's mouth was skewed wide open, and with her head tilted back, Henry could see the top set of her teeth, right to the back of the mouth.

He frowned and had to peer to confirm what he saw.

Then, taking his time to walk back alongside the body on the opposite side, he came back to the head.

There was a dirty laugh behind him – the pathologist and his assistant chuckling about something inappropriate, probably.

Henry angled his head slightly to try and pick up what they were saying. He grinned and bent forward to inspect the dead girl's mouth, carefully pushing back the frozen lips to expose the teeth with his fingertips.

They hadn't been a good set to start with. Misaligned, discoloured, possibly from a deprived upbringing and a poor diet, several missing from both upper and lower jaws. Henry's forehead furrowed as he racked his brain, thinking about the missing teeth, and what mention, if any, had been made of them on the file. He couldn't recall anything, but that wasn't to say it wasn't there.

The thought dissipated as he honed in on the reason why his attention had been grabbed by the girl's top set that he could see looking up from her feet. There it was.

He pushed her mouth further open, easy, but unpleasant. He heard broken bone scraping sickeningly against bone in her jaw.

He saw a gold filling in one of the molars right at the back of her mouth – juxtaposed against the poor condition of her other teeth.

Henry stood upright and pouted – though this could not be seen because of the face mask – then glanced thoughtfully across at the pathologist, who was still dissecting the old man's brain and giggling at some shared joke with his assistant, making his thin shoulders wobble.

*　　*　　*

Steve Flynn was already regretting his hastiness in saying yes to a friend in need. Not because of the task, or the reason he'd said yes, but simply because of the weather.

In the five or so years he had been resident in Gran Canaria, the most southerly of the Canary Islands, Flynn had become a diehard sun bum. Whilst respecting the ferocious power of that hot ball in the sky, he loved being in it. He loved everything about the consistently high temperature in which he lived, from the early morning stroll to buy fresh bread rolls, to the often steaming midday heat when even he wasn't silly enough to venture out unprotected, to the long languid evenings sitting outside, eating and drinking with friends or clients from the sport-fishing boat he skippered, when it wasn't even necessary to put a thin jumper on at midnight.

It had been a long time since he had woken up shivering – since his last visit to the UK, actually. He tugged the sleeping bag more tightly around himself, not wanting to get up.

He could even see his own breath. A rare phenomenon in Gran Canaria, all too common in Britain.

But finally he knew he had to move, this being the first day of the new job he'd agreed to do. Temporarily, that is.

He kicked the sleeping bag off and sat up on the – supposedly – double bed and looked down the full length of the canal barge on which he had spent his first night back in England, following his early-hours arrival by air from Las Palmas.

He shivered and rubbed the goosebumps covering his arms, making his hairs stand on end.

It was a superbly appointed boat, however. Lovingly restored by his friend from just a bare shell. A friend now in hospital, ready to undergo surgery that day in relation to bowel cancer.

Flynn cringed at the thought. Poor guy, but at least it seemed the disease had been caught in time and a full recovery, minus a third of a bowel, was forecast.

Still feeling grimy from the travel, ducking his head he stepped into the tiny tiled wet room and showered until the hot water ran cold, then shaved and got dressed before making down to the galley where, as promised, there were bacon, eggs, bread and filter coffee.

At home, as he now thought of Gran Canaria, his usual

breakfast was a croissant and strong coffee, but the bacon and eggs enticed him, so a fry-up it was. He worked hard at perfection at the gas rings: crispy bacon, fried eggs with just-right runny yolks, a nice filter coffee and two slices of buttered toast. Proud of his achievement he took the plate out to the seating area on the rear deck. Though it was very chilly, he wanted to eat al fresco, the hot food contrasting wonderfully with the weather. It went down well.

The canal boat was tethered about two hundred metres east from the actual start of the Lancaster Canal, which began at Glasson Dock. From where Flynn sat, sipping his second coffee, he could see all the way down that straight stretch of water to where the canal merged with the yacht marina at Glasson, beyond which was the sea lock. This lowered or raised vessels down to, or up from, the dock itself. From there the dock opened out into the estuary of the River Lune and beyond to the Irish Sea.

Flynn knew the area well. He was a Lancashire lad and had been a cop in the county until circumstances forced him to leave. He knew Glasson Dock from being a youngster, on day trips with his parents, and when he was a cop. In uniform, very early in his service, he'd been here during the 1984 miners' strike, when Glasson came back to life as a working port, bringing in coal supplies from abroad. This had attracted striking miners and there had been a few confrontations that Flynn had been part of policing.

Then, as a detective in the drugs branch, he had once arrested a high-level drug-runner who had been using Glasson as a landing point for his imported contraband.

Now he was back to help a sick friend.

Henry Christie slouched against the outer wall of the mortuary building, sipping from a cup of coffee bought at the hospital cafe.

He was ruminating about the dead girl and what he would have to do to reinvigorate the investigation into her murder which, in more ways than one, had gone stone cold.

Obviously he had known about the murder, but at the time his mind had been on much more pressing matters – such as the fast-approaching death of his wife, Kate, from a particularly aggressive strain of breast cancer. Although he had ostensibly been at work throughout the fight for life, he might as well not have been as his head was firmly up his arse. The girl's murder, although it had occurred in the geographical area Henry was responsible for covering, was taken on by one of the other SIOs in FMIT – Detective Superintendent Joe Speakman. But Speakman had suddenly retired not long after the girl's body had been discovered, taking everyone by surprise, and the investigation had seemed to dwindle off to nothing.

Henry had also been considering 'putting in his ticket' – retiring – but Speakman had beaten him to it. This meant that the SIO team was now down to three detective superintendents. In terms of proposed budgetary cuts this was a 'good thing' and had been on the cards for a while. It also meant that the possibility of Henry quitting was now much more distant because whilst the force was happy to run FMIT with just three supers, and therefore increase their already crippling workload, they couldn't manage with two because if Henry went there was no one in line to replace him.

Henry was amazed to have been approached by the chief constable, begging him to stay on – 'Another year at least, eh, mate?' – and, 'Oh, by the way, you've just inherited all of Joe's ongoing cases and his other responsibilities.'

Henry had said yes, even though he'd made the chief squirm just a little bit. He could have refused and retired. No one could stop him doing that, and whatever the chief said, the force would have to manage. It always did because it had to, and Henry had never overestimated his position within it, just another disposable cog in the machinery. All that his staying on did was give a bit of breathing space for the force to train up the next few SIOs.

Also, he wasn't sure what he would have done if he had retired.

He could have drawn his lump sum and his pension and life would have been OK, but he hadn't made any plans as to how he would occupy his time. He knew he couldn't be one of those who sat and did nothing all day, every day. Some of the time was fine. But mostly he wanted to be doing something, just hadn't quite worked out what.

Maybe another year was about right. Time to get his head

around some planning . . . and see how his new 'relationship' would pan out. That had quite a bearing on everything.

He smiled at the thought of the woman who at that moment was making him very happy indeed. Nice thoughts . . .

He sipped his coffee and shivered. It was a cold morning.

A voice behind him said, 'I believe you want to talk to me about dead people and teeth?'

Midweek and Glasson Dock was quiet.

Flynn sauntered down the canal path, the yacht marina to his left on the opposite side of the canal, up to the dock itself, enjoying the stroll despite the chill. He was wrapped in a thick windcheater, jeans, trainers and a scarf thrown rakishly around his neck. He could not remember the last time he'd worn a scarf.

The large static caravan serving brews and snacks situated close to the swing-roadbridge spanning the sea lock was open for business. A couple of overweight middle-aged leather-clad bikers clutched mugs of coffee and exchanged pleasantries about their very hairy looking hogs parked nearby.

A double-masted yacht was in the lock and the water level was falling. Flynn watched the pleasant sight wistfully for a moment, then bore diagonally across the road to a row of buildings behind which was the River Lune. The tide was high, but Flynn could see it had begun to ebb. At one end of the row was a pub called the Victoria and at the opposite end was what used to be a pub – the Caribou – but was now converted into apartments. Between the two was a terrace consisting of houses and Flynn's destination: the chandlery.

He entered the shop, inside much more spacious than the exterior suggested, and what was an Aladdin's cave of all things relating to small boats and yachts.

Flynn had entered a little corner of heaven. Boats – in particular sport-fishing boats – were his world.

In Gran Canaria he was employed as the skipper of a sport-fisher called *Faye2* and he had left her behind with reluctance to return to the UK, only because of the serious illness of his friend who owned this shop.

He approached the lady behind the counter, who was head down, frowning at some paperwork.

'I think I've died and gone to heaven,' Flynn said.

She looked up, her face instantly breaking into a smile, brightening up all at once. She came out from behind the counter and hugged Flynn, who patted her shoulder blades, and they parted with pecks on the cheeks.

'Did you sleep all right?'

'Pretty good . . . woke a bit chilly, though.'

'I know . . . sorry about that. Later I'll show you how the heating system works, and where everything else is.'

'Sounds good.'

'Steve, I know I said it last night on the way back from the airport, but we are really grateful to you. Colin could only think of you and you dropped everything to help out.'

'He's an old mate and you're a friend too, Diane. Least I could do.'

'How did you square it with your boss?'

'He likes me . . . but I've got ten days, max, then I have to get back. There's a few repeat parties booked in on the strength of my ace personality,' he said humbly. He gave Diane a wink. 'So how is he?'

'I haven't seen him today, so far, but he goes into pre-op this morning, then down to surgery, which will last two to three hours minimum . . . but he's keeping bright.' She gave a helpless shrug, then her face seemed to implode and she burst into tears.

Flynn took her tenderly in his arms and held her just tight enough so she had room to sob and get it out of her system, before drawing back and wiping her eyes with the balls of her hands. She wasn't wearing make-up, so there was nothing to smudge.

'Sorry,' she apologized.

'Hey, no problem.'

She regarded Flynn critically. 'Steve, you really are a good man, aren't you?'

'Some say otherwise.'

'No – you really are.'

'Aw shucks,' Flynn said, breaking the moment. He gestured with his hands at the shop. 'My task . . . the one I've accepted . . . is to look after the shop whilst you're otherwise engaged . . . where do I start?'

Diane checked her watch. 'You start today . . . but I haven't got time to show you any of the ropes just now, if you'll pardon the expression. I want to be with Colin before he goes into pre-op . . . hand-holding and such like . . . then stay for the operation itself.' Her face creased a little at the prospect but she held it. 'Which means I'll be back here around three, probably. Then I'll show you how it all works. In the meantime, the shop will be closed, but I'll leave you the key and you can mooch around the stock, see what we have. Just kill some time however you like until I get back.'

Henry had recognized the pathologist in the mortuary as Professor Baines, the Home Office pathologist he had known for many years now. They had often met each other over the dead, then continued to discuss the dead over a pint or two.

Baines was at the mortuary to keep his hand in on more mundane matters than his usual murder victims. He was performing a post-mortem on a run-of-the-mill sudden death, an old man who hadn't been seen for a few days and whose neighbours had alerted the police because of the terrible odour creeping out from his flat. This was the body that Henry had seen sliced open on the slab.

Baines had been so engrossed in his task – and impressing his lady assistant – that he hadn't even noticed Henry, but Henry had recognized Baines and asked him for some advice about the dead girl. Whilst waiting for Baines to finish, Henry had got the slightly creepy mortuary technician to put the dead girl back into the chiller then bought a coffee and killed time.

The two men were now standing either side of the tray jutting out from the fridge while Baines carefully eased open the dead girl's mouth and inspected the inside with the help of a mini Maglite torch.

Baines was an acknowledged expert on dental pathology, having single-handedly amassed a database about teeth over a long period of time. It was a little obsession that had begun when he'd spent time in Bosnia with NATO, investigating and trying to ID some of the thousands of people who had been murdered and dumped into mass graves. One of the main means was via dental records, which were mostly woefully inadequate. This frustration had been the starting point for Baines's database of dentists, dental practices and methods for use in pathology. His work had resulted in him being awarding an OBE for his services to dental forensics.

Henry, who had never yet had to plumb this knowledge, knew that one day all this would come in useful as Baines peered knowledgeably into the dead girl's mouth cavity, then looked up at Henry, then at the mortuary technician.

'Sort her out and slide her back in,' Baines told the technician. Then, to Henry, he said as he removed one of his gloves, 'Time for another brew? I'll just get washed up and be ready in five. Fancy a stroll into town?'

'Alison, that's the name of this one, isn't it?' Professor Baines said to Henry, who nodded. 'Any others on the go?' Baines asked hopefully.

Henry shook his head and Baines seemed crestfallen. He had always been intrigued by the twists and turns of Henry's love life and been devastated when Henry had remarried his long-suffering on-off-on wife/not-wife/wife, but only because it brought Henry's tasty romantic shenanigans to a crunching halt. He had been pleased for Henry, of course, but he did enjoy a certain vicarious pleasure in Henry's romps. When Kate had died, although genuinely upset for Henry, Baines held out a hopeful return for the old ways. Unfortunately, when Henry started a new relationship that seemed serious and stable, Baines was gutted.

Henry grinned. 'She's fantastic,' he told Baines.

'And a landlady! I knew there was a silver lining.'

Henry chuckled and thought pleasant things about Alison Marsh, who he'd met a while back in Kendleton, a quiet village in north Lancashire, where she ran a country pub called the Tawny Owl.

'Is it serious?' Baines probed.

'I hope so,' Henry admitted. 'We'll see.'

The two men had walked the quarter of a mile or so into Lancaster and found a nice cafe on Thurnham Street close to the police station. They served up a Kenyan filter coffee that really hit the spot.

'The gold filling is what interests you?' Baines said, bringing the conversation back to a more professional level.

Henry was puzzled for a moment, then said, 'Now you're talking about a dead girl.'

'She's still unidentified, I believe.'

Henry nodded.

Baines pondered. 'There is a possibility I could help . . . there is other dental work in there, too. Older, concrete fillings, but not much left of them. Wasn't a dental analysis done anyway?' he asked, referring to the already completed PM.

'I'm not certain. I know it should have been, but I'm not taking it for granted.'

'I would've thought Professor Broad would have done it . . . but you never know.'

'Professor Broad?'

'Yes, the pathologist who performed the PM on the poor girl.'

'How did you know he did it?'

'The stitching . . . we all do it our own way. Our little signatures, if you like.'

Henry pulled a face. 'Fancy.'

'So this is your case, is it?'

'It wasn't, but it is now.'

Flynn spent an hour familiarizing himself with the chandlery stock, enjoying every moment of it. For the past five years he had been on a boat virtually every working day, and being on the water was an integral part of his life. Although he skippered a sleek sport-fishing boat, he appreciated all forms of water craft – from the canal boat he'd spent the night on, up to the most luxurious yachts and everything in between. As a consequence he also loved all the bits that held them together and made them work, hence his appreciation of Colin and Diane's chandlery.

Colin and Diane were retired cops in their fifties and Flynn had met them while he was still in the job. Colin had been a traffic cop and Diane had been involved in child protection. They had become good friends with Flynn and his then wife, Faye, and occasionally went out as couples, with the men talking boats all the time. Back then Colin had restored two canal barges and owned a small power boat, whilst Flynn was merely an enthusiast who helped out when he could.

Colin and Diane retired about the same time and opened the small chandlery in Glasson Dock. Colin continued to refurbish and sell canal boats, one of which was the one Flynn had spent the night aboard. It was due to go up for sale shortly but would be Flynn's accommodation whilst he stayed in the UK.

Although he could only commit a short time to staying, Flynn hoped it would be enough to help the couple through a tough patch and assess the success or otherwise of Colin's operation.

If the prognosis was good, Flynn knew the business would continue. If not, it would close without having really got going.

By 11.30 that morning Flynn could probably name every item of stock on the shop floor. What he did not know was how to run the shop or even how to use a till, which is what he needed to learn from Diane before welcoming in customers.

Flynn thought he had plenty of time before Diane came back from the hospital in Lancaster, less than five miles up the road.

Peering out through the front door of the shop he saw that the weather had brightened a touch. The smell of food being cooked at the static caravan wafted across to him, making him suddenly hungry again. A bacon sandwich called. He locked up and walked across, bought the said sandwich and a mug of tea, devouring both on one of the picnic tables in front of the caravan. Then, fortified, he set off for a walk.

His plan was to do maybe twenty minutes along the old railway track, now a public footpath and bridleway that ran parallel to the banks of the Lune all the way up to Lancaster.

Flynn enjoyed the quite desolate views north up the river, still one of the country's finest salmon and trout rivers.

The tide had ebbed further, exposing treacherous sand, mud and grass banks and water channels as the water level receded.

He walked away from Glasson, bearing left along the footpath, seeing not another soul. He reached the old single track rail bridge at Conder Green, under which the tiny River Conder emptied into the Lune estuary. He paused here, looking inland towards the Stork, a pub by the A588, which he planned to visit at some stage during his stay. Then he turned outwards, looking west across the river.

It was a very wild, untamed location and he liked it very much.

His eyes drew back until he was looking straight down into

the muddy water, flowing quite quickly away underneath his feet, like a plug had been yanked from a drain.

Which is when he spotted the body.

TWO

The body floated underneath the bridge, dragged by the fast-retreating tide, along the main channel of the River Conder. Flynn watched it, slightly mesmerized initially, as it rolled gently in the water, limbs moving as though doing some kind of lazy swimming stroke.

At first the body was face down, head under water, but as it emerged fully from below the bridge and the tug of the tide altered, it swished around onto its back. From less than twenty feet above, Flynn saw it was a female, maybe mid-thirties, dressed in a short jacket and black jeans with a cut-off Wellington boot on the left foot, the right foot bare. The skin of the face was tight, white-blue, the features distorted by its time in the water, maybe even starting to rot away now. But the eyes were still there. Open.

With a gush and a slurp of the tide, the body increased speed. The legs seemed to kick, the whole body spun around so it was now heading feet first towards the Lune estuary.

Flynn cursed.

He looked at the geography between himself and the main channel of the Lune. There was every chance the body might lodge in one of the many muddy channels. Also a chance that the tide would suck it out into the Irish Sea, never to be seen again. Or drag it back up on the next tide to be deposited somewhere completely different.

It could go any of those ways.

Flynn ran to the end of the bridge and scuttled down a short set of rusting iron steps onto the harsh grass exposed by the tide fall. It was wet and soft – but not as wet and soft as the sandbanks.

He leapt across two tight channels, by which time the body

was even further away. He took two more with the agility of a mountain goat and found himself on a clump of grass next to the main channel of the Conder, about three metres away from the body, just out of reach even stretching. He knew he would have to enter the water if he was going to grab it.

He knew something else, too: This would not be like stepping into the warm Atlantic waters at Amadores beach, Gran Canaria.

He was right.

As he carefully eased his trainer-clad right foot into the water, holding his balance whilst feeling it sink into the slurpy mud, the sheer coldness of it hit him and seemed to swarm up the veins in his leg, like a jolt of freezing electricity.

The body wafted further away.

He knew he could not hesitate, otherwise it would be gone. He trudged forwards, both feet now in the water, so incredibly cold. In a moment he was calf-deep, then knee-deep, and with his feet in the mud, it was a huge effort to actually take a step. It was like walking through molasses.

Ahead of him, the body did a quick spin.

Flynn then felt the power of the tide at the back of his legs, pushing his knees – but he forced himself on, keeping upright and walking like a toy robot as he dragged his feet.

Then the body twisted into an ugly angle and ran against a muddy bank, pausing as if to take breath. The head seemed to pop up at a loose angle and look at Flynn.

He saw his chance. He pushed himself on, trying to run before the body moved again out of reach. He lunged to grab hold of a sleeve, missed, lunged again and this time grabbed the dead woman's left hand, which felt terrible, cold, delicate and awful.

Flynn's face creased in horror, but he held on, conquered the urge to recoil, and pulled the body towards him and took hold of the neck of the jacket.

He waded back against the flow of the tide, but felt like he was losing hold, so, as unpleasant as it was, he scooped her up into his arms as though she was a corpse bride, then stumbled across the channel and up the nearest bank to lay her as delicately as possible on a grassy mound and sank down on his sodden knees alongside her.

*   *   *

Having gone as far as he had, Flynn thought it only right and proper to finish the job and carry the body up onto dry land, to a point where the emergency services could easily get to her. Not that she needed an ambulance now, but paramedics usually turned out to such incidents and did the job of transporting the corpse to the mortuary. The cops would definitely come, too.

She was quite light and for a moment Flynn had the horrible thought that her lolling head might drop off as he made his way from grass bank to grass bank, leaping over the narrow channels, so he cradled it in the crook of his arm to stop it flopping about.

His eyes were drawn to her face, the skin wrinkled from immersion in water. He noticed the remnants of fine white foam and mucus under her nostrils and at the corners of her mouth – one of the few external indications of drowning, though he was no expert in such matters.

Not so long ago, he guessed, she would have been very good-looking and her long black hair would have been quite spectacular. Now clods of it had fallen out and she had some ugly bald patches on her head.

'What a shame,' he breathed.

She was wearing a variety of rings on her fingers that looked expensive, he also noted. Including a wedding band.

He stumbled up to the side of the road that led to the picnic area he had been planning to walk through, and placed her gently on the grass and exhaled.

Not that he was out of breath. Five years of playing and landing big game fish, some marlin in the region of 1,000lb, and most heavier than this woman, had made him into a fit, strong guy.

He shuffled out his mobile phone and tapped out treble-nine, standing by the body as the line connected.

Her eyes were still wide open, but now they seemed to be staring imploringly at him.

Henry had mentally switched off.

Professor Baines, foolishly prompted by Henry, was now on a roll, explaining energetically to the detective about his lifelong obsession with the teeth of dead people.

'Problem was, you see, there was, is, no internationally

accepted standard for ante-mortem dental records and there are several hundred types of dental charts used around the world . . . no consistency . . . which is where I came in and then got my gong, as it were,' he spouted proudly.

A blank-faced detective superintendent sipped his coffee.

'Symbols and designations were – are – by no means standard, and, of course, the general record-keeping of overworked dentists is pretty appalling too. And some use their own systems anyway . . . so I devised an ID database that cross-checks between all known ways of cataloguing records.'

Baines went on to triumphantly explain the intricacies of the system he had been researching and devising for over twenty years.

'Still not foolproof, of course,' he admitted. 'Human error, bent and lazy dentists and all that. But it's still pretty good and from my own research and knowledge I'm pretty certain I can already put some geography on what I've seen in the girl's mouth.'

Henry suddenly perked up. 'Really?'

'Which could help to pinpoint exactly where she came from. I'd put her as Eastern European, possibly Russian or one of its surrounding states. I'll do X-rays and take a sample from the fillings, the gold one and the concrete ones, and look at the other dental work in there.'

'Russian?' Henry queried with arched eyebrows.

Baines shrugged enigmatically. 'First guess.'

'I'm impressed.'

Henry's mobile phone rang before he could ask Baines the next question. His ringtone was a jaunty James Blunt number all about sunshine and making love, reflecting his currently happy state of mind.

'Detective Superintendent Christie, how can I help?'

It was the Force Incident Manager, or FIM, based in the communications room at police headquarters at Hutton, just to the south of Preston. The FIM was the officer who contacted and turned out SIOs. Henry got a lot of calls from that source.

The FIM, a uniformed inspector, outlined the nature of the incident and asked Henry if he wished to attend.

He said yes. There was rarely an occasion when Henry refused to have a look at a dead body. He finished the call with an estimated time of arrival and looked across at Baines with a grin. Who better to be having a coffee with at such a time than a Home Office pathologist?

Henry and the professor made their way back to the mortuary where Henry climbed into his car, a Mercedes coupe, and Baines said he would follow on a short while later when he'd finished in the office. Leaving the mortuary car park, Henry was instantly on the A588 and by turning right and travelling south a few miles he was soon at Conder Green. He slowed and turned off the road in front of the Stork and drew up in the car park at the front of the pub.

From where he was, he could see activity about a hundred and fifty metres dead ahead at the old railway bridge over the River Conder. There was an ambulance, a marked police car, a couple of other vehicles on the grass verge and a huddle of people.

Henry went to the boot of his car, where he always kept the bits and bats of paraphernalia that a good detective always carried. This included the water-and-windproof jacket that he hunched into and zipped up. Even in the few moments exposed to the weather here he had shivered at the cold of this bleak location.

He always preferred to approach the scene of a death on foot if possible. He thought it gave him some sort of psychological insight into what might have happened, although he had no evidence to back this up. Not that he had any reason to suspect that this death was anything more than a tragic accident and his presence at it was simply a procedural thing.

That said, he never made the assumption that any sudden death was straightforward. He always thought murder, then back-tracked from there. A thought process that had been ingrained in him since the year dot – ever since his first-ever lesson about dealing with sudden deaths at the police training centre when he was but a 'sprog', the derogatory term used to describe probationer constables.

And death by drowning was always worth a proper look, even though few such deaths were the result of homicidal foul play, which is why he had been asked to attend. If anything was amiss, he could kick-start the appropriate level of investigation.

He had only been given sparse details.

The FIM had told him that it was more than likely the body in the water was that of Jennifer Sunderland. She had been missing from her home for three days and it was thought she might have fallen into the River Lune, close to where she lived – further upriver in the village of Halton. The night she had disappeared had been stormy, the river high and running fast from heavy rainfall up in the hills, and if she had gone in she could easily have been swept away out to sea and never seen again.

The day after the disappearance the police had organized searches at ground level along the banks of the Lune accessible by foot, and with the force helicopter, but to no avail.

But the currents of the Lune estuary are unpredictable as well as dangerous. Henry had known of people being washed away and never seen again, others who had been half-drowned but survived, and others whose bodies had been deposited on sandbanks one day later, or ten days later. Sometimes they were in good condition – if dead and drowned could be described as good – others rotted away, chewed by fish and in a terrible state.

There were no set rules. The river and the sea made the running. In places like this, nature was the boss.

Up to the body being found, the disappearance of Jennifer Sunderland had been treated as an urgent but run-of-the-mill 'missing from home' enquiry, run by the local uniformed section and overseen by the detective inspector at Lancaster section.

There was every chance it would be wound up in the same way, with the uniforms supervising the post-mortem and all contact with the coroner. Not a job for FMIT.

Henry hoped it would pan out this way: just a tragedy, but not one he needed to be concerned about.

He locked his car and started to walk towards the scene. As he came off the car park another car pulled off the main road and parked alongside his Mercedes. He did a quick check to see it wasn't too close to his pride and joy and irritably wondered why the driver hadn't stopped somewhere else in the virtually empty car park. Other than that, he didn't really give it much heed, other than to notice it was a big high-spec Range Rover with two men on board. He assumed they were going to the Stork, which was open for morning coffee.

The DI from Lancaster detached himself from the huddle of cops and paramedics and met Henry halfway. His name was Ralph Barlow.

'Boss,' the DI said, obviously knowing Henry, who knew every detective of rank in the county. The two men shook hands. 'Nothing here for you, I'm afraid,' the DI went on. He was a very experienced detective, mid-forties. He and Henry had crossed paths a few times, but Henry didn't know much about him, other than he tended to grate a little and there were various unconfirmed rumours about his gambling habits. He was a brittle, self-opinionated man who Henry tried not to dislike. That said, he was a sound detective. 'I actually told the FIM not to bother you. I'm quite capable of dealing with a drowning,' he said grumpily.

'Well, he did, but I'm here now . . . so I'll just go through the motions.' Henry understood the DI's point of view. No doubt he was eminently capable.

'Whatever,' Barlow muttered.

'What've we got, then? I know the general scenario.'

'Aye, well, looks like she went in the water three days ago and turned up today.'

'Yeah, got that much, Ralph. Did she fall or was she pushed?'

Henry watched Barlow's mind tick this over for a second before saying, 'Husband said she was a bit depressed, but not necessarily suicidal. No talk of ending her life.'

'So who is she?'

'Jennifer Sunderland . . . wife of Harry Sunderland?' Barlow said this as if Henry should connect the dots. Instead he just looked blank. 'Harry Sunderland, local, but big businessman? Haulage, property . . . you name it.'

'As in Sunderland Transport?' Henry guessed.

'One and the same.'

'Ahh.' Henry had seen their lorries all over the place. Not as numerous as a company like Eddie Stobart, but still quite noticeable. And with a big international operation. Henry hadn't made the connection, but there wasn't any reason why he should have done. He wasn't local to this area. 'You've seen the husband, then?'

'Yeah, when she went missing. She . . . er . . . went out in the rain, never came back.'

'You happy about that?'

'Why wouldn't I be?' Barlow said shirtily.

'No reason. Just a question I'd ask of any detective, Ralph, and expect them not to get uptight about it . . . So what's the crack here?' Henry gestured to the hive of activity.

'Guy out for a stroll spots the body swishing about in the tide and drags her out.'

'And we're sure it's Mrs Sunderland?'

'Oh, yeah . . . I knew her,' Barlow said, then stopped himself.

'You *knew* her?'

'Well, only in passing. Seen her with hubby at one or two golf-club shindigs, that's all.'

'Oh, OK.'

'Yeah, they have quite a high profile around here,' Barlow explained smoothly. 'Charities, businesses and all that shit, y'know . . . Hey, thinking about it,' he said, changing the subject, 'you'll know the guy who dragged her out of the water. I don't know him, but he's an ex-cop.'

By the time Barlow had said this, they were almost at the scene and Henry could see a half-covered body on the ground, feet sticking out, one with a Wellington boot on it. He had also spotted the biggest man in the group. His heart lurched slightly.

'He's the fella that was involved in all that stuff up in Kendleton a while back. The stuff you were involved in, too.'

'Oh, yeah,' Henry said. 'I know him.'

Flynn decided he'd had enough questions from the two keen young PCs now. Their eager enquiries were beginning to annoy him and because the weather was getting colder as a sharp wind increased from the west and zipped around, he was getting very cold. His trainers and jeans were soaking, as was the front of his jacket where he'd carried the dead woman. And this was all a bit of a problem because he hadn't brought a change of footwear or jeans with him from Gran Canaria. Having travelled very light, not expecting to have to wade knee-deep in unpleasant, cold, muddy water and recover bodies, he'd thought that one pair of jeans would be enough to sustain him for at least a week.

At the very least, he needed to warm up.

'Look, guys,' he said, holding up his hands, 'I've done my duty, you've got my current address, my mobile number and my details. I need to get out of these clothes, otherwise I'll contract hypothermia and you'll have another death on your hands. If you want to come to the chandlery about three this aft, I'll happily give you a written statement . . . but first, change of clothing . . . somehow,' he added wistfully and eased his way past the bobbies.

As he walked by the rear of the ambulance that had turned up, he caught the eye of a female paramedic and she smiled at him pleasantly. But then he glanced sideways, right into Henry Christie's face.

Henry smiled grimly – very much the opposite of the paramedic. 'Mr Flynn,' he said, 'we meet once more . . .'

Flynn emerged from the gents' toilet, having spent a few minutes directing the hot-air flow from a wall-mounted hand drier downwards onto his jeans legs and socks. He had to perform a precarious dance/balancing act, lifting up one leg, then the other, in an effort to dry himself off. He had little success and came out carrying his trainers and socks and walked barefoot across the bar to where Henry Christie was sitting at a table by the roaring fire.

At Henry's insistence they had retired to the Stork for a chat and a warm.

Flynn plonked himself opposite Henry and dropped his sodden trainers on the hearth with a splat. He laid his equally wet socks on the mesh of the fire guard. They started to steam immediately.

Henry had bought each of them a coffee and Flynn took a sip of his, grateful for the warmth.

The two men eyed each other suspiciously. Their pasts were intertwined. Flynn blamed Henry for hastening his departure from the police, a grudge he had borne for quite a few years, until he worked out that his own perception was skewed by the whole sorry affair. It had really been his own paranoia that had been his downfall. Flynn had also been involved in the blood-soaked scenario at Kendleton – through no fault of his own – and, more recently, had furnished Henry with some details he had stumbled across regarding terrorist activity in the UK.

Henry, for his part, had suspected that Flynn had helped himself to a share of a million pounds of drug-dealer's money in a police raid that had gone spectacularly wrong. Since then, he'd come to believe it had actually been Flynn's then partner who'd snaffled the money and disappeared and Flynn hadn't seen a penny of it.

That didn't make them friends, though, and they rarely saw eye-to-eye willingly, and tended to grate one another when they met up, which was fortunately not regularly.

'Good coffee,' Flynn said.

'Yes.'

Henry glanced past Flynn's shoulder and clocked the two men he'd seen arrive on the car park earlier in the Range Rover. They were tucking into an all-day breakfast, as he'd guessed they would. The sight of the food made Henry feel very empty.

Bringing his eyes back to Flynn, Henry said, 'What brings you back to these parts?'

'A friend in need.'

Henry arched his eyebrows. 'Do you have a collection of people who need you to help them out?'

Flynn grinned. 'Believe it or not, I still have a few friends, and if they need help, I'll try and give it.'

'You're a real trooper,' Henry said sarcastically.

Flynn glared at the detective, feeling a reddening of the neck. 'I'm assuming all you'll need from me is a statement?' he said coldly. 'All I did was drag a body out of the drink, after all. I presume this' – he indicated the coffee – 'is just a social brew between mates and not an interrogation.'

'Suppose so. And to say thanks for doing what you did. Good stuff,' Henry conceded.

'Anybody would have.'

'No they wouldn't.'

'So what's the poor woman's story?'

Henry shrugged. 'Not sure. So far it's just a uniformed issue, not CID. Might stay that way, but I'll have a look at the circumstances leading up to her going missing. It could just be one of those things, a fatal slip.'

Flynn took a long drink of the coffee and set down the mug. 'I really need to get dried out properly, maybe even go into Lancaster for some new gear.'

'I'll give you a lift,' Henry volunteered.

'You're a real trooper.'

Henry cracked a smile. 'Touché.'

'But a lift back into Glasson would be helpful. I'll take it from there.'

Flynn watched Henry drive away, leaving him standing outside the chandlery. He had a tight expression on his face as he thought about Henry, then dismissed him from his mind and let himself into the shop. Although he'd considered going into the city for some new togs, he'd realized there was no need because the chandlery had a fair selection of clothing that would do just fine. It wouldn't exactly be his favourite Keith Richards T-shirt and baggy three-quarter-length pants, but it would have to suffice.

He selected a shirt, trousers, socks and a pair of stout shoes that he packed into a large carrier bag. He thought his best course of action would be to get back to the canal boat, work out the heating system for himself, have his second shower of the day, then get changed. He would get lunch at the cafe on the other side of the sea lock – fish and chips – and get back to the chandlery to meet Diane for more induction as arranged.

Flynn locked the shop and made his way along the canal in his wet clothes.

The canal boat was still cold inside, but he managed to fettle the vagaries of the heating system, stripped off and hung his clothes over a rail and re-showered.

Afterwards, changed into his new togs, comfortable and practical rather than stylish, he sat next to the gas fire in the living area, surprised at how efficiently it had warmed up.

He sat back, flicked on the small flat-screen TV and found a news channel.

The warmth permeated him until he was glowing. Then the combination of a late-night flight, early morning arrival and the excitement of dragging a body out of the river seeped over him like an anaesthetic. He could not have stopped himself if he'd wanted and before he knew it his head had lolled forwards and he was asleep.

By the time Henry returned to the scene from dropping off Flynn, Professor Baines had arrived in his pristine E-type Jaguar.

He was at the body, squatting down, carefully examining the head. He was speaking in low tones through the side of his mouth into the barely visible microphone that looped down from his ear and was linked to a voice-activated recorder inside his jacket.

He rose as Henry arrived and stood on the opposite side of the body. They nodded at each other. Henry tilted his head, inviting Baines to speak.

'I pronounce life extinct,' Baines declared, checking his watch and reading out the time.

'I was pretty sure of that one,' Henry said.

'Needs to be said and done,' Baines said loftily.

'And beyond that?'

'Looks to be a drowning. External signs are what you would expect. She does have head injuries, but they could have come after immersion. Not unusual for a drowning person to have injuries like that, especially one drowned in these circumstances. River debris, tides . . . she could easily have struck something hard.'

'But you'll be able to tell?'

Baines gave him a withering look. 'I am a pathologist.'

'So they say.' Henry turned as a crime-scene van pulled up nearby. 'A few photos, then back to the mortuary. How soon can you do the PM?'

'As soon as you get this woman identified, I'll put knife to flesh.'

THREE

After the crime-scene photographer had recorded the minimum necessary, plus a few shots of the landscape, the woman's body was bagged and heaved into the back of the ambulance. The paramedics would take her to the mortuary, even though they were not obliged to do so. They could have been awkward and insisted she be removed by an undertaker, but as usual they were helpful.

Henry and DI Barlow had a short conversation with the result that Henry said he would follow the ambulance and body, to maintain the chain of evidence just in case it became something more than a drowning. Barlow – much to his facial disgust – was told to go to the police station in Lancaster, get the 'missing from home' file and bring it to the mortuary. The details in the file, which included a photograph, would be helpful to confirm the identity of the deceased.

Behind the ambulance was a little convoy: Henry, Barlow, Baines and two marked police cars. One of the police cars stayed with the ambulance as it turned into the hospital grounds just south of the city, whilst the other, and Barlow, carried on.

The ambulance reversed up to the mortuary doors, which were opened from the inside by the pre-warned creepy mortuary technician, waiting with a trolley that he manoeuvred expertly up to the ambulance doors. The bagged lady was slid onto it and then reversed into the mortuary, the double doors then closed to keep the outside world at bay from this strange, unsettling, but vital world.

Once inside, the body bag was reclaimed by the paramedics, who washed it with a hose, then took their leave. Henry, the uniformed PC who'd come along to help and the technician looked at the drowned body.

'You want me to strip her?' the technician asked, slightly gleefully, Henry thought, snapping on a pair of medical gloves.

He nodded and Henry watched as the soaked clothing was

removed. He supervised the recording and bagging of each item by the constable. The outer jacket, jeans, blouse, underwear and the single polka-dotted cut-off Wellington boot. Henry visualized the missing one to be somewhere out in the Lune estuary, maybe getting washed up further down the coast at some stage. He doubted it would ever be recovered and if it was it would probably be left where it was found. Just another item of flotsam and jetsam, of no significance whatsoever.

Once naked, all that remained was the woman's jewellery. The rings on her fingers were carefully screwed off by Henry and handed to the constable, who bagged each one separately. There were four, each distinctive and expensive-looking, including the wedding ring. She also wore a gold necklace with a pendant, and bracelets on each wrist. They were described, as is usual police procedure, as 'yellow metal' – just in case they weren't actually gold.

Henry inspected each item in the clear plastic bags, held up the wedding ring and peered closely to see if it was inscribed. He saw '*To J*' next to a tiny love heart etched inside the ring.

'Jennifer,' he thought.

Another ring also had an inscription. This looked like an eternity ring with '*J*' and '*H*' inscribed and intertwined by another heart.

'Jennifer and Harry,' he thought, a great detective's mind at work, piecing all the clues together.

There were no markings on any of the other pieces of jewellery, so he turned his attention to the body, looking but not touching. He peered closely at the crown of her skull and saw a deep cut which formed a parting in her hair, the injury Professor Baines had already noted. Henry raised his eyes and saw her body was not showing any signs of other wounds, but the skin was what he described as 'curdled' after being in the water for so long, and smelled like a blocked drain. There was nothing more he could tell, but he gave her a last glance and thought what a shame it was to have died so early. The thought made him shudder for a moment. The fairly recent death of his wife, Kate, zipped through his mind.

He swallowed back his emotion and packed it away in a separate brain compartment, then turned to the bags into which the dead woman's clothing had been placed.

As the constable had recorded it, he had also gone through the pockets and found nothing.

Henry gave each piece a quick squeeze and was satisfied: nothing.

'Should I wash her down?' the technician asked brightly.

'No, let's wait until the pathologist has had a look first . . . he's somewhere, not far away.' At which point Baines entered the mortuary, having parked his beloved E-type at the far end of the car park and purposely across two bays to discourage others from pulling up too close. He was already removing his jacket and replacing it with a green overall, walking across to the body and circling it for the close visual inspection. He was recording his observations via the mike fitted to his ear.

Henry watched and listened, although the man's voice was fairly quiet, and eventually Baines turned to him.

'Nothing of real note, certainly nothing I wouldn't expect to see on someone who has drowned in such circumstances.'

Henry nodded. He was glad this was getting a little further away from him, still hoping it would turn out to be a tragic but ultimately run-of-the-mill death that the uniformed branch could deal with. Nothing to bother him.

Baines moved to the woman's head, placed a hand carefully under her neck and tilted it backwards, using his hand as a fulcrum. Her mouth sagged slackly open. With his other hand he pulled her jaw wider and looked inside, pulling her cheeks wide and inspecting her teeth.

'Nice set,' he commented. Then frowned. Something caught his eye, so he tilted her head slightly to the right to get the light working better for him and said, 'Fancy.'

'Fancy what?' Henry said.

Baines shrugged. 'Gold filling in a pre-molar.'

'And?' Henry shook his head.

'And . . . don't know yet, maybe nothing,' Baines said, but Henry could see the man's mind flicking through its internal Rolodex.

'Anything for me?' Henry said.

'Hard to say yet . . . need a closer look.'

Henry pouted with disappointment. He was going to say something, but his words were cut short when the muzzle of a gun was screwed painfully into the back of his neck at the point where his skull balanced on his spinal column.

*   *   *

The gun was removed. The man holding the weapon backed off, keeping it aimed at Henry, who turned slightly and saw there were two of them, both armed, having entered the mortuary through the public entrance which should have been locked.

They arced their guns threateningly across the four people in this section of the mortuary – Henry, Baines, the PC and the technician.

The gun that had been jammed into Henry's skin was a large-calibre pistol of some sort; the other gun was a black, ugly looking machine-pistol, very deadly in this enclosed space, capable, with one short burst, of cutting them all down.

The men were dressed in black jeans, black zip-tops, trainers and balaclava masks, with latex gloves on their hands. Henry thought there was something familiar about them.

'What the . . . ? Henry started to utter angrily. He'd not yet had the chance to get frightened.

But then he wished he hadn't opened his mouth.

The man with the handgun, a big, heavy-framed guy, stepped quickly forwards and slammed the pistol across his face like he was doing a backhand smash in tennis.

Henry's head jerked sideways, his whole face distorted with the strength of the impact. His jaw crunched, his teeth catching the inside of the mouth. He staggered with a 'Ungh' noise and pain seared diagonally across his cranium like a knitting needle had been hammered into him. His knees buckled as all communication between brain and spine was disconnected. He crumpled over, even though he tried not to.

The next moments were just hazy and confusing for him, as though he was drowning in dish water. Then a dreamy sensation of being dragged across the tiled floor, his cheek stretching, a trail of blood dribbling from his mouth. He heard shouting, a scream of agony, the voices unrecognizable and distorted, then nothing but blackness as he passed out.

Then his eyes flickered open. He knew instinctively he had not been out for long. His brain clicked into gear as he found himself lying on his side in the recovery position, this time on a carpeted floor. He could feel the weave of the carpet against his cheek. And taste blood in his mouth.

He didn't move. Tried to work out what was happening, but for the moment that conundrum was beyond him, even though his mind was functioning. He moved his face slightly and looked up with one eye into the concerned face of Professor Baines kneeling down over him.

'Henry, old man, are you OK?'

Henry squinted and moved his mouth, the salt-taste of his own blood on his tongue. He tried to speak, but could not manage the words. Instead he manoeuvred himself onto his hands and knees. His head drooped between his arms and he spluttered blood out from his lips, the whole left hand side of his face creased with pain.

'What happened?' he asked fuzzily.

'They locked us in here at gunpoint,' Baines said.

Henry raised his head painfully and looked around. 'Where's here?' He was having a bit of trouble focusing.

'The viewing room. They locked it from the outside so we couldn't get out.'

Henry twisted carefully around, but his elbows gave way and he thumped arse-down on the floor with a groan. Exhaling carefully, he moved his head and tried to make sense of where he was and who was with him. Baines knelt by him, there was the uniformed PC, the mortuary technician and two more mortuary employees, a man and a woman. Henry's eyes descended on the constable for an answer.

'They ripped my PR off,' he blurted, but held up his mobile phone. 'I called it in . . . backup's on the way.'

'Good lad. Anybody else hurt?' Henry's eyes were beginning to work a little better now and he checked the terrified faces of the mortuary staff. He saw a woman tending to the mortuary technician sitting on one of the chairs, dabbing something on his eyes.

'They sprayed something into the tech's eyes,' Baines said 'CS spray, I'd guess. His eyes are streaming, but he looks like he'll be OK.'

They had been herded (or in Henry's case, dragged) into and locked in the viewing room. This was the room to which relatives of deceased persons were brought to either view a body in a casket in the room itself, or to look through a large curtained window on the other side of which was an anteroom where trolleys could be pushed, the curtains drawn back and they could see through the glass. It all depended on the circumstances and the state of the body.

Henry rattled the door handle.

Correct, it was locked from the other side by twisting an inset bolt which could be released from this side if they'd had a big, flat-bladed screwdriver. Like being locked in a toilet cubicle.

Baines had risen to his feet with Henry, now reaching his full, spindly height of over six feet. He was still watching Henry with concern, who was working his jaw, assessing the damage done.

The cuts inside his mouth and cheeks where his teeth had connected with the flesh were still bleeding. He touched them gingerly with his tongue.

'What the hell do they want?' Henry uttered.

Baines shrugged. 'Stealing from dead bodies?' he suggested.

'Or stealing from a particular one,' Henry said and crossly rattled the door handle again.

The constable's mobile phone rang and he answered it. 'Yeah . . . in the viewing room . . . they locked us in here . . . right . . .' He ended the call and looked at Henry. 'Backup's here – but the bad guys have gone.'

'You need to go to A&E,' Baines said firmly. He was following Henry around with his arms open, ready to catch him if he suddenly fell.

'I know,' Henry agreed, the tip of his tongue still touching the inner mouth cuts and also finding a loose tooth. He felt the side of his face with his fingers, carefully pressing the new swelling under his eye. He'd broken his cheekbone once before and it had taken a long time to heal, and still gave him gyp. He hoped it wasn't bust again, but his face was very tender and sore, reminiscent of the pain from the previous fracture.

He and Baines were standing next to the gurney on which the drowned woman lay . . . or at least the woman who'd been pulled out of the river lay. Only a post-mortem could establish for certain how she had died. And because of the events of the last fifteen minutes, Henry now wanted to be one hundred per cent positive she had drowned.

Suddenly his head went muzzy.

He fought it and leaned both hands on the edge of the trolley, hoping to disguise what was happening to him. He might well have needed to go to A&E, as Baines suggested, but he didn't want to go.

His mind started working again.

The armed men had assaulted Henry probably as a show of their capabilities so no one was in any doubt that they meant business. He hoped it wasn't anything personal, just something to encourage everyone else to follow their orders.

Briefly unconscious as he hit the floor, he hadn't been privy to what happened next. According to Baines and the constable, the men had yelled and screamed and herded everyone at gunpoint into the viewing room. They had made the constable and the mortuary technician drag Henry – one leg each – in with them, then ripped the PC's personal radio off. They'd sprayed the technician when he'd stood up to them.

Henry's blood was smeared across the tiled floor, then along the short carpeted corridor to the door of the viewing room, like a leopard had dragged a gazelle across the jungle.

Then they were all locked in, including the staff who'd been working in the examination room.

Ripping the constable's PR off him had only really been a gesture, Henry thought. The intruders must have realized that at least one person amongst their captives would have a mobile phone. The only thing achieved by grabbing the police radio was that it cut off a direct line of communication to the police control room. Using a mobile phone, even on a treble-nine, would be far slower than a PC screaming for assistance down a PR.

So the men had bought themselves some time. Not much, but presumably enough to achieve their goal.

Which was what? Henry asked himself.

His eyes – one gradually closing to a hazy squint as his cheek swelled – moved to the bags containing Jennifer Sunderland's property that he and the PC had been recording.

They'd been ripped open and the contents tipped onto the floor, and scattered as the men searched through them.

So this was the answer: they wanted something that she possessed, or thought she possessed. And whatever this something was, they were prepared to be utterly ruthless in finding it. Ruthless enough to smash a gun into someone's face. And maybe kill if necessary.

The captives had been released from the viewing room by the first officer on the scene. Now more cops had arrived and were being a bit aimless, like they were playing bumpsy-daisy. They needed some direction, as there wasn't much for them to do here, so Henry took charge and told them all to get back on the streets. The offenders had gone before the first officer had arrived, therefore Henry wanted cops out on the streets pulling any vehicles with two or three men on board. It was more miss than hit, he knew, but he wanted to get things moving and keep the scene of the crime as pristine as possible for the CSIs.

When all the uniforms had dispersed, that left him, Baines and the PC who'd been helping out with the property, as well as the mortuary staff, who had all retreated to a refreshment room, drinking tea, traumatized by the events, unable to do any work in the foreseeable future. They all had to be interviewed and statements taken. Henry also guessed they'd all need counselling, too. Par for the course. He didn't even consider that luxury for himself.

If it hadn't hurt his head to do so, he would have shaken it in despair.

Baines and the PC, however, seemed pretty unaffected by it all, fortunately.

'Right,' Henry said, 'let's see if anything's missing.'

Other than having been scattered everywhere, the clothing and possessions were as Henry and the PC had recorded. It seemed the only thing taken was the constable's PR.

'I suppose it's possible I might've missed something in a pocket,' the PC admitted.

'Or sewn into a seam,' Henry added – but he knew he and the PC had run their fingers carefully over each item of clothing and unless they'd missed something tiny, maybe the size of a SIM card or smaller, they'd missed nothing. They had searched the property diligently, and Henry assured the PC of this.

They hadn't even taken the very expensive-looking jewellery.

Which was a mistake, Henry thought, because that turned the incident into something more sinister.

If they had taken the jewels, then it was more than likely the police would have looked on it as just a robbery. Leaving the good stuff gave it a whole new twist, which unsettled Henry.

A wave of pain and nausea, beginning at the very top of his head, rolled through him.

He had been squatting down by the property bags, but as he cranked himself up, the sensations hit him. He staggered a little, keeping a grip, then caught sight of himself in a wall mirror and shivered in horror.

His face was a contorted mess. He already knew that, but what made him extra cross was the amount of blood down and over his jacket and shirt, which were ruined.

'Shit,' he said. 'I think I'll go and get patched up.'

The first thing the triage nurse did when Henry presented himself at casualty and explained what had happened – and that he thought he'd passed out for short time – was to sit him in a wheelchair and get a porter to push him down to the X-ray department.

Baines accompanied him.

'All I want is a plaster and some Savlon,' Henry moaned ungratefully as he was wheeled along the corridors.

'I've been waiting a long time to say this,' Baines chuckled, 'but you need your head examining.'

'Ho bloody ho,' Henry grunted as they arrived at X-ray.

Then the waiting began, during which time Baines told him that the doctors would probably want to keep him in overnight for observation. The news cheered Henry no end.

'I don't have time to spend a night in a hospital. I don't have time for this.' He grumbled a few more things, then looked at Baines. 'You need to go, too. People to dismember.'

'They can wait . . . they're dead, after all.'

'No,' Henry insisted. 'You have things to do. I'll be OK . . . and I'm not staying the night unless I collapse of a brain aneurysm.'

'Don't joke,' Baines said seriously. 'But I will go . . . I've

some mouths to look into, but I don't see me doing Jennifer
Sunderland's post-mortem until tomorrow at the earliest.'

'That's fine. I need to speak to the coroner anyway and she
needs to be formally identified.'

Baines rose, then hesitated. 'That was pretty frightening, Henry.
Y'know – the guys with the guns thing?'

Henry's good eye squinted at him, which meant both eyes
squinted. 'Soft fucker.'

'Knew you'd understand,' Baines grinned.

'I'm sure I would've been frightened too.'

'If only you'd been awake.' Baines touched Henry's shoulder,
in a tender, but still manly gesture, turned and left, passing DI
Barlow shoulder to shoulder through the swing doors.

Barlow regarded Henry's bashed-up face. 'Jeepers – you OK?'

'Exactly how do you want me to answer that one?' Henry
winced.

'Uh, sorry. Hell of a thing . . . everybody's running around
like blue-arsed flies at the moment.' Barlow leaned against the
wall. 'What do you reckon it was all about?'

'No idea, Ralph, other than to guess . . . and then go and ask
the grieving husband what the hell his dead wife had in her
possession that it took two armed men to try and find.'

'Do you think they found what they were after?'

'Again, I don't know. Maybe.' Henry indicated the file
Barlow had in his hand. 'Is that Sunderland's MFH file?' he
asked. Barlow nodded. 'Does everything match up, file to body,
et cetera?'

'It's definitely Jennifer Sunderland.'

'Right, we need to speak to hubby, then.'

'Leave that to me, eh, Henry?' Barlow swept his hand around
to indicate their present location. 'I can sort him.'

Henry glanced at the scrolling LED sign above the X-ray
reception desk. It informed him, and the other people in the
waiting area, that there was a three-quarters of an hour wait for
the next X-ray.

'No, I'm coming,' Henry said, seeing Barlow's face fall.

'But, Henry, I'm quite capable of . . .'

'I know you are. That's not the issue.'

'What is, then?'

'I've got a fresh shirt in the back of my car and if I wear my anorak instead of my jacket, I can get away with my appearance.'

'What's the issue?' Barlow persisted.

'I want to look Mr Sunderland straight in the eye and tell him we've found his wife – dead. Well,' Henry amended this, 'look him in the eye as straight as possible in the circumstances. My curiosity has been aroused.'

FOUR

F lynn jolted awake, feeling worse than he had done before, cursing for having made the fatal error of falling asleep in the middle of the day.

He groaned, shrouded by the warmth thrown out by the canal boat's central-heating system, which was proving far more efficient than he could have imagined. His eyelids flickered heavily and even though he wanted to wake up, he could not seem to stop himself from dozing, his brain mushed by the mid-afternoon nap.

Combating the urge, he inhaled deeply and forced himself to stand up. He glanced at the wall clock.

'Oh – *what*?' He could not believe that more than an hour had slipped by.

From their box, he pulled out the sturdy new boots he'd acquired from the chandlery, quickly threaded the laces and slid his feet into them. They were a good, comfortable fit.

'Shit,' he uttered, extremely annoyed at himself.

He was late for the arranged meeting with Diane, who had enough on her plate to contend with, without an unreliable friend who had promised to help out. He switched the heating off, locked up and jumped off the barge onto the canal side. He jog-trotted back to the shop, his mind still not having woken up fully.

Diane was already there and Flynn entered awkwardly. She was leaning on the counter, looking through some order forms. Flynn crossed the shop floor quickly and said, 'Sorry I'm late, Diane.'

She raised her eyes at him. They were red raw with tears and she seemed to have aged ten years since he last saw her.

He hardly dared pose the question.

But he did. 'How did it go?'

Her lips worked soundlessly for a moment as the enormity of the last few hours seemed to hit her like a sledgehammer. 'I . . . I . . .' she stammered. Then she burst into tears.

Flynn shot around the counter and took hold of her, walking her back into the private office where he kept hold and held on whilst she cried out her emotion with big, gulping sobs and a runny nose and tears. Finally it subsided and she eased herself away from him, looking up through eyes filmed with moisture.

Flynn braced himself for the worst.

She struggled to find the words. 'I . . . they said . . . oh, God, I don't know . . . they said . . . the doctor said it went as well as could be expected . . .'

Flynn exhaled in relief.

'They won't know for certain for a while and there's a long way to go and we probably won't know for weeks how successful it was . . . or not.' A long blob of phlegm dripped out of her nose and she wiped it away with a chuckle, but then her lips quivered again, her mouth on the verge of collapse. 'It was horrible, Steve . . . the worst moments of my life . . . waiting around . . .'

'I take it you've seen him?'

She nodded. 'Just briefly . . . I wanted to be there when he came round. He opened his eyes for a few seconds, but that's all . . . and he . . . he managed a smile, then he went back to sleep. They said to get back about five.'

Flynn squeezed the top of her arm, trying to avoid saying any of the trite but reassuring lines people say in circumstances like this. Things like, 'He'll be fine,' or 'He's a fighter.' Phrases that seemed meaningless and were often wrong in the end. Flynn knew how serious Colin's condition was and could only hope that the operation had caught the cancer in time, that it hadn't spread, wasn't going to ambush his body three months down the line.

Instead, he drew Diane towards him again and held on to her with another embrace before easing her away and saying, 'Have you eaten or had anything to drink?'

'Not hungry.' She blew her nose. 'Couldn't eat anything. Need a brew, though.' She smiled feebly at him. 'Thanks for being here.'

'Least I could do – how about that brew, then?' He picked up the kettle and filled it from the tap in the small loo at the back of the shop. As he plugged it in and switched it on, he said, 'Had a bit of an adventure myself in your absence.'

'Oh?'

'Heaved a dead body out of the river.'

'You what?' she gasped.

Flynn told her his tale and included how he'd helped himself to a new wardrobe from the chandlery afterwards to replace his soaking wet clothes.

When he'd finished, Diane said, 'Who was she?'

He shrugged. 'Cops didn't tell me anything.'

'Probably Jennifer Sunderland.'

'Who?'

'Jennifer Sunderland . . . she went missing a few days ago. It was in the local paper and on the radio . . . it was thought she might have slipped into the river.'

'Did you know her?'

'Phh . . . sort of vaguely. Colin knew her husband. He did a bit of driving for him when he retired from the police, and we bought this place from him. But I wouldn't say I knew her – or him, really.'

'Oh,' Flynn said absently. When he glanced into the tea jar he found it empty, neither was there any coffee or milk. And the kettle had just boiled.

'Sorry – a bit scatterbrained at the moment,' Diane said.

'I'll get some supplies from the shop across the way.'

'OK – then I'll try and show you how the shop works – even though you've already found your way around the clothing department.'

Operating with one good eye, Henry cautiously drove his Mercedes from the mortuary car park to the police garage at Lancaster nick and parked in the already overcrowded premises. He didn't want to leave his car unattended in the hospital grounds, which had a poor record for car crime. He was also a touch reluctant to leave it in the police garage, where the cars were jammed tightly together and there was every chance a police motorbike would topple over and cause extensive damage. It was the lesser of two evils.

Ralph Barlow waited impatiently for him in the CID Astra. Henry dropped in alongside him, already regretting his decision to go AWOL from the hospital without getting his face X-rayed. It had swollen up even more and was bruising nicely purple now, throbbing like a pump, sending out pulses of agony. Definitely a cheekbone broken.

Now he was suffering. The adrenaline that had flooded his system at the time of the incident had dissipated and all he wanted to do was place his head on a soft pillow. But no. He'd been too keen, didn't want to miss anything even though he knew he could easily have let the DI deal with Harry Sunderland, which he was more than capable of doing.

But Henry had an insatiable desire to witness people's reactions to bad news first hand. He believed it was an intrinsic part of being a detective to judge how people dealt with things and the only way to do that properly was to deliver the news personally, watch, read, assess and feel. Especially in this case, as there was clearly not something right with the situation.

From what he'd skim-read on the MFH file, Jennifer Sunderland had gone out for a walk, as she often did, apparently, down to the bottom of her garden and along the banks of the River Lune. It had been a bad night weather-wise, so the theory went that she must have slipped and gone into the fast-flowing, deep water . . . with something in her possession that two armed men wanted.

Henry was therefore looking forward to seeing Harry Sunderland's reaction to the news of her death confirmed. That was purely from a professional point of view. Not because he enjoyed delivering death messages. In fact that was an aspect of the job he had never been comfortable with. He had done it many times during his police service, but more frequently as an SIO, since it usually fell to the senior investigator to deliver the message because, sometimes, it would be to the actual murderer.

He touched his face gingerly.

'You OK, boss?' Barlow asked. 'It looks really bad. Let me take you back to X-ray.'

'No, it's fine,' Henry shook his head. 'I need to see Harry Sunderland's reaction . . . then you can take me back and I'll throw myself on the mercy of the nurses.'

'They don't like people disappearing on them.'

'I know.'

Barlow pulled away from the police station and eased the CID car into the traffic gridlock that was Lancaster's one-way system.

'Where are we going?'

Barlow said, 'To Sunderland's haulage depot out at Slyne. He's most likely to be there. If not we'll go to his house . . . you sure you don't want me to ring ahead, Henry? Tell him we're coming?'

'No. I want to see his unprepared reaction.'

'You think it's more than a simple drowning accident?'

'I'm making no assumptions – but you know the score: always think murder, then you don't make a tit of yourself.'

'Yeah, yeah.'

'I like to see the whites of their eyes.'

Barlow skipped from lane to lane to make progress through the city. Soon they were heading across Greyhound Bridge, which spanned the River Lune, taking westbound traffic out of Lancaster towards Morecambe. Henry's one eye got a good view of the river as he looked across to St George's Quay and south down the river itself, under Carlisle Bridge, which was just a footbridge. At that moment the river was fairly low, but ebbing quickly, and he thought of the terrifying vortex of a journey Jennifer Sunderland must have had in the river. If she had fallen in at the Crook o' Lune, where her house was – maybe a mile and a half north of Greyhound Bridge – she had been dragged and dumped five miles away at Glasson on the estuary.

'I wonder at what point she gave up struggling and accepted her fate,' Henry mused out loud. She could have gone a long way, gasping and fighting, hoping to get snagged on an over-hanging branch or washed up on the bank. Henry was reasonably familiar with the general geography of this area – as he was for most of Lancashire – and knew she had passed under seven bridges, including an aqueduct, and over a weir. She had been on a hell of a journey. 'Unless she was unconscious before she went in,' he added. 'Or maybe she didn't struggle at all. Maybe she just jumped in and killed herself intentionally.'

Barlow filtered across more lanes of traffic and picked up the A6 to head north out of Lancaster. He did not reply to Henry's first stabs at forming a hypothesis.

Flynn trailed Diane around the shop, both of them with a mug of tea in hand. She showed him the ropes, literally and meta-phorically, of how the chandlery operated. From how to use the till and credit/debit-card machine, to how items were priced, how stock was recorded and even how to bag up goods for customers, how to smile, make small talk, make them feel important, all that customer focus stuff.

He was amazed at how much stock there was and the value of it, running to tens of thousands of pounds. Upstairs there was a large storage room that was once a bedroom, jam-packed with boxes and crates, plus an upstairs toilet and shower, but they didn't go up there.

He let her chatter on and could tell she was enjoying being distracted from the main issue in her life, which would very soon return to the forefront when she went back to the hospital.

After this introduction and the opportunity to deal with a couple of customers, they sat at the back of the shop with new brews.

'I never asked how you are,' Diane said. 'I mean, pulling a body out of the river, for goodness' sake.'

Flynn blew out his cheeks. 'Not really bothered,' he said. 'Done it before a few times – y'know, back in the day, as they say,' he spoke wistfully. 'I've even hooked my fair share of bodies out of the Atlantic . . . boat people from Africa, you know. Thousands come ashore in the Canaries . . . and hundreds don't make it.'

'That must be awful.'

Their conversation ran on for a while, going around the houses, studiously avoiding the important issue. Flynn could sense what was going on, so he said, 'Do you need to go back to the hospital now? You can leave the place with me . . . I'll muddle through. You do what you need to, Diane.'

She stared at her tea, then raised her eyes. 'Will you come with me?'

The glaze of her tears did it for Flynn. He always considered

himself to be a hard man, and in most instances he was. But
Diane got to him and he had to swallow back his own tears.

'Course I will.'

Slyne village lay a couple of miles north of Lancaster, straddling the A6. Henry knew it a little, that it consisted mainly
of dwellings and rural businesses because this part of Lancashire
was predominantly countryside. Years ago he'd been to the two
pubs on either side of the A6, but hadn't visited the place
recently.

Barlow turned off the main road, left the houses behind and
drove into the rolling hills, then swung a tight right into
Sunderland's haulage depot. It was a huge operation with at least
four massive warehouses, surrounded by smaller units, and a
long line of HGVs parked in a regimented row, all bearing the
Sunderland Transport crest. Henry counted twelve, plus two
pulled up at the doors of warehouses being filled with goods. He
guessed there were a hundred more out on the roads. There were
also possibly over fifty container units stacked high.

The place had once been a farm. Some of the buildings were
converted barns and the main office block had once been a large
farmhouse.

Barlow drew into a visitor's parking bay and got out.

To their right were some designated parking spaces, one taken
up by a sleek silver-grey Aston Martin with a personalized number
plate. It didn't take a super-sleuth to make the connection between
the registration plate and the owner of the company, Harry
Sunderland.

Henry climbed slowly out of the CID car. He and Barlow
walked to the office entrance and through the revolving doors.
There was a small foyer with a large desk where a female receptionist sat tapping away at a computer keyboard. It was a nice
modern set-up inside an old house.

As they entered, the receptionist glanced up from her work
and her eyes instantly clocked Henry's battered face. Her jaw
dropped slackly and her lipstick-covered lips popped open.

Henry rooted out his warrant card and flipped it for her to see.

'Apologies for the appearance,' he said as he introduced
himself. 'We'd like to speak to Mr Sunderland, please.' Henry

saw that her name badge said Miranda, so he added, 'Miranda.'
The personal touch.

'I'm afraid he's busy at the moment.'

'I'm sure he'll want to see us,' Henry said firmly.

'Could I enquire what it's about?' Miranda's hand hovered
over the telephone.

'Very personal and urgent,' Henry said.

Miranda got the message. She picked up the phone.

At that moment a door behind her opened and a man spun out
from the office beyond with a mobile phone clamped to his ear.

'Look, I said no, OK?' he insisted down the phone. 'The
consignment will be delivered as soon as practicable . . . Can't
be done any sooner . . . You have my word . . . Yep, yep . . .'
His face was angled down as he spoke, his head bobbing, his
free hand gesticulating with annoyance.

Harry Sunderland, Henry guessed . . . and not quite what he
was expecting.

He was dressed in a cheap white shirt, no tie, sleeves rolled
halfway up his forearms, and dark grey trousers that reminded
Henry of a school uniform. His shoes – black and scuffed and
unpolished – looked like lads' shoes as well. His hair was blond,
unkempt.

Henry had been expecting more of an executive look, but
seeing Sunderland and linking him to the type of business he
ran, he immediately nailed him as a man who had made his
money through hard graft and getting his hands dirty – literally
– and didn't give a stuff about how he looked. He was in an
industry where appearances probably didn't matter. Haulage
wasn't exactly banking.

Sunderland was, however, a good-looking man in a charming,
boyish way. Mid-forties, a bit stocky, the blond hair accentuated
by a tan.

He finished his call and slid the phone shut with the words,
'Fuckin' basic.'

Only then did he look up and take in the two detectives standing
at reception. He came up behind Miranda, who had swivelled on
her chair to look at him, then positioned herself so she could
point at Henry and Barlow.

'Mr Sunderland,' she began hesitantly.

Sunderland's eye darted from one man to the other, trying to weigh them up. Henry spotted a flicker of recognition when he looked at Barlow that went as soon as it came. Sunderland's brow knitted, then his face crumpled in horror.

'You're cops, aren't you?' Before either could answer, he uttered, 'It's about Jennifer, isn't it?'

FIVE

They retired to Sunderland's office behind reception. Henry sympathetically outlined the finding of a woman's body in the river and that all indications – from clothing, other property and photographic comparison – were that this was his wife, Jennifer. It just needed a formal identification – and Henry was, of course, deeply sorry for his loss.

Sunderland seemed stunned and his features became granite-like as the news permeated. Henry studied him carefully, but tried not to draw any hasty conclusions from the way the man took the news.

There was no set of rules as to how people should respond. Henry had seen everything, from hysteria to cold-blooded anger and shouting; others were detached and practical. Most veered between extremes.

Henry had much experience in delivering awful news both to the innocent nearest and dearest and to those who knew exactly what was coming – the killers of the deceased. The way these people took it was often over the top. Much weeping, wailing and gnashing of dentures, vowing revenge – reacting in a way they thought people should behave on hearing the devastating news. Often, they were very convincing and it was only subsequent good coppering that unearthed the truth.

So what was Harry Sunderland going to do?

If he'd pushed his wife into the river, then he would be mentally ready and would probably have rehearsed his reaction.

If he hadn't and still harboured hopes of her turning up alive, or even if he feared the worst, he would have given

no thought to how he would take the news and it would be
spontaneous, whereas if he was her killer it would appear to
be spontaneous. There was a subtle and not very obvious
difference and Henry had to try to work out which was which.
Prepared or unprepared? Guilty or not? He watched Sunderland's
mouth, his eyes, any facial tics, the general body language . . .
but he had to admit he couldn't reach any firm conclusion. He
was not Sherlock Holmes, after all.

'When did you find her?' Sunderland asked.

'Two hours ago, maybe?'

For the first time he made direct eye contact with Henry and
said softly, 'Thank you for coming to tell me.' Then he noticed
Henry's injuries. 'What happened to you?'

'I'll come to that.'

Sunderland looked confused. 'Is it something to do with my
wife?' he asked. 'Your injury?'

'In a way . . . look, Mr Sunderland, because this is a sudden
and unusual death . . .'

'Unusual?' he butted in.

'Not that many people drown,' Henry said. Sunderland nodded,
understanding. 'As I was saying, because of the circumstances,
we will need you to do a formal identification and we will
have to ask you some questions and the coroner will want an
inquest.'

'Some questions?'

'About the night your wife went missing, what went on, that
sort of thing. It will have to be quite detailed.'

'I told the bobby everything who reported it . . . and this
detective has also been to see me . . .' He indicated Barlow, who
was standing by a window that overlooked the nearest warehouse
unit.

'I'm aware of that.'

'So what then? It was obviously accidental . . . clearly she must
have slipped into the river . . .' His voice trailed off wistfully. 'She
liked walking by the river . . . and the tides must have washed her
into the Conder.'

'I know what you're saying,' Henry began, then stopped
momentarily and shot a quick glance at Barlow, before coming
back on track and continuing, 'All drownings have to be thoroughly

investigated and I know you told the reporting officer what happened, but we need a statement from you now.'

'From some questions to a statement, is it now?'

'Is that a problem?'

'No . . . no, it isn't . . . sorry for being abrupt. It's just so much to take in. I sort of thought the worst, but hoped for the best, y'know?' His face was tight with emotional pain. 'It's starting to hit me, I guess.' He dropped his chin to his chest, rotating his jaw, clearly holding back the urge to break down. His bottom lip wobbled. If he was acting, it was pretty good.

'First things first, though, eh?' Henry said. 'We do need that formal identification and I'm afraid it'll be a tough call, but I'd like you to come down to the mortuary now.'

'Now?'

Henry said, 'We'll give you a lift down, if you like.'

'I'll drive myself, I know where it is.'

'Do you have a relative or close friend who could accompany you – give you some support?'

Sunderland shook his head. 'No one I'd care to bring along,' he said sarcastically.

'OK. In that case, how do you feel about coming down in an hour? That way we'll have a bit of time to get things ready.'

He nodded.

Henry considered asking what his wife might have had in her possession that would end up with two violent men turning up at the mortuary. But he held back for the moment. He wasn't sure how important it was, but the cynical side of him – the side that didn't believe a damn thing anyone said until it was proved to be the truth, the side that made him a half-decent jack – thought it might be wise just to hang fire. It was a feeling, nothing more, maybe the ace in the ankle sock.

He turned to Barlow. 'OK?' he said, and gave the DI a stare that was unequivocal. *It was OK.*

'Y-yes, boss.'

They left Sunderland alone in his office.

'Seems straight up,' Barlow said.

Henry paused. 'Yeah, suppose so.'

'You don't think so?'

'Well . . . let's do the job by numbers and see what transpires,' Henry said. 'And to that end, will you sort out the ID with him and then arrange to take a statement at some time, depending on how he's handling it. If he's in pieces, put it off until tomorrow, but arrange to do it at the nick and not his home.'

'Will do.' Barlow understood the reasoning behind that. Police-station interviews gave the cops the psychological upper hand, and in cases of suspicious deaths, it was always best to have home advantage where possible.

Henry eased himself into the front passenger seat of the CID car, Barlow got behind the wheel.

There was a moment when Henry was going to say something. He actually turned square to him and opened his mouth, but stopped as Barlow looked at him and smiled. Henry hoped his transition was smooth, and instead of saying what he was going to say, he said, 'I'll try and get back into the X-ray queue because my face is actually killing me. Not that they'll be able to do anything if the bone's broken, other than to ply me with painkillers.'

'Yeah, no problems . . . were you going to say something else?' Barlow had obviously realized Henry was about to say something, then halted.

'No,' Henry said.

And, as the saying goes, his arsehole twitched: 'Half-crown, sixpence.'

He was meek, mild and apologetic to the hospital staff and by overuse of his well-practised, but now slightly crooked and frankly scary, boyish and endearing grin – made so by his facial injury – on both male and female nurses, he was logged back into the system with just a mild reprimand.

Barlow had accompanied him back to A&E and hung around for a few minutes whilst Henry worked his frazzled charm. Then they walked back to X-ray – no wheelchair this time, that boat had sailed – whilst Henry ran through a few points he wanted Barlow to cover with Harry Sunderland, the ID and the subsequent statement. He also told him he wanted to get an update on how the operation had gone to find the robbers.

Barlow nodded patiently until Henry realized he was being a

bit patronizing to a seasoned detective who knew his job. So he stopped yapping.

They had reached the double doors to the X-ray department.

'OK, boss, I'll go and sort him out and see what's happening elsewhere.'

'Thanks, Ralph.'

The DI turned away, but Henry said, 'Oh, just one thing.'

Barlow paused. 'Yeah?'

'How well *do* you know Harry Sunderland?'

'Not at all . . . like I said, just in passing at golf club events and such.'

'But you have talked to him at these events?'

Barlow shook his head. 'Not specially.'

'Mm, OK . . . just wondering,' Henry said airily. He put a hand on the door. 'See you later.'

Barlow looked at him for a second, then walked away down the corridor. Henry half-stepped into the doorway, watching the back of the DI, who fished out his mobile phone and put it to his ear, then turned out of sight.

Henry's mouth screwed up. He would have squinted thoughtfully, but his left eye was now as good as closed and he would have blinded himself had he done so. He shrugged, then peered at the warning sign on the door forbidding the use of mobile phones in the X-ray department.

Before he went through he had to make a personal call of his own.

Flynn drove Diane up to the hospital in her tiny Smart Car, into which he had to fold himself tightly, his knees almost under his chin. He walked with her to the post-operative unit in which Colin was being cared for and monitored following the surgery. He was in a poor and drowsy state, hardly aware of what was going on around him.

Flynn was shaken by Colin's appearance. They had known each other for many years as cops. Flynn had taken the detective route, but Colin, keen on all things motor vehicle, had gone on to traffic and motorcycles. Despite this divergence they had remained good friends. In fact Colin was one of the few people Flynn had been able to confide in when his own career went down the toilet. During the time when he was suspected of stealing a million pounds of drug-dealer's money, when the whole organization treated him like a pariah – including Henry Christie, who Flynn had thought hammered the final nails into the coffin that was his career – Colin had remained a good mate.

They shared a passion for sea fishing and boats and it was the least Flynn could do to help out in this hour of need.

Flynn also knew Diane well. Also a retired cop, she and Colin had hooked up on their initial training course over thirty years before and been inseparable since.

'Someone here to see you,' Diane whispered to Colin, who stirred and opened his eyes, which were opaque and unfocused. He was attached to various machines, pumps and drips. The bed clothes were drawn back almost as far as his groin and a large dressing covered the lower half of his stomach where the operation had been performed.

Flynn swallowed at the sight, as Colin looked blankly across the room, Flynn thinking he couldn't see at all and was surprised when he said, 'Hey, Steve,' and raised a dithery right hand off the bed, which Flynn shook, feeling the bones.

'Hey, man, how're you doing?'

'Another day above ground,' he said croakily. 'Gotta be good, eh?'

'Can't argue with that.'

Colin exhaled painfully and closed his eyes. Flynn and Diane exchanged glances. Then Colin's eyes opened again. 'Thanks for coming . . . y'know, the shop and all that . . . appreciated.'

'Not a problem.'

A great weariness seemed to enshroud him and he closed his eyes and fell asleep instantly.

Diane sat on a chair next to the bed and took her husband's hand. She looked desperately at Flynn, who did not know how to react to the expression.

'Bugger,' he said.

'Yeah,' she agreed.

'Look, I'll go and have a mooch around and be back a bit later to see where you're at, eh?'

She nodded.

'Shit,' Flynn said under his breath as he walked out of the unit with one last glance at Colin.

Following an interminable wait for an X-ray, Henry was back in the casualty unit for an equally long wait to be seen by a consultant. He sat miserably in the waiting area, but fortunately the pain was ebbing slightly after he'd been given some analgesics. He was eventually summoned to a curtained cubicle where he was told to lie on an uncomfortable couch and wait for a doctor who would be along soon. The whole unit was moderately busy, but being short-staffed, everyone was chasing their tails doing several jobs at once.

He tried to relax, lying back and thinking through the day.

It seemed such a long time since he had looked at the frozen body of the unknown murder victim, and he hadn't given her any consideration since. She had lain unforgotten for such a long time, he almost thought that another day would not make any difference. The more urgent incidents that had happened seemed to insist on being dealt with first . . . but Henry dismissed that idea.

Her death had to be investigated properly and it wasn't going to wait any longer. It would be all too easy to let the new stuff take precedence – after all, it was new and it had resulted in him being battered, and he was fuming about that – but he would not allow that to happen. Just by having her drawer pulled out of the fridge, he had obliged himself to get to grips with her murder.

Not that anyone would be bothered even if he did nothing for another two weeks. Except it did matter, would matter to her family, whoever and wherever they were. She deserved to be treated properly and professionally, and so far it looked as though that was not the case.

And that was one of the things Henry prided himself on . . . fighting for the dead.

Then he started to think about Jennifer Sunderland and what little he knew about her and her husband, Harry. Rich people, good life – on the surface. But what was there underneath, what would Henry find when he scraped away the veneer?

'Behind closed doors,' he heard himself say and thought about

Harry Sunderland, whose reaction to the news of his wife's death did seem genuine . . . except for one niggling thing . . . which was giving Henry a very strange sensation.

Could I be wrong? he wondered. But if he was right, what significance did it have?

He didn't know.

His face hurt – a lot – and all of a sudden he didn't care.

All he wanted was to get out of hospital and go to bed.

He opened his good eye when he heard the curtain swish back – and the most beautiful sight in the world stood before him.

'Babe,' he whispered.

'God, Henry,' Alison Marsh gasped on seeing his battered face. She swooped across the gap towards him, her eyes taking in all his injuries. 'You didn't say you were hurt this badly,' she complained.

'Looks worse than it is,' he lied.

'I don't believe that,' she said, cutting through the fib. 'I was a military nurse, you know.'

Alison Marsh was Henry's 'lady-friend'. He wasn't exactly certain what the correct term was. 'Girlfriend' seemed inappropriate, 'partner' not quite right, because they didn't live together, yet 'lady-friend' sounded like something from a Jane Austen novel. Whatever . . . the fact was they were together, madly in love with each other, and the future looked as bright as it could be.

Alison was the landlady-owner of a pub called the Tawny Owl in Kendleton, a village deep in the countryside far to the east of Lancaster. Henry had met her when he stumbled into the pub and the middle of a blood-soaked stand-off between rival gangsters.

Henry and Alison began their relationship tentatively after Kate's death, fully aware of the sensitivities surrounding it. Even now, several months after Kate's death and months after they had started seeing each other, Henry was still getting untold grief from his youngest daughter, Leanne; his eldest, Jenny, was much more sanguine about the matter.

Despite this, Henry and Alison were moving forward.

He guessed that one day, in the not too distant future, the question of marriage might be raised. Surprisingly for him, it didn't faze him at all. The prospect of living in a country pub was very appealing. As well as being with Alison, who he adored, of course.

'Is there any part of you I can kiss?' she asked.

'Lots of parts,' he said, 'but here will do nicely for the moment.' He puckered his lips and she kissed him softly, before sitting on the edge of the examination couch and gripping his hand.

The curtain was yanked back and a young Asian doctor appeared with an X-ray of Henry's head in his hands.

'I'm going to stay the night. The nurse has told me there's a room close by and I can get some sleep if I need to.'

'That's fine,' Flynn nodded to Diane. 'Is it OK for me to keep hold of your car? You can call me any time – and I mean, any time – to get picked up or whatever you need. Middle of the night . . .' He grinned stupidly.

'Thanks.'

'Do you need anything now?' he volunteered.

'No, I'm fine.' She patted the bulky shoulder bag she had brought along with her. 'Night essentials just in case.'

'Just let me know. I'll go and get something to eat now, probably down at the Victoria, then I'll bed down for the night in the boat, then open up the shop tomorrow and hold the fort.'

'You're a love,' she smiled weakly. 'An alley cat with a mushy heart. At least that's what Colin calls you.'

'I've heard worse.'

'But look – I'll be here all night and I don't want to tie you down to the end of a phone line. And I'll bet you're gagging for a pint, so just go back, enjoy a drink with your meal and don't worry about me. I'll call you in the morning.'

Flynn gave her a peck and a hug and watched her walk back into the post-op unit to be with her husband.

'Snapped like a desiccated twig,' declared the doctor gleefully, holding up the X-ray and pointing. 'Even through the swelling, the X-ray has managed to pick out the fracture. See!'

'Oh, yeah,' Alison said, peering. 'Look, Henry.'

Henry could not see the detail, but he was fascinated by the X-ray that clearly showed his skull – cranium, jaws, teeth. Pretty ugly and an unsettling insight into what he would look like once the maggots had eaten away his flesh.

The doctor lowered the sheet. 'There's not much we can do about it, unfortunately. Can hardly put a plaster cast around your head, can we?' he chuckled. 'It'll be down to time and good pain relief.'

'Like last time,' Henry said.

'It's been broken before?' Henry nodded and the doctor examined the X-ray closely again. He sighed. 'Can't see the previous break, so it could be in exactly the same place. But it should still heal well.'

'Didn't last time.'

'I'm sure it will this time,' the doctor answered him.

A few minutes later after being given a prescription for a string of painkillers, Henry was discharged. The suggestion that he might have to stay in for overnight observation was thankfully not raised, and he didn't remind them.

Hand in hand, he and Alison walked towards the exit, discussing what to do about his car. Because of the size of the swelling and the fact it had closed one eye, he had been advised not to drive. The prospect of leaving the Merc in the police garage wasn't appealing, though. It would be safe from thieving, but not damage – and Henry didn't want to abandon it there.

Alison pulled Henry to a jarring halt. 'Look, I'll drive you to the Owl in my car and we'll collect yours in the morning when the swelling might have gone down,' she insisted.

'I can drive. One eye's plenty good enough. I know where I'm going.'

'The country roads have no street lights – so you can't.'

'I can so.'

She gave him her best look of disdain, then shook her head at his stubbornness and glanced down the corridor to see a figure walking disconsolately towards them from the surgical wards. She was about to give Henry a piece of her mind, but did a double-take.

'That looks like . . . oh my God, it is. Steve Flynn.'

'Is it?' Henry reckoned to peer at him.

'Yes, it is . . . Steve,' she called.

If there had been stones or pebbles on the floor, Flynn would have been kicking them forlornly along. He stopped and raised his head at the sound of his name.

'Alison?' he said uncertainly.

She released her grip on Henry's hand. 'Steve . . . it's so good to see you,' she said genuinely, pacing away from Henry and giving Flynn an enormous hug, the sight of which opened Henry's good eye with infuriation. Flynn had met Alison at the same time as Henry in Kendleton.

'You look really well,' she said, drawing away and inspecting him from tip to toe. Flynn always looked well. A deep Canary Island tan on a well-proportioned and extremely fit body, six-two, and looks to match. 'What are you doing here?'

'Hasn't he told you?' Flynn indicted Henry with a sneer, then a double-take as he saw Henry's face.

Alison gave Henry an accusing look. 'No, he hasn't.'

He responded with a wimpy shrug. 'I haven't had time – and why would I, anyway?'

Flynn scowled at Henry, but instantly changed his expression to pleasant when Alison looked at him. 'I'm just here helping out a poorly mate,' he said, then frowned. 'So . . . you two?' He pointed at them, his finger rocking back and forth.

Alison's face softened proudly. 'Yes – us two.'

Flynn wasn't the best of men to read lovey-dovey body language, but he couldn't help it in this instance as it was clear that Henry and Alison were very much an item. What he didn't understand was why they were so brazenly public about it. Flynn thought Henry was married.

'Oh, right, nice one,' he said quickly. To Henry he said, 'What happened to you since I last saw you?'

'Bumped into a door,' Henry said shortly, no desire to enter into a discussion with Flynn about anything.

'No he didn't,' Alison said, knowing full well the two men did not rub along nicely. 'He's been assaulted.'

'Well, fancy that.' Flynn stifled a laugh. 'Can't imagine anyone wanting to hit you.'

Henry held Flynn with a one-eyed stare, then said to Alison, 'Time we were going.'

'How long are you here for, Steve?' Alison asked, ignoring him.

'Not sure. Not long.'

'If you get the chance, come out to the Owl. Have a meal and a drink and I'll put you up for the night. All the bedrooms have been refurbished now. They're really nice.'

'And the bloodstains wiped up?'

A shadow crossed Alison's face at the memories evoked by the remark. 'Yes, they've gone,' she said darkly, then bucked up. 'Done wonders for trade, actually. Appeals to people's dark side, I guess. Seeing where murders took place. Anyway . . . it'd be nice to have a catch-up.' She placed a kiss on Flynn's cheek and Flynn saw Henry's bristling reaction to it, like a male lion being challenged by an upstart. So Flynn returned it with a kiss of his own and gave Henry a smug sideways grin.

Then, to add insult to injury, he said to Alison, 'I'll definitely come.' He gave a quick wave, but Henry stopped him from going.

'Quick word.' He edged Flynn out of Alison's earshot.

'Is this a warning to steer clear of her?'

'Not necessary . . . that woman you dragged out of the water?'

'Oh yeah?'

'Did you take anything from her?'

Flynn's face hardened instantly, offended. 'What are you suggesting?'

'Did you take any property from her? I'm asking. I'm doing my job – remember?'

Open-mouthed, Flynn said, 'Do you want the other side of your face to match up?'

'Just answer the question . . . did you take anything from her?'

'How dare you ask me that, Henry? Fuck off!' He spun away and stalked through the sliding door of the main hospital entrance, furious that Henry had the nerve to ask the question.

Henry watched his back and muttered, 'He doth protest too much.'

SIX

B y the time Flynn re-entered earth's atmosphere, having been flung fuming and furious into orbit by the insinuation of Henry Christie's question, he had driven the Smart Car all the way back to Glasson Dock. He'd parked outside the chandlery and was halfway through a bar meal at the Victoria, which was accompanied by a very chilled pint of Stella Artois and a Glenfiddich chaser.

The food was good, simple and filling. The lager was excellent, the whisky tremendous . . . the ideal combination to re-enter from the stratosphere without completely burning up.

It was only as he cleared his plate, sat back and started to sip his second pint and chaser did his emotional temperature start to fall.

Such was the effect Henry Christie had on him. Although Flynn had initially laid most of the blame on Henry for hastening his departure from the force and he had learned the truth of the matter later – that Henry had actually covered up a lot of the incriminating stuff he'd unearthed about Flynn – the damage to their relationship was pretty much done. They just didn't like each other, never would.

The two men had come into contact a few times in recent years, in situations not compatible with endearing themselves to one another. It didn't help that when they'd met up in Kendleton, Flynn had thought he'd had a chance at getting something together with Alison. Circumstances and geography dictated otherwise – not least that Alison did not fancy him – but to find Henry walking hand-in-hand with her, like two lurv-struck teenagers, really piqued him. That Henry knew he fancied his chances with Alison and was probably now having a 'right good chuckle' to himself, also made him seethe.

He sipped his beer and as he thought about things, he realized his problem went far beyond simple jealousy.

Yes, he was envious of Henry, but what really irked him was his own inability to find and keep someone for himself.

He had been in love once recently, the only time since his acrimonious divorce some years earlier. But it had ended in tragedy and he had been unable to pick up the pieces since.

Now he was starting to get worried about facing a future alone.

The big, rough, tough man of action wanted a serious relationship.

'Diddums,' he thought to himself.

What falling in love had taught him – after vowing never to do so after his divorce – was that it was wonderful, confusing, compelling – and something he needed. He thought he could handle being alone, indeed had done so for a few years, but now the prospect of hitting sixty and single frightened the crap out of him, more than swimming with a hammerhead shark.

Sixty was a long way away, but time flew, and you got old before you knew it.

'Bastard,' he hissed quietly into his beer. 'How did he get someone like her? Wonder what his wife thinks about it?'

The beer went to his lips and half of it slid down his throat.

He glanced around the pub, which was moderately busy. A few couples and a few single oldish men propping up the bar. Flynn's eyes paused on the couples, before tearing away and returning to the drink in front of him. He finished it in one fell swoop, then the chaser.

Actually, he reasoned, life wasn't that bad. He enjoyed his life in Puerto Rico in Gran Canaria, had made some good friends, had regular sex with a few 'no strings attached' ladies, and had a great job he hoped he would do for the rest of his life. Skippering a sport-fishing boat was an awesome way to make a living and his plan was – eventually – to buy his own boat.

Lots of blokes would leap at the chance of leading his life.

Suddenly he felt better after his inner pep-talk.

He stood up, went to the bar, bought a couple of bottles of beer and went out into the night, which was cold and dark.

'Boss, I thought you'd want to know – it's definitely Sunderland's wife,' Ralph Barlow said. 'Jennifer.'

Henry was sitting in the warm lounge of the owner's living accommodation at the back of the Tawny Owl. On the journey across from Lancaster in Alison's car, he'd got a call from Barlow but the signal had gone before they could talk – not uncommon out in the sticks – and he hadn't been able to return it. He had called Barlow using the landline in the pub.

'Thanks for that,' Henry said.

'He was pretty cut up about it. It must have hit him.'

'Genuine?' Henry asked.

'Think so.'

'What about a statement and interview?'

'I've left it loose. Some time tomorrow.'

'Might as well get the PM done first anyway. See if anything comes of that.'

'Yeah, I thought that.'

'Did you mention the robbery thing, the armed guys?'

'You said not to.'

'Yeah, I did, didn't I?'

There was a slight pause as Henry's brain ticked over whilst he mentally rechecked his list. Had everything been covered? Could everyone sleep tight tonight?

'Boss?'

'Just cogitating . . . anything on the two robbers yet?'

'Not as such . . . but there could be some CCTV footage from the hospital cameras.'

'Leave it for now, we'll have a look tomorrow.'

'Tomorrow? You not reporting in sick, boss?'

'Things to do.'

'But you're well hurt.'

'I'll be fine after an ice-pack, some JD, more pills, food and sleep . . . I'll be in at nine-thirty.'

Henry hung up. The door opened and, as if on cue, Alison entered the room with a small ice-pack from the freezer, wrapped in a tea towel. She sat alongside him and brought the ice up to his face. He winced at the contact, but bravely hung in there, then took it from her, moulding it tenderly around the contours of the swelling.

'You're not really going to invite Flynn round, are you?' he asked.

'Yes.' It was a firm answer. Although she had no romantic ideas where Flynn was concerned, the two did have a bond that would connect them for the rest of their lives. She had saved his life and in so doing had been forced to take someone else's. Flynn had covered it up but Alison was secretly aware that Henry knew what had happened but had never voiced his suspicions. She hoped he wouldn't raise the subject now that Flynn was back on the scene. 'You were a bit harsh with him, I thought.'

'I wouldn't trust him as far as I could chuck him, love. Y'know there's over a million quid missing from a drugs raid he botched, years ago . . .'

'I know, I know . . . let it go, will you?'

'And, and,' Henry went on, about to mount a very high horse. 'All right, maybe he didn't steal it, but his bloody cop-partner did and the money and his partner have vanished somewhere in the ozone layer.' He looked at her.

'Finished?'

'And I know he fancies you,' Henry admitted dully.

'Ahh, the truth will out. The old green-eyed monster.'

Henry's look became a guilty frown. 'He's a good-looking bastard,' he said. 'Tanned, fit . . . smooth.'

'And I'm so easily seduced. Is that what you're saying?'

'You were by me.'

'Henry, I love you . . . end of.' It was a statement that broached no further argument.

'Yeah, well,' he muttered. 'I need to make a few calls.'

'And I need to get back to the bar, the locals are thirsty tonight.' She touched the back of his hand gently, then left.

Henry picked up the phone and dialled with his thumb, a number he knew well.

'Hello, Marina, it's Henry Christie . . . is Jerry about?' he asked.

'One moment. I think he's just distilling the home brew . . . Jerry!'

Henry held the phone away from his ear as she bawled out the name. Henry was calling DC Jerry Tope, who worked in the Intelligence Unit at headquarters. Tope had done a lot of good work for Henry over recent years, was an excellent Intel analyst. He was also an expert at hacking into computer databases – usually illegally. Tope had been headhunted by the FBI, so impressed were they after he'd drilled into their computer network, but Henry had managed to block the move. He guessed it would only be a matter of time before he left the cops for more lucrative pastures. For the time being, Jerry Tope was his and because he was so talented and useful, Henry tolerated the fact he was a grumpy bastard who showed little respect for rank.

There were a lot of rustling noises, some whispering, and suddenly Tope's voice came on the line. Abruptly he said, 'Two things. First it's gone nine and I'm off duty. Second, I'm just sterilizing my wine bottles.'

'And third,' Henry cut in, 'I'm your boss, you're a DC, and if you don't shut it, you'll be on a school-crossing patrol in Bacup on Monday. Promise.' It wasn't really a promise or a threat, but part of the little ritual he and Tope often went through to kick off their conversations.

Tope grunted, 'Whaddya want?'

Henry explained the two things. One was a fairly straightforward piece of research, the second something a little more delicate that required Tope's computer skills and sensitive links with the Telephone Unit, because Henry wanted this doing via the rear entrance.

Tope did his usual 'umming', but didn't ask why. The first request was easy, the second less so. He said he would get back to Henry next day.

Before hanging up Henry said, 'Incidentally, I bumped into an old friend of yours today . . . Steve Flynn.' Tope emitted a loud groan. 'Just to warn you,' Henry said. 'I know he fishes for information from you, because of what he has on you. Don't be tempted.'

Henry was certain he heard Tope's Adam's apple rise and fall in his throat. He hung up with a smirk – one that hurt his face.

Then he stretched out, tilted his head sideways and balanced the ice-pack on his cheek, and settled down for the night.

The wind slapped the halyards on the rigging of the yachts in the marina, making a lovely clanking noise. Flynn paused to listen to the sound that made him smile. He sighed, wishing he was back in Gran Canaria. It was in the same zone as the UK, difference being if he had been there he would have been dressed in a T-shirt, three-quarter-length pants and flip-flops, cruising from bar to bar in Puerto Rico's commercial centre. The evening would still be young – and warm.

Instead it was bone-chilling, the wind zipping in up the Lune estuary.

He hunkered down and walked alongside the canal up to the barge, stepping over on to the rear deck. He immediately saw that the door leading to the living area had been smashed open and was hanging off its hinges. The door was pretty substantial and to smash it off must have taken some doing.

In spite of the beer and whisky, he became alert, although he had no reason to suspect this was anything other than the work of kids. He placed his beer bottles on the deck and walked to the door. He did not expect anyone to be inside but if there was he had already alerted them to his presence when he came noisily aboard.

Three steps led down to the door. He went sideways down them and pushed the door away from him. Although the interior of the boat was in darkness, Flynn's eyes were fairly well adjusted from having strolled back from the pub and he could immediately see the disarray inside. Galley cupboards were open, pots, pans and utensils were scattered around, and the furniture overturned.

Flynn swore. He bowed his head and ducked in order to get inside and fumble for the light switch that was somewhere to his right. His fingers ran down the wall, his arm stretched out.

It was at that moment the two men moved in for him – one from behind, one from the front.

Flynn saw the blur of movement ahead of him. A dark shape, a hooded man moving quickly, and also the swish of something moving through the air, a stick or a bat, perhaps. It connected to his outstretched forearm, smashing against his ulna, sending a jarring spasm up past his elbow to his shoulder.

He didn't see the man behind him, just felt the flat-footed kick against the base of his spine that jerked his whole body and catapulted him onto his knees down the steps, crashing hard on to the wooden floor, where he sprawled out at the feet of the man in front of him.

The mistake the attackers made in those first, brutal moments was that they didn't hit him across the head, to at least disorientate him, so by the time Flynn hit the floor, he was retaliating.

Using the forward momentum of being kicked down, he went for the man's legs in front of him, finding purchase with his own foot against a cabinet and propelling himself forwards.

He grabbed the legs and in a moment the guy was toppled over onto his back and Flynn was scampering across him, chin in, head down, working on his strategy as he went.

There wasn't much choice in the matter. It had to be this one, then the other. The one on the floor had to be dealt with instantly, then maybe used as some sort of shield against the other.

Flynn dropped on him, chest to chest, face to face, combining the fall with a powerful head-butt. Head-butts were not the best means of attack. There was no escaping the fact that the move entailed the clashing of two heads and if the deliverer of the blow didn't connect accurately – forehead to bridge of nose – both parties suffered.

Flynn had delivered his fair share of head-butts in his time, mostly well aimed and timed, and, of course, in his younger days when he was faster and sharper.

So even though this head-butt was powerfully delivered, the man underneath saw it telegraphed and dinked his head sideways. Flynn connected with fresh air, missed him completely. This man was faster. Big realization.

By this time, still only a few seconds into the conflict, the man behind who had kicked Flynn into the boat was moving quickly to help his mate and Flynn lost his advantage – the advantage he had hoped to achieve by showing them this was no pushover and they'd bitten off more than they could digest.

Flynn's head came back, and, angled slightly so that his face gave a perfect target, the men made up for their earlier mistake of not putting him down straight away. Something hard, heavy and metallic was smashed down hard across his head. It was like being hit by a frying pan – in fact, it could have been a pan from the galley. Flynn tumbled sideways off the man, who spun and rolled up onto his feet with ease, whilst Flynn's brain was sent into free-fall by the blow.

Then the blows began to connect.

He rolled into a foetal ball, forearms covering his head, trapped tight against a bench seat, unable to do anything now but cower and try to protect himself.

They hit him hard, one with a baseball bat, the other with the butt of a gun.

Then they stopped. Next thing Flynn was hauled roughly into a half-seating position and the barrel of the gun – it was a machine-pistol of some sort – was rammed underneath his chin, then forced upwards so he looked along it, along the hands and arms of the man holding it, who squatted in front of him, up to his ski-masked face.

The ski mask. One of the simplest forms of terror inducement that existed. A hood with eye holes and a mouth hole. An innocent garment that, worn under the right circumstances – usually during a violent robbery – was so terrifying that it immediately gave offenders a massive psychological advantage over victims and witnesses.

The eyes behind the mask. The obscene mouth.

Flynn's head was swimming from the blow, but he also felt fear.

'Jeez . . . what . . . hell!' he gasped, trying to give the impression of total incomprehension, although he was trying to work out the angles and odds now.

The man pushed the muzzle of the gun deep and hard into the soft flesh under the V of Flynn's jaw.

'OK, tough guy, you finished fighting?'

'Yuh,' he said and his brain clicked: accent.

'Good.' The man's head moved closer to Flynn's face. Flynn could smell his breath and sweat and cheap deodorant. An unpleasant combination.

Flynn looked to his right and saw the other man standing there slapping a baseball bat into the palm of his hand, a corny but effective gesture.

'Now . . . where is it?'

'What? Where's what?' Flynn sneered.

'Whatever you took from the dead woman. We want it.'

'I didn't take anything.'

The gun was jammed further into his throat and in a concurrent line of thought, Flynn worked out that if the trigger was pulled, the bullet would rip up through his tongue, behind his teeth, up through the roof of his mouth. His brain would be removed, the top of his skull would explode outwards and there would be a hell of a mess inside the boat.

'You did. Do not lie!'

'I'm not in a position to lie,' Flynn protested. Then he lurched forward instinctively and grabbed the man's ski mask and ripped it off, and stared directly into his face.

The man laughed harshly, said, 'Fool,' and slammed his weapon sideways across Flynn's face with such force that it had the instantaneous effect of knocking him into oblivion.

Henry shifted on the settee, settled, closed his eyes – then almost leapt out of his skin when his mobile phone, left in his trouser pocket, vibrated as a text message landed.

It was unexpected because he'd forgotten the phone was there and with the signal in this area being so poor and unreliable, it was rare for anyone to get through anyway.

He pulled it out and slid it open, peering at the screen. He visualized the text having been sent, then loitering in space for a while before suddenly seeing a chance to swoop down to his phone. This was the same person who was convinced that a text could be sent with a nifty wrist-flick of the phone, like throwing a Frisbee, but not actually letting go of the phone. Henry had a fairly childlike view of the new age of technology.

The sender was Professor Baines, the Home Office pathologist. It read simply, 'Call me.'

Henry had been on the verge of serious slumber. The ice-pack had helped stem the expansion of his swelling and the painkillers plus a second JD had made him sleepy.

He forced himself into a sitting position, picked up the landline phone and dialled Baines's number, gently touching his face as the call connected.

'So they didn't keep you in overnight?' Baines said immediately.

'No, I've got my own nurse, free, on tap, works behind a bar . . . all the best attributes of a good health-care worker.'

'Lucky you . . . how are you feeling?'

'Grog and cross,' Henry muttered. 'What can I do you for?'

'Well, I haven't done any post-mortems yet, but I have found something that might be of interest to you.'

'Are you still at the mortuary?' Henry asked incredulously, his eye glancing towards the fireplace clock.

'Death never sleeps,' Baines said mysteriously. 'Yes, I am still here, surrounded by the dead – and from the looks of the mortuary assistants, the undead too. But needs must.'

'What have you found?'

'As you know, I'm a tooth man. I look at dead people's teeth for various reasons, mainly selfish.'

'Hence the OBE.'

'And maybe a knighthood, if rumour is to be believed.'

'Don't hold your breath.'

'OK – banter over. These days I tend to head straight for the mouth first. Which is why I had a peer into the mouth of the woman who was pulled from the river, who has now been identified, I believe. Post-mortem now scheduled for ten-thirty tomorrow, by the way.'

'Great.'

'She'd had some bridge work done, some fillings.'

'Not unusual.'

'Not in itself, but what I consider to be unusual is that there are now two dead bodies in this mortuary who have had work carried out by the same dentist.'

Henry waited.

'The work done in the mouth of . . . ahh . . . Mrs Sunderland was done by the same dentist as the work carried out in the mouth of the unidentified girl, the murder victim we looked at earlier. Now what do you think about that?'

Flynn was woken by a combination of two things – smell and heat.

The smell was that of petrol.

The heat was from the fact that the petrol had been set alight and flames were whooshing up, along and around the interior of the canal boat.

Flynn was face down, cheek pressed into the wooden floor.

The smell was horrendous, invading his nostrils.

He moved his head, opened his eyes and looked down the length of the boat, burning with intense heat, bright flames crackling and heading quickly in his direction.

He attempted to raise himself, but slid back down on weak, rubbery arms that would not hold his weight.

'Bastards,' he groaned.

They'd set the boat alight with him still in it, unconscious.

Flynn pushed himself up again, head swooning, disorientated slightly, but knowing he had to crawl backwards to the door.

Then his brain cells started working again and he realized that he hadn't been left in the position where he'd been bashed unconscious. The men had dragged him through the galley area, along the floor, through the living room, the full length of the boat and into the bedroom where he'd been dumped. Then they'd doused the boat in petrol and lit it.

Leaving him trapped by the flames.

To get out of the door would mean running through a tunnel of fire, thirty feet long, which was now fearsomely hot and would roast him instantly.

Flynn rose to his knees and peered through the flames at the door beyond, the one which had been kicked off its hinges by the men, and had been loosely pulled back into place when they left.

He felt heat on his face, scrambled backwards against the bed. He kicked the bedroom door closed, and smoke hissed through the gap underneath it.

Now the situation had slightly changed.

Instead of being burned to a crisp, he was probably going to die in the way most people do when trapped by fire – by inhaling noxious smoke. Both were gruesome, terrible deaths.

The bedroom door, thin and not very substantial, even started to glow.

Flynn scrambled across the bed, which almost filled the small room. He ripped the flimsy curtains away from the window, unlatched and opened it and started to squeeze himself out like toothpaste in a tube. It was a very small window. But in his haste to escape the flames he'd forgotten the geography of the boat. It was only when he was halfway out of the window did he realize he should have crawled out of the one on the other side, which would have given him the chance to drop onto the canal bank.

Instead, as he slithered out he dropped straight into the

ice-cold muddy waters of the Lancaster Canal just as the flames
in the galley burned through the rubberized taps that connected
the gas cylinder to the cooker and the boat exploded.

SEVEN

enry was about to pour his third generous measure of
Jack Daniel's when the phone rang. He picked it up,
instinctively checking the time as he did – that ingrained
reflex hammered into cops from day one: '*Time, time, time.*' It
was one of those simple but fundamental things that can always
be challenged. If you got the time wrong, what else did you get
wrong? A good defence lawyer could easily slide his stiletto into
that crack and prise open what should have been a watertight case.

He saw it was 11.12 p.m. Mentally noted it.

He recognized the voice of DI Barlow at the other end and
exclaimed, 'Why are you calling me?' He didn't mean it nega-
tively, just that he expected Barlow to be home by now, off duty.

'You know how it is,' he said. Henry knew. Detectives worked
ridiculous hours. It was in their nature and, mostly, didn't even
get paid for the overtime worked. They did it because they liked
it. 'I just happened to be earwigging the PR when a job came
up. I recognized the name and wasn't a million miles away, so
I checked it out.'

'Job being?'

'That guy Flynn, the ex-cop?'

Henry's heart lurched at the mention of the name. 'Go on,' he
said guardedly.

'Says he's been attacked and that the canal boat he's been
staying on has been blown up.'

'Are both statements true?'

'Well, I'm standing here on the canal side. Flynn looks a mess
and there's bugger all left of the boat . . . and he's demanding
to see you.'

'Bloody drama queen,' Henry thought.

*   *   *

Despite Alison's protestations, he commandeered her four-wheel-drive monstrosity, and with her gentle but insistent haranguing echoing in his ears, he picked his way along the jet-black country lanes, realizing just how hard it was to drive safely with only one good eye and two JDs. Street lighting began to appear spasmodically as he motored into the environs of Lancaster with a sigh of relief, finally dropping into the city from the fells.

He felt haggard and tired and knew he should have left it until morning. He could easily have delegated it to Barlow and the local CID and nothing would have been spoiled or lost. But Henry was insatiably curious, even more so the older he got. He loved to know, see, feel things first hand. This trait actually made him a poor, but popular, manager, always leading from the front, never asking someone to do something he could not tackle himself.

He knew that 'real' managers delegated, got others to do the dirty work. They dealt with strategy, not tactics, but Henry loved being hands-on, loved 'playing out' as he called it. So far, by dint of a careful balancing act, he'd managed to survive as a detective superintendent, but occasionally he'd had words in his lugholes from his own bosses. Rein back, let others do.

On that night he knew he could have let others 'do'. Maybe should have done. But couldn't, especially when Steve Flynn's name was in the pot. To have him involved twice in one day . . . a coincidence even Henry found hard to swallow.

Traffic in Lancaster at that time of night was almost non-existent, in complete contrast to its daytime state of total gridlock. Henry made it through easily and less than ten minutes later was at Conder Green, near to where Jennifer Sunderland's body had been heaved out of the river. Passing the Stork, he then turned right onto the road that led directly to Glasson Dock.

This was a place Henry knew well, somewhere he had a personal history. A place where, over a dozen years earlier, he'd almost died when he came face to face with a Mafia hitman who'd been after his blood.

He shivered at the memory. Even though it was so long ago it occasionally still came back to haunt him. Not simply because of the personal danger he'd faced, but because of the jeopardy his wife Kate had been put in, through no fault of her own. She too had been lucky to survive.

Mentally shrugging off the cloud, he drew onto the rough stone surface of the large car park adjacent to the yacht basin and parked the nose of the four-wheel-drive facing the water.

He climbed stiffly out and was immediately struck by the biting, unforgiving wind coming in from the estuary. It was tinted, though, with a whiff of smoke and petrol which he could smell clearly even through his facial injury.

He palmed a couple more paracetamols into his mouth, swallowed them using saliva and hoped they would complement the painkillers he'd already taken that night. Last thing he needed was to overdose.

Then he started to walk the hundred or so metres to the point where the yacht basin and the Lancaster Canal joined.

There was a line of emergency vehicles nose-to-tail, crammed onto the canal towpath, together with emergency lighting. Two fire tenders headed the queue, so wide they virtually blocked the path. Two marked police cars were behind, then a plain car and then an ambulance on the grassy area at the end of the car park. Lots of blue lights flashed, lots of people scurried around, and it was apparent that the explosion had brought out most of the local population, eager to see some fun. A police crime-scene tape had been stretched across the path to keep the onlookers back.

A little further on, just out of Henry's eye-line, thick, heavy smoke plumed upwards into the atmosphere, visible even against the dark night. He assumed this was from the remnants of the barge.

He walked towards the ambulance which had its back doors open, activity going on inside. As he got closer he could see two people, a female paramedic, clad in the usual hospital green overalls, and a casualty: Steve Flynn.

Flynn was leaning back on the bench seat inside the ambulance holding an oxygen mask over his face whilst the paramedic squatted in front of him, gently dabbing the side of his face that Henry could not see with an antiseptic cloth of some sort. Henry recognized the paramedic as one of the two who had been at the drowning scene earlier and he wondered quickly what sort of hours they worked.

'That's nice – cool,' Flynn's muffled voice said through the mask, commenting on the work being done by the paramedic. He didn't seem to have noticed Henry yet.

'You really should let us take you to hospital . . . you need looking after,' the lady paramedic said. The last four words were spoken with more than an undercurrent of suggestiveness and, maybe, Henry thought sourly, a little unprofessional.

'You're doing a great job as it is,' Flynn said. 'Lovely touch.'

'Thanks,' she gasped and dropped her face so she had to angle it at Flynn with a look of lust tempered with shyness.

Henry, trying not to vomit, cleared his throat.

The paramedic's head turned quickly, guiltily.

Flynn turned less quickly and Henry realized he'd known he was there all along and was just winding Henry up by flirting with the lady medic. Henry saw the injuries to Flynn's face and saw they looked similar to his own, though clearly not as serious.

'What happened?' he asked.

The blast had ripped the canal boat apart. The roof had been blown off, scattering debris across a wide area, and what remained of the boat, basically just the hull, had keeled over and sunk into the canal, which was about six feet deep at this point. It reminded Henry of the German merchant vessels that had been blown up in Bordeaux harbour in a commando raid in World War Two. The boat had slumped over, torn apart by a ferocious blast, and was obviously beyond any sort of repair.

Henry had listened to the early conclusions of the chief fire officer at the scene, which supported Flynn's version of events, at least as to the cause of the explosion, if not what happened beforehand.

A combination of accelerant, gas from the bottle underneath the sink and deliberate ignition equalled big BOOM.

And if Flynn's story was true, he was lucky to have escaped with his life. If he hadn't regained consciousness in time, he'd have been vaporized.

As Henry surveyed the mess, Barlow came towards him.

'Boss, I take it you've spoken to Mr Flynn?'

'At the ambulance. You think he's telling the truth?'

'Not sure. He wouldn't tell me much, wanted to speak to you. What did he say?'

Henry pulled a face. 'Not much, either,' he replied, uncertain as to why he wanted to keep Flynn's story under wraps for the time being. Detective habit, possibly. The old-fashioned state of mind, knowledge and power, coupled with the mental jigsaw of bits of evidence and information slowly coming together, gradually forming a picture.

'Surely he must've said something?' Barlow insisted.

'Well, yeah, something . . . just remembers waking up and finding the boat on fire, so he squeezed out of a window. It was a bit jumbled, though. He must've cracked his head.'

'You think it's something to do with Jennifer Sunderland? It sounds like it was started deliberately.'

Henry shook his head. 'Nah – doubt it. Why should it be?'

Barlow gave a little shrug and said, 'Dunno, just a thought. What then?'

'Don't know,' Henry said.

The paramedics could not persuade Flynn to let them take him to hospital, so when another emergency call came up, they had to leave quickly.

Henry witnessed the parting of Flynn and the lady paramedic, heart-rending to nauseating. She was clearly smitten by Flynn, even though he estimated Flynn was at least double her age.

The refusal to go to hospital meant Flynn was left abandoned next to the canal, shivering, with an ambulance blanket wrapped around his shoulders, and no home to go to.

Henry felt no sympathy for him, even if his predicament was not of his own doing.

'What's your plan?'

Flynn shook his head. 'I'll crash down in the shop.' He jerked a thumb in the direction of the chandlery.

'When are you going to tell them about the boat?' Henry asked, referring to the friends he had come to help.

'On top of their already massive problems . . .' Flynn's voice faded out and he sighed, deflated. 'Maybe in the morning . . . Diane's spending the night at the hospital.'

Henry regarded him. Already he had briefly considered offering him a room for the night at the Tawny Owl, knowing that there were two unoccupied ones, but he'd dismissed that idea, wanting to keep his distance from Flynn, and also keep him away from Alison. But he could already hear Alison's voice ringing in his ears if she ever learned that he had left Flynn out in the cold.

With a reluctant change of mind, Henry said, almost under his breath so Flynn might not hear, 'You're welcome to stay at the Owl tonight.' His voice sounded like someone else was saying the words. Henry, doing something nice for Flynn. It was like he'd been taken over by some benign spirit.

Trouble was, as much as it irked him, he knew it was the right thing to do. Even so, it made him shiver with repulsion.

Flynn gave him an incredulous look. 'Seriously?'

Henry nodded. 'You want to follow me back in Diane's car?'

'Breakfast, too? Full English?'

'Don't push it,' Henry growled.

'I just need to nip into the shop, though – and liberate some more clothes.'

An hour after arriving at the Tawny Owl with Flynn in tow, and Alison meeting, greeting and fussing over them both (did she fuss more over Flynn, though, Henry wondered), Henry was still up trying to chill out with the help of that third JD, but found it hard as his brain churned over the events of what was now yesterday.

His face pounded with pain, which also served to keep him awake.

Alison – once Flynn had been shown to his room (did she take too much time up there with him, Henry's suspicious mind asked) – came back down, but was unable to tempt Henry to bed because of the spinning thoughts. Eventually she admitted defeat and left him sitting in front of the fire, glass in one hand, bottle in the other.

The owner's living room was also the dining room and after a few minutes' thought, Henry picked up his briefcase and shifted himself across to the dining table.

He clicked the locks open and took out the folder inside, which he opened and tipped out the contents.

This was a copy of the file regarding the unsolved murder of the unidentified young woman he'd been at the mortuary to look at. The murder investigation that had got nowhere almost six months down the line.

He placed glass and bottle on the table, started to read.

Flynn was impressed by the standard of the refurbishment and thanked Alison profusely. He asked her to pass on his thanks to Mr Grumpy, too.

'Not a problem,' she smiled.

'Do you think our lives will be forever entwined, Alison?'

'They will, but only you and I will ever truly know what happened that night.'

'You're right.' She'd saved him from a killer and he'd saved her from the complexities of an ugly justice system that didn't always work for real justice. But he also knew that Henry Christie had slotted the pieces together.

Meaning the three of them shared a very big secret.

'I love Henry, by the way,' she said, having seen a certain look come into Flynn's eyes as they wished each other good night. 'Madly.'

'I can see that. He's wild about you, too.'

'We're good for each other and nothing will get in our way,' she said determinedly.

'Point taken,' Flynn conceded, even though he was dying to ask what Henry's wife thought about the situation.

They had a quick hug and Alison left him to it.

First thing he did was head for the well-stocked minibar to liberate three Bell's whisky miniatures which he poured into a glass and downed in one. This made him cough and bring something up from the back of his throat which was like a lump of black snot when he spat it into the toilet, result of smoke inhalation.

Then he peeled off his wet clothes and had a long shower which felt incredible after his immersion in the Lancaster Canal.

Dried off, heated up, and wearing the provided robe, he sat on the bed and helped himself to another whisky, which he sipped this time without coughing and mulled over his day.

His eyelids started to droop and he wasn't far off sleep when it hit him.

'The bugger,' he said angrily. But there was nothing he could do about it at that moment. Instead he removed the robe, slid in between the wonderful cotton sheets and closed his eyes, thinking lustful things about a female paramedic.

Well rested and with his head feeling very clear, which surprised him after having been unconscious, even if it was for such a short time, and wearing his second set of new togs within two days, Flynn sauntered down for breakfast at eight next morning. His face was very swollen, cut, a puffy mess, but the pain was being kept chemically at bay by the painkiller slipped to him by his favourite paramedic – whose name he had failed to get.

A few other guests were at tables in the dining area, having breakfast served by Alison's stepdaughter Ginny. When she saw Flynn, her face brightened. She gave a squeak of excitement and rushed toward him with a big hug, after which she perused him critically, her face wincing slightly at his injured visage.

'Mum says you can have breakfast with us, if you like.'

'That would be great.'

They exchanged pleasantries as Ginny led Flynn through to the private accommodation at the back of the pub, where Flynn found a jaded-looking Henry Christie slumped at the dining-room table, munching a croissant and drinking coffee, the unsolved-murder file open next to him. Something he closed as Flynn entered.

He looked at Flynn as though he hoped last night's magnanimous gesture was just a bad dream and was devastated when it wasn't.

Alison emerged from the kitchen and, just to wind up Henry, Flynn planted a smacker on her cheek and said, 'Mornin', lover.'

'Stop it,' she said with a smirk.

Henry watched, annoyed, especially when Flynn gave him a wink.

'Take a seat and I'll get you food. Full English?'

'Love that,' Flynn said, raising his eyebrows at Henry. He sat down at the end of the table, ninety degrees to Henry.

'Help yourself to coffee,' Alison added over her shoulder as she disappeared into the kitchen. There was a filter coffee machine

on the table and Flynn poured himself a steaming mug full of
the superbly smelling brew, to which he added a dash of milk
and sipped it appreciatively.

'Morning, Henry.'

'Morning, Steve.'

'Sleep well?'

'No – you?'

'Like a tot plied with Calpol.' He sipped his coffee. 'You think
I might call Diane? I'd better do that sooner rather than later.'

Henry indicated the handset on the table and said, 'Help yourself.' He picked up the remains of his croissant and folded it into
his mouth.

Flynn called Diane at the hospital. She sounded exhausted and
slightly bewildered. When Flynn said he had some bad news for
her about the boat, it didn't seem to register, so he didn't push
it. He did learn that Colin had slept well and that she was being
picked up by her sister to get some sleep at her place and that
Flynn could keep the Smart Car for the day. He thought it would
probably be better anyway if he told her face to face that her
beloved canal boat had been destroyed. And there was every
chance she would hear it from another source anyway.

As he hung up Alison came back bearing a wonderful breakfast,
the likes of which Flynn hadn't seen for many a year. He gave
an appreciative whistle.

'All locally sourced, everything within a two-mile radius,' she
boasted proudly.

'Fantastic. Thank you.'

Alison looked at both men and chuckled. 'You could be
bookends.'

'What do you mean?' Henry said.

'With your faces. Sort of matching. But opposite.'

The men glanced at each other, neither enamoured by this
idea, and Alison backed off, seeing she had hit a bum note.

Flynn chewed the end off a pork sausage. He said, 'Henry?'

'Mm?'

'Tell me how you got your injury – y'know, your face.' He
pointed a fork at the detective.

'Why?'

'Seems hellish similar to mine, doncha think?' Flynn leaned

over and closely inspected Henry's wound, part of which still bore the faint imprint of the weapon that caused it. 'What was it? An automatic pistol of some sort? Two men?' Henry kept shtum and let him speculate. 'I know it was two men because it's been on the local news. Just been watching it on TV in my room.'

Henry sipped his coffee.

'Circumstances are a bit vague . . . something to do with the mortuary and the police spokesperson really had no answers as to why you were assaulted, but that two violent armed men are being hunted. Well, they didn't give your name, but it was you, wasn't it?'

Henry sighed. Waited. Deductions always intrigued him.

'And if that's the case, when exactly were you going to reveal to me that we were beaten up by the same men?'

'If it ever became a necessity.'

Flynn bit another chunk of sausage. 'You think you know me, don't you?'

'Slightly.'

'Well in that "slightly", you should know something.'

'What?'

'That no one attacks me and destroys what is essentially my home, and property belonging to two dear friends of mine and thinks they'll get away with it.' The words were said very flatly, matter-of-fact. Which made them all the more scary. 'Now – you can let that happen and when I catch those two guys, and I will, Henry, there'll be some very fucking unpleasant business you'll have to clean up. You can go a long way to prevent that – if you want.' He shoved the last segment of the sausage into his mouth.

'Is that a threat of some sort?'

'Just pure fact, Henry. I nearly died last night and, to put it mildly, I'm fuming about it. But I'd rather you just did your job, caught them and dealt with 'em. Which means us maybe doing some sharing of information.'

'How exactly do you propose to get any leads? They were masked, they took you by surprise, they knocked you out . . . and also, there's nothing to say they were the same men who attacked me. You surprised two burglars on the boat. The ones who attacked me did so openly.'

Flynn snorted. 'Don't insult my intelligence, Henry.'

The two men glared at each other.

It was Flynn who relented. 'Look, tell you what – you show me yours, I'll show you mine. Let's stop pussyfooting around, eh?'

'You first,' Henry said.

'OK.' Flynn cleared his throat. 'They wanted what I'd taken from Jennifer Sunderland.'

'And that was . . . ?'

'I dunno, because I didn't take anything.'

'Did they say what they were after?'

'No, I had to guess.'

'So what did you take?'

Flynn burst his fried egg, wishing it was Henry's face he was driving his fork into. 'I won't even grace that with an answer. Now show me yours.'

'They were after something in her property.'

'I assume they didn't find it.'

'Not if they came knocking on your door later.'

Flynn concentrated on his breakfast, Henry his coffee.

Flynn broke the uncomfortable silence. 'Have you spoken to Mr Sunderland?'

'I have – but I haven't asked him the obvious question.'

'Is it in your plans to do so?'

'Duh – yeah. I want to get the PM done first, though. See if that throws up any nooky questions for him. He's due to be seen later today.'

'I'd like to get involved in some way,' Flynn said. 'After all, I did see one of them when I yanked his mask off, even though it was only for a second before I got knocked out.'

'Would you recognize him again?'

'I think so.'

'What about spending some time with a police artist?'

'Give it a go.'

'But I think that's as far as your involvement should go,' Henry said. 'And about what you've just said, if you take the law into your own hands, I'll get you, Steve.'

Once more the men stared rigidly at each other.

Thing was, Flynn believed him.

'And anyway,' Henry said more brightly, 'don't you have a shop to run?'

The phone rang and Henry answered it. 'Tawny Owl, can I help?'

Flynn smirked as he heard this. Henry sounded like a Girl Guide leader. Henry shot him another chilling stare.

It was Barlow calling from Lancaster nick. 'Yes, it is me, Ralph,' Henry said. 'Not good . . . Face still sore, swollen . . . Look, Mrs Sunderland's PM is scheduled for ten-thirty this morning, can you cover it for me? I want to have a look at something and then speak to someone on my way in. It's . . . I've been asked to take over that unsolved murder . . . Yeah, the young girl . . . I think you worked that, didn't you? Hm, yeah . . . I want to check out the scene and also see Joe Speakman on the way in . . . Yeah, he lives in this neck of the woods . . . I know he's retired, but I virtually pass his house on the way in, so I'm going to call on spec, get his perspective on it . . . Bye . . .' Henry hung up.

'What was that?' Flynn asked.

'A cold case I'm reviewing.'

'One of Joe Speakman's? I know him, he used to be my DCI way back.'

'Well, he retired earlier this year, without much notice.' Henry suddenly had a thought and snatched up the phone and jabbed in a number. 'Prof? It's me, Henry – I've asked DI Barlow to attend Jennifer Sunderland's PM in my stead . . . look,' he dropped his voice conspiratorially, 'I'd be obliged if you didn't mention the teeth thing to him . . . Cheers . . . Don't ask.'

Henry hung up and turned back to Flynn, who had a knowing smile on his face.

'Keeping secrets?' Flynn said.

'Oh shit,' Henry said.

'What?'

'My car! It's at Lancaster nick . . . and there's no way I can use Alison's . . . it's cash and carry day today.'

'If you can fit your fat arse into the passenger seat of a Smart Car, I'll give you a lift,' Flynn said, an offer accepted with bad grace by Henry.

EIGHT

S he had died a brutal death. Savagely beaten in a frenzied
attack – particularly about the head – half-strangled, as
Henry had seen at the mortuary. The strangulation had not
killed her, but the brain trauma from the assault had.

The day before visiting the mortuary he had only half-perused
the murder book, but had then read it thoroughly in the early
hours of this morning before tumbling into bed with Alison and
falling deeply asleep for the next few hours, before taking a
convivial breakfast with Flynn.

Joe Speakman, the retired detective superintendent, had
been SIO in charge of the investigation into the murder of the
unidentified female.

Henry had got on well with Speakman, who was then one of
the four detective superintendents heading FMIT. With all the
swingeing cost-cutting going on, the chief constable had been
looking at the possibility of reducing the number of superintendents
on FMIT from four to three and Henry had been right in his
cross-hairs. Slightly ahead of the other three in length of service,
he was ripe to be pushed into retirement.

It had been a bit of a shock when Speakman had put his ticket
in out of the blue. And a pleasant surprise as far as Henry was
concerned. It gave him some breathing space. He didn't want to
retire just yet, had found a new lease of life as regards the job
and personal life and was happy to be considering his options
without the chief breathing down his neck.

But Speakman's sudden departure had left quite a lot of unfinished business which had to be divvied out amongst the remaining
detective supers and Henry had been dealt an unsolved murder.
Which was absolutely fine by him.

His reading of the murder book – the book in which the SIO was
required to maintain in every murder enquiry, recording decisions
made, actions taken, reasons for doing things and a whole myriad
of other things relating to the murder – left him slightly puzzled.

Not that there was anything intrinsically wrong with it. It just seemed . . . listless, lacklustre . . . Henry could not quite find the right word. It was like Speakman was bored by what he was doing.

Murder books were usually fascinating reading. As events unfolded, evidence was uncovered, suspects were identified, people arrested . . . whatever . . . they could be as compelling as a thriller and often gave an insight into how the mind of the SIO worked.

Speakman's murder book was just a bit sparse in every detail.

Maybe it was because he was winding down to retirement that only he knew about. Maybe his heart wasn't in it and he was just contemplating how to spend his lump sum. Henry had half-heard that he had invested in property abroad.

Henry could not say . . . which is why he wanted to drop in on Speakman unannounced on his way to Lancaster and chat things through.

As he wriggled into the passenger seat of the Smart Car, trying not to look too embarrassed by its lack of street cred, his mind flipped over the contents of the murder book and the other related items he'd been reading.

The young woman's body had been discovered by a dog-walker in Moss Syke wood, a smallish copse within metres of the south-bound carriageway of the M6, south of junction 34, which was the Lancaster north exit. The wood was accessible by a lane that ran off the A683, the main road into Lancaster that Henry would eventually be driving along that morning.

She had been dragged a few metres into the woods and discarded there, but with no real effort made to hide or bury her. It was obvious she would be discovered sooner rather than later and the pathologist's estimate was that she'd probably been left there for perhaps twelve hours and had been murdered about four hours prior to that in a different, unknown, location, probably indoors.

That was the first thing that struck Henry: no real effort to hide the body. What did that say about the killer?

Confidence, Henry guessed. Confident that even though the body would be found, he – or she – would not get caught and that, possibly, she would remain unidentified.

So if the killer knew that, what did it say about the victim?

Henry's initial thoughts turned straight to people-trafficking, or perhaps migrant workers. Many nationalities came to work the cockle beds on Morecambe Bay, for example, not just the unfortunate Chinese people who had been caught up in the disaster a few years back when twenty-odd immigrant cockle-pickers were drowned after being caught by the fast-rising tides.

If she wasn't local, and possibly she came from Eastern Europe, as the dental work suggested, then was she here illegally? If she was, then identifying her would be seriously hard. Her fingerprints had already been checked without success. And if she couldn't be named, that always made a murder investigation much harder.

'Fuck,' Henry thought.

And what was the link with Jennifer Sunderland, or was the dental aspect merely just a coincidence? He wondered what the odds were. Two women met violent deaths within, say, ten miles of each other and six months apart, and both had their dental work carried out by the same person.

'Slim.'

'What was that?' Flynn said.

'Did I say that out loud?'

'You surely did.'

'Sorry.'

'That's OK.'

They had reached the junction with the A683 at the village of Hornby. Turning left would take them towards Lancaster, passing through and under the bridge that formed junction 34 of the M6.

Flynn had told Henry he did not mind going around to Joe Speakman's house on the way into Lancaster, then dropping Henry off at Lancaster nick where he could pick up his car.

As Flynn joined the main road in the Smart Car – not a car designed to carry two strapping men in comfort – Henry said, 'Look, there's something else I'd like to do before seeing Joe, so I tell you what, just drive me to the nick, I'll pick up my car and then you can get on with what you have to do. I'll contact you later if there are any developments. And thanks for the lift.'

'What do you want to do?'

'Check out the murder scene re this cold case.'

'Is it nearby?'

'Slight detour, but on the way.'

'I'll drive you there,' Flynn said brightly. 'Just direct me and tell me all about the case if you want.'

Less than ten minutes later, following Henry's directions, Flynn slowed the car and turned left into Grimeshaw Lane, nothing more than a narrow, rutted track off the A683 which ran at a south-westerly angle, but virtually parallel with the M6. The lane passed Moss Syke woods, after which it veered right and crossed the motorway on a narrow bridge.

Diane's tiny car thudded unhappily, but gamely, in the ruts, until after a few hundred metres they reached the woods, just a few acres of tightly compressed trees, nothing spectacular. Far enough away from any prying eyes, because there were no buildings nearby, but handy enough to dump a body.

Henry had the murder file on his knees and shuffled out the crime-scene photographs, trying to compare them to where he was now and also in relation to a plan-drawer's map of the location. He kept peering at the documents and glancing up as Flynn drove at a snail's pace on the track.

'Stop here,' Henry said and got out of the car.

The woods were across to his right. Henry leaned on the car roof and took it all in. The motorway was a hundred metres beyond the far perimeter of the woods, but out of sight because of a small hill rise. Traffic noise could clearly be heard, thundering up and down, north–south.

He looked to his right, back down along Grimeshaw Lane towards the A683, which he could see in the distance.

To his left the track carried on to the motorway bridge, beyond which it became Ridge Lane and went on to the Ridge Estate in Lancaster, a fairly middling council estate. The road over the motorway bridge was nothing more than a track, servicing the farmland either side of the motorway. Henry turned to look at the vast area of countryside behind him to the east. Then he turned back and looked at the woods.

Flynn got out and joined him.

Henry pointed. 'She was discovered just in there.'

Flynn nodded. Henry hadn't told him very much – hardly anything – about the girl's murder, even though he had asked, but he said, 'Victim, location, offender . . . usually a link of some sort.'

Henry nodded. It was a standard quote, one right out of the Murder Investigation Manual. 'Unfortunately only the location is known in this case.'

'Still,' Flynn pulled a ruminative face, 'the location usually says a lot . . . I take it she wasn't murdered here, though?'

'No.'

'Not a place you'd trip over by accident,' Flynn said.

No, it wasn't, Henry thought. Whoever dumped her here would probably have had local knowledge.

'Are you going into the woods today?' Flynn asked.

'Maybe later. Let's call on Joe Speakman first.'

Henry had once been to Speakman's house, a few years earlier for a party of some sort, but for the life of him could not remember the event clearly, because he had been drunk. Possibly a fortieth, but he did recall where the house was and could direct Flynn there. It was not far from Moss Syke wood, but he attached no importance to that.

Flynn did a six-point turn in the tiny car and bumped it back down Grimeshaw Lane without ripping the sump off it. From there it was almost straight across the A683 into Denny Beck Lane, then over the River Lune via Halton Bridge into the village of Halton itself. Then he bore right, travelling east with the river on his right, up to Halton Green, where he found Speakman's house. It was large, detached, with quite extensive private grounds, bordered by Leylandii trees and high fencing.

Flynn gave an appreciative whistle. 'Nice one. Obviously supers are paid too darn much.'

'Not nearly enough,' Henry said. 'I think it helps that his wife is, or was, something big in local government, on a similar whack to him.'

Flynn pouted and did the arithmetic. One-fifty grand plus per year. A nice little earner if you can get it.

Flynn drove up the curved drive and stopped at the front of the house alongside a TVR Tuscan in a silvery-purple colour that changed and sparkled depending on how you looked at it. He gave another whistle.

'Literally,' he said, 'they don't make 'em like that any more.'

'What do you want to do?' Henry asked him.

'I wouldn't mind saying hello. Then I'll keep out of your way.'

Henry nodded, got out and went to the front door and rang the bell on the door frame. He stood back and surveyed the front of the house with admiration. He was joined by Flynn, doing much the same thing.

But there was only so much admiring they could do before getting bored, as no one had yet answered the door. Henry pressed the bell again in a way which he hoped conveyed his impatience. He could hear it ring hollowly inside. Somewhere at the back of his mind he recalled that Speakman owned a dog of some sort. He remembered it being a noisy beast . . . but maybe it had died. It was a long time since he had been here and he still couldn't recall the reason for the party. Had it been a twenty-first?

'Maybe they saw you coming and hid,' Flynn suggested. 'Like my gran used to do when the rent man came.'

'Maybe they saw you.'

Henry was about to hold his thumb on the doorbell again when he noticed that the door, though it appeared to be closed, was just pushed tight against the frame and there was a tiny gap all around the edge. He gave it a gentle nudge. It swung open easily onto a wide hallway.

And Henry froze, instinctively shooting out his right arm to prevent Flynn from entering.

One of those sensations of utter dread shimmied through him from chest to toe as he saw the reason why the dog had not barked.

It was a red setter, one of those daft, bouncy, never exhausted dogs that went through life with an optimistic, never-say-die attitude, backed up with little brain.

He remembered the dog's name in that instant: Carlo.

Carlo, the red setter. If it was the same dog, that is.

But Carlo was now splayed out dead in the tiled hallway, half its head blown away, lying in a pool of thick treacly looking blood. One of the dog's back legs jerked, then stopped moving.

'Holy shit,' Flynn hissed in Henry's ear.

Henry was still frozen to the spot, but his mind was moving.

Flynn was right up by his shoulder and the two men exchanged a glance.

'I'll make my way around the back,' Flynn whispered.

Henry nodded. Flynn split away.

Henry sniffed up and even through his damaged face could smell the reek of cordite. He stepped into the hall and moved to the edge, trying not to step in the blood, but also trying to listen hard, his senses on fire, heart slamming, palm clammy, forehead starting to sweat. His throat was dry and saliva did not want to form as he tried to imagine what hell he had blundered into here.

The stairs to the first floor ran up from the centre of the hallway up to a landing that split in two directions.

Henry moved forward, remembering that dead ahead was the door to the kitchen at the back of the house, a large open-plan room with a dining area leading out to a massive conservatory. It was all coming back to him now.

To his left was the door to the main lounge, which was closed. Over to the right were doors to the downstairs loo, another to a smaller hallway, off which were two further ground-floor rooms, a study and a small lounge converted to a music room with a big sound and vision system.

Ahead was the open kitchen door.

Henry went to it, stepping over blobs of blood, and halted on the threshold.

The kitchen was as he recalled it. Huge enough for a central island with an extractor hood hanging above it.

It was silent in here.

Then Henry saw a pair of feet jutting out from the far side of the island. Slippered female feet, not together, but apart.

He stood there for a few more seconds, not breathing. Looking, listening . . . and only then did he step into the kitchen, again keeping to the edge by the cupboards, and manoeuvred himself into a position from which he could see the rest of the body which lay half-propped against the island.

The injuries caused by a shotgun were horrific. A stomach shot, punching a hole the diameter of a mug into the stomach, and one straight in the face. Close range, instantly fatal, and although Henry could not see the exit wounds, from the amount of blood he knew they would be huge.

It was Joe Speakman's wife, Stella.

Dead, having been shot and then staggered back against the island, and slithered down to her current position.

She was wearing a dressing gown over a nightdress. On the work surface by the sink was a kettle and two mugs. Steam wisped out of the spout of the kettle, only recently boiled. Henry glanced into the mugs. Instant coffee in each, ready to be made into a brew. Next to these items was a toaster with two pieces of toast popped up, ready to be buttered.

Stella Speakman had been preparing breakfast for two and had been shot to death in her own kitchen. It didn't take a detective to put that one together.

Henry's instinct was to squat down and have a closer look, but he could see everything he needed from where he was.

The hairs did rise on the back of his neck as he asked himself the next questions: Where was Joe Speakman? And had he done this?

Had there been some horrendous domestic dispute here, one of those 'murder all the family, then commit suicide' scenarios? Or had a burglar called?

Henry backed slowly out of the kitchen into the hallway, wondering where Flynn had gone. He pivoted on his heels, eyes pausing on the dead dog, then at the other doors off the hallway, each one closed. He listened hard – not easy because of the pounding in his ears.

A squeak, a scratching noise from upstairs. Or not?

It was tempting to go up, but he had to check the remainder of the downstairs rooms first, horribly aware that someone could be hiding, still armed with a shotgun.

He did the rooms quickly. They were empty. No bodies. No gunman.

Then he was at the foot of the stairs, behind him the dog. It had stopped twitching.

He went up slowly, feeling a second gush of adrenaline. The steps were carpeted and did not creak, so he could move silently.

At the top he turned to the door to his right, knowing it led into the main bedroom. He recalled collecting his coat from the bed when he was leaving the party. He pushed open the door gently. The entrance to the en-suite was on his left, then beyond the room opened out into a very large bedroom with a sitting area and French windows leading out to a balcony. The view from the balcony, he recalled, was stunning, sweeping down the fields to the river.

He went past the closed en-suite door into the bedroom area. The huge bed was rumpled and unmade and there was no sign of anyone.

He breathed a sigh, then back-tracked to the en-suite door, which he pushed open with his fingernail. It swung easily to reveal an expensive-looking fully tiled room, half of which was a walk-in shower.

In which was the naked body of an adult male, crumpled up.

Henry edged across to look into the shower cubicle properly.

Like his wife, Joe Speakman had been blasted to death by a shotgun. Blood, brains and water mingled down the pure white-tiled walls.

Henry was putting all this together.

Speakman showering. The wife preparing breakfast. A run-of-the-mill domestic scene. Not a murder-suicide, because Speakman had not blown his own head off.

Someone else had.

Henry heard something behind him.

He spun.

And the hooded man filled out the bathroom door, a sawn-off double-barrelled shotgun pointed directly at Henry's chest.

Flynn saw the dead dog at the same time as Henry. Up to that point he hadn't really been too concerned about proceedings. Visiting the scene of a six-month-old murder that he knew zilch about, then going on spec to see a retired SIO, even though he was vaguely curious to see what his old boss was up to, held no great interest for him.

His mind had been on plenty of other things. Primarily the fact that he'd been almost killed the night before – and was still hacking up smoke-tinged phlegm – and how he could start tracking down the two bastards who'd left him to die in a blazing inferno. Something he was planning on doing with or without Henry's help.

Then he had to think about Diane and Colin and how he would

tell her properly about the fate of the canal boat. He had tried when he phoned her earlier, but it wasn't a successful attempt at passing a message. She had not been 'with it' at all.

And also the shop. It had to be opened for business, which was the main reason for him being in the UK in the first place . . . and also his need for accommodation. Now he had nowhere to bed down. The thought of crashing out nightly at the Tawny Owl was very appealing, even though it was hardly in the most convenient of locations. Maybe he'd get one more night out of it, but anything beyond that would be very unfair to Alison – and Henry, he supposed. At some point he would have to pay and that was money he didn't have. He was not a wealthy man at all.

But when he saw the dog, his rusty but still functioning cop instincts surged to the fore.

He had been a good detective. Maybe not in Henry's league, he was reluctantly forced to admit, but one rung above competent and hard and ruthless with it.

He made his way around the perimeter of the house on the gravel path, carefully looking into each room and seeing nothing.

Then he found himself at the kitchen window, where he saw Henry looking at something on the floor. From his position, he could not quite see what, but the expression on Henry's face was grave and thoughtful as he backed out of the kitchen without even spotting Flynn at the window.

'Ten out of ten for observation skills,' Flynn muttered, about to move away from the window – until he saw the door to the utility room open slowly at the far end of the kitchen.

A man emerged.

Henry had once been winged by a shotgun blast, dozens of pellets hitting his shoulder like pebbledashing. After the numbness and disbelief, the pain had been incredible, right off the scale. But he'd survived.

He knew he would not survive this one.

Whatever was loaded in the shotgun would hit him in the sternum and drive a massive hole through the centre of his body and shatter his spine on the way out, after shredding his heart and lungs on the way.

As he faced the man in the door and his mouth dropped open, and the thought about taking a shotgun blast in his chest went through his mind, he was already throwing himself sideways.

Then there was a roar and a blur combined as Steve Flynn powered into the man, roaring like an attacking lion and using all his brute strength to take him down. But in so doing the shotgun jerked up and a barrel was discharged, splattering shot at an upwards angle into the top corner of the en-suite shower room.

Henry saw the men disappear and roll through to the bedroom.

The man held grimly on to the shotgun as he and Flynn tumbled untidily across the carpet, Flynn completely aware that the weapon between himself and the gunman was still loaded with one barrel.

They hit the floor and rolled, grappling desperately for control of the weapon, the man trying to tilt it away from him just enough so he could take Flynn's head off; Flynn, totally knowing this was what he intended, and fighting the opposite way. The man had one big advantage, though: his right forefinger was hooked into the trigger guard.

Then they struck the corner of the bed hard and they came apart.

Flynn knew it was over.

The man still held the gun. He contorted, trying to aim the weapon, but Flynn saw that his finger had come out of the trigger guard. He reacted. In that nanosecond before the finger once against instinctively found its place on the double trigger, Flynn's right hand shot palm-out and smashed the barrel upwards just as the finger jerked on the trigger.

The sound of the blast was incredible.

Flynn's face was only inches away from the discharge. He heard the hammer connect and hit the cartridge. He felt the kickback of the explosion within the chamber, but at that exact moment he was forcing the gun hard against the man's chest, so it was pointing upwards under his chin.

Flynn cowered away as the man's face disintegrated, completely removed by the force of the blast that went straight up into his lower jaw and lifted his mouth, nose, eyes and forehead away from the rest of his head.

Flynn rolled away, came up on to his knees, gasping, horrified, but unable to tear his eyes away from the bloody, faceless mask, who, although twitching horribly, and his right forefinger was still pulling back the triggers, was dead.

NINE

'Here.' Henry handed Flynn coffee in a mug. Flynn took it with a murmur of thanks and had a sip. It was hot and bitter. Good. 'How're you feeling?'

Flynn was sitting half-in, half-out of Diane's Smart Car, still parked in the driveway of Joe Speakman's house, now surrounded by an array of police vehicles of various descriptions.

He pouted and considered Henry's question.

There was no doubt about it, Flynn was a tough guy.

As a teenager he had served as a Royal Marines Commando in the Falkland Islands conflict with Argentina and beyond that in various well-known and not so well-known campaigns.

In his subsequent police career, on the streets and as a detective in CID and the drugs branch, he had mixed it and faced up to some of the hardest, meanest guys out there, people to whom violence was second nature. Flynn's physical prowess, courage and sheer determination – and delight at confrontation – had always seen him through. He had once been led away by two very professional hit men for questioning and then a bullet in the brain. He had emerged victorious and their bleached bones lay undiscovered, and probably would for another hundred years.

Not much got to him. He could dole it out and take it.

But a shotgun going off between himself and a man he was fighting to the death had made him a bit dithery.

Had the weapon been angled a few more degrees in his direction, it would have been his face removed, not the attacker's. He would have been dead and no doubt Henry Christie would also have been dead.

'I'm fine,' Flynn responded. He took another sip of the coffee and the tiny shake of his hand was noticeable to no one except

himself. He eyed Henry and wondered, 'Are you going to arrest
me for murder? I'd expect nothing less from you.'

'Mm, good point,' Henry toyed with him. 'Are you going to
do a runner, leave the country?'

'Course I am . . . I live in the Canary Islands, not here.'

'Will you make a statement before you go and then come back
for any court hearings?'

'Yep.'

Henry shrugged. 'In that case, no arrest.' His face became
serious in a way that Flynn had never seen. He touched Flynn's
shoulder. 'I know what you did. Thank you.'

'I'd have done the same for any arsehole.'

'I know you would.'

They held each other's look for a deep and meaningful moment
but broke it off before it became embarrassing.

'I will need your clothing for forensics.'

'You want me to strip now? I'm kinda running low on things
to wear . . . I'm down to socks and underpants and I don't think
it would be a good idea to help myself to anything from the shop
again. Running up a bit of a tab there.' Flynn glanced down at
himself. 'Although I think I'm going to have to.'

Even though the shotgun had gone off away from him and the
force of the blast was also away from him, he had been splattered
with blood as though someone had flicked a big paintbrush full
of red paint across his upper chest.

Henry said, 'If I get someone to follow you to the shop with
some forensic bags, can you get changed there? How does that
sound?'

Flynn nodded. Good idea. He had expected Henry to be
awkward and demand he strip right there and get into one of
the paper forensic suits and slippers that balloon out like the
Michelin Man.

'I'll have that,' he said. Then, 'So – who is that up there minus
his head and what is this all about, Henry? Because he ain't no
burglar, that I do know,' he concluded.

'I don't know who he is,' Henry admitted.

'And,' Flynn pushed on, 'how is this linked to Jennifer
Sunderland's death?'

Henry blinked. 'I don't know that it is. Why do you say that?'

'Because . . .' Flynn pointed to the house, 'that is one of the guys who tried to fry me up last night. He's the one whose mask I ripped off.'

It was going to be a very long day at the scene. Fortunately, because the house was detached and a little isolated, it was easy to seal off and the police were under no pressure to hurry up any processes and get the job done because someone was waiting. They took their time – and Henry made certain nothing was missed.

He turned out the whole circus: forensic and crime-scene investigators, search teams – including dogs – and detectives. Uniformed cops were tasked with house to house in the village.

Henry made it all happen with ruthless efficiency and once the wheels were in motion he appointed a detective inspector from FMIT to manage the whole scene and secure and preserve evidence.

At ten that morning, Professor Baines rolled up in his E-type Jaguar at about the same time as Ralph Barlow arrived in the CID Focus.

Barlow sought out Henry and said, 'I've put the post-mortems on hold, like you asked, and I've told Harry Sunderland we'll get back to him as soon as we can. I said something major had come up and he seemed to understand.'

Henry thanked him, then walked over to Baines, who was easing into a forensic suit over his clothes from his supply in the boot of the E-type.

'Morning,' Baines said, grim-faced.

Henry said, 'Do you mind?' He picked up one of the unopened forensic suits from the boot and ripped the packet open, started to climb into it.

When they were both suited, Henry gave him a nod and said, 'Shall we?'

It was time to walk through the crime scene with the pathologist.

By 6 p.m., the bodies of the Speakmans had been transferred to Lancaster mortuary and their dog taken to a vet – to be examined later by Baines and the vet. In order to avoid any allegations of evidence cross-contamination the as yet unidentified body of the gunman had been taken to the mortuary at Blackpool Victoria Hospital, a decision Henry made. He had also decided that a cop would stay and guard it for the time being.

The scene at the house was still undergoing scrutiny but everyone was coming close to wrapping up for the day. It would be sealed and guarded overnight and the examination would continue next day.

By then Henry was feeling pretty rocky.

He had powered himself through the day, focusing on the crime scene, pulling everything together in terms of a murder squad – even though it seemed the murderer had been apprehended. He wanted to ensure he went through the motions and setting up a Murder Incident Room would ensure that happened, even if it was only short-lived. He also had the press to deal with, issuing a holding statement to keep them off his back for a few hours, and his own bosses who had to be briefed, all of whom knew Joe Speakman and his wife well. Some had been good friends.

He had not allowed his mind to wander to the possibilities of what might have been if Steve Flynn hadn't bravely rugby-tackled the shooter and put his own life on the line. It didn't bear thinking about, so he hadn't.

But there was a dark shadow at the back of his mind that kept telling him it would hit him at some stage, that all the little brain barriers he'd erected would come tumbling down.

It didn't help him that as the day progressed his face hurt more and more, despite the painkillers. What had begun as a controlled pulse grew steadily into a throb like a bass drum, especially as he became more tired and stressed.

At seven he was at Lancaster police station, having cadged a lift there from a section patrol.

He slid into the DCI's office, the usual incumbent nowhere to be spotted, and settled into the comfortable chair behind the desk.

He exhaled, causing his face to twinge, and found a couple of tablets in his jacket pocket which he tossed into his mouth and swallowed with water from a bottle he'd bought from a dispensing machine.

'Jeez,' he hissed, all the energy draining out of him like air from a punctured tyre. He tried to concentrate again and not dwell on the fact that instead of sitting in an empty office he could easily have been laid out naked on an ice-cold mortuary slab with his friend Professor Baines about to perform a post-mortem on him. Sat there, he realized he wasn't a particularly brave man.

'It's no good,' he intoned to himself, 'I'm here, I'm alive, I'm not dead – OK, same thing – and the bad guy is dead. So c'mon, move on.'

He sat forward and pulled a sheet of paper out of the tray in the desktop printer and hovered over it with pen in hand, marshalling his thoughts. There was a lot to do, to consider.

He scribbled five headings: VICTIM, OFFENDER, LOCATION, SCENE FORENSICS, POST MORTEM.

He divided the sheet into five columns, one underneath each word, and started to jot down some lines of enquiry, firstly under the heading of 'Victim'.

—Lifestyle

—Routine

—Associates

—Relationships

Then he threw the pen down and leaned back in the chair, unable to prevent his mind from wandering, sifting over everything that had happened over the last couple of days. Starting with the cold-case review, the unidentified girl in the mortuary. Then Jennifer Sunderland's drowning – if it was! The attack by masked men at the mortuary, the same two – probably – who almost murdered Steve Flynn in an unimaginably horrendous way, destroying his friends' canal boat at the same time. The visit to Harry Sunderland . . . and the 'something' that wasn't completely right about that . . . teeth . . . and stumbling on the double murder (triple, if dog included) and Steve Flynn's claim that the guy with the shotgun was one of the two who'd tried to kill him the night before. Flynn said he was the one whose ski mask he'd ripped off. And if that was the case, he was also one of the two men who'd smashed Henry in the face at the mortuary searching for something that Jennifer Sunderland might have had with her when she drowned.

Dead girl. Teeth. Jennifer Sunderland. Robbers – one still at large. – Joe Speakman/wife. Harry Sunderland.

Henry scribbled it all down, hoping he hadn't forgotten anything.

There was another name he was tempted to add, but did not want to commit it to paper. Yet.

He sat back again in the DCI's chair, which was nice, big and comfortable, knowing his day was not yet over.

Then a grim thought hit him. He quickly got out his mobile phone.

The display showed many missed calls, the ones he'd chosen not to take, including four from Alison, together with three unread texts from her, and a voice message, all asking him to call.

Guilt cascaded through him and he punched his face mentally. One of the many ways in which he'd failed his late wife was that he did not keep in touch, keep her updated as to where and what he was up to, when he would be home, or when he was actually on his way home. He would get so engrossed in his work, so blinkered that everything else simply went out of the window. He didn't want to make those mistakes again, or any of the others because he didn't want to lose this gem . . . but a ghastly feeling came over him as he looked at the list of missed calls and texts.

Maybe the leopard couldn't change its spots.

He called the number and it was answered quickly. Almost as quickly Henry said, 'I'm really sorry. It's been a hell of a day, but no excuses.'

'Maybe you'd better tell that to my mum,' came the frosty voice of Ginny, Alison's stepdaughter. 'Shall I put her on?'

'Better had.' Shit.

The phones changed hands. 'Henry?'

'Babe, I'm really sorry . . .'

'Just wanted to know you're OK . . . I've seen the news. It looks awful, and you looked exhausted when you were talking to that TV reporter.' She didn't sound too furious.

'I'm OK . . . I just got sidetracked . . . and there was a bit more to it than was on the news,' he said. The police had held back the details concerning Henry and Flynn for the time being. 'I'll tell you when I get home.'

'When will that be?'

'Late, I expect . . . need to sort out staff and a room and stuff like that.'

'Have you eaten?'

'Er, no.' Food was something else he'd forgotten about, too. Coffee – fully leaded, as he called it – was what had kept him on the go.

'Get a snack and I'll have something hot and ready for when you land,' she ordered him.

Henry considered making a quip about the double-entendre but decided against it. 'Thanks, darling.'

'Darling! That's a new one.'

'Did I say that?'

'Yes, you did.'

'Meant it.'

After a further selection of lovey-dovey exchanges, Henry brought up the thorny subject of Steve Flynn. He asked if it would be possible to accommodate him for a few more nights at the Owl. With surprise in her voice, Alison said it would be fine but could not resist asking why he was even asking. After all, didn't he despise Flynn?

'Yes, course I do . . . but . . . I'll explain it when I get there.'

The office door opened and DI Barlow poked his head around it. He mimicked a phone call, thumb to ear, little finger to mouth.

'Got to go, sweetie . . . Yeah, you too . . . No I bloody won't bloody say it!' He hung up, aware of the redness creeping up past his collar.

Barlow gave him a knowing look.

'And?' Henry demanded.

'Joe Speakman's son is on the line.'

'Can you put him through to this number?' He pointed at the DCI's phone.

Barlow retreated and Henry had to wait for the call, wondering how he was going to handle it. The Speakmans had two kids, son and daughter, both late twenties or early thirties. The son had moved to Cyprus and the daughter lived somewhere in the south of England. Steps had been taken to trace them and obviously the first to be contacted was the son.

The phone rang. Henry said, 'Mr Speakman, I'm Detective Superintendent Henry Christie . . .'

'I know who you are . . . we met once way back, when I was a lot younger. What's happened?'

'I'm truly sorry to tell you this,' Henry began, the words not coming easily.

After dropping his blood-splattered clothes into the forensics bags, which were taken away, Flynn re-attired himself from head to foot from the clothing stock in the chandlery, then opened up for business, thinking this was the best thing to do for himself and Diane.

He was surprised by the number of customers and a good deal of money was taken in the first couple of hours from local yacht-people. He closed for lunch so he could buy a sandwich from the static caravan caff and also had a trot along the canal to have a look at the canal boat.

The sight made him shiver at the memory of his close call . . . the first of two close calls, as it happened.

Daylight revealed the true extent of the damage. The boat was beyond any sort of repair, blown apart beyond hope.

'Please be insured,' he said to himself.

Henry was frowning – not an uncommon facial expression for him – but this time there was a good reason for it as opposed to him just being a grumpy swine.

Another death message delivered. And once more a reaction to it he felt he could not criticize, but which did puzzle him slightly.

With much care, he reversed his Mercedes inch by inch out of the police garage, relieved it hadn't been scratched in the tight space, then pulled onto the streets of Lancaster, intending to drive back to the mortuary where the bodies were piling up for the pathologist.

The frown stuck on his face all the way there.

Inside, the bodies of Mr and Mrs Speakman were on trolleys next to each other on the floor space by the refrigeration unit. The creepy mortuary technician was looking them over, scratching his slightly misaligned chin thoughtfully. He appeared to have fully recovered from his face-full of CS gas, or whatever had been sprayed at him. Henry asked him how he was doing and they had a short conversation about the attack.

Henry went into the office to find Baines sitting at the desk, working on his laptop, transcribing notes from his portable tape machine. He gave a little gesture with his finger for Henry to take a seat, then another which meant, 'Just hang on, I need to do this.'

Henry sat. Frowning.

Because of something Joe Speakman's son had said. Three little-ish words: 'Probably deserved it.'

Three words – but three words too many because when Henry instantly queried them, 'What do you mean by that?' the line went dead and he could not get a reconnection.

Probably deserved it, he mulled, eyes narrowing, lips pursing, and as he stared dead ahead but unfocused at a diagram of the human body on the office wall, he didn't realize that Baines had finished and was looking intently at him.

'Face still looks a mess,' the doctor observed.

Henry turned his head slowly. 'As ever, your diagnosis is spot on.'

'Cheers.'

'Any news for me?'

Baines shook his head. 'Only that I'll be starting the post-mortems shortly.'

This caused Henry to check his watch. 'Now?'

'If I don't, they'll stack up and it'll become impossible to catch up. And knowing you, if I don't get them done, there'll be a whole new batch tomorrow.'

Henry chuckled, then sighed.

'Well, I'll do one, anyway,' Baines said. 'I reckon four hours for each.'

Henry nodded.

'But I do have some news – in between the crime-scene walk-through and now, I did Jennifer Sunderland's PM – which is what I'm typing up.' Henry waited for the bombshell. Baines said, 'Drowned. Plenty of inhaled river debris. Lungs saturated.'

'So she was alive when she went in the water?'

Baines cocked his head at Henry. 'Didn't I just say that?'

Henry smirked. 'What about the head injuries?'

'Inconclusive, but not especially serious and certainly not the cause of her death, and impossible to say whether she received the blows before or after immersion.'

'So she could have been hit and fallen in?'

'It's a possibility.'

'OK. Can I make a suggestion?'

Baines waited expectantly.

Henry checked his watch again. 'Been a cruelly long day, so why don't we start fresh tomorrow. There's nothing spoiling – so long as there's enough room for the bodies in the chiller . . . and, of course, there's also the body to sort in Blackpool.'

Baines stretched wearily. 'You're probably right.'

'Selfish, too . . . I need to spend some time getting my head around stuff and do some planning – not least how I'm going to deal with Harry Sunderland.' There was a huge amount to do, including the things that were nagging at his brain.

He had started the 'to do' list in the DCI's office, then got sidetracked by his own thoughts and calling Alison, then talking to Speakman's son – who was supposedly in Cyprus, but in reality could have been anywhere.

'I need to straighten a few things out here first,' Baines said.

'What time tomorrow?'

'I'll dig in at ten.'

That was fine by Henry. He had already decided to get home, partake in whatever food had been prepared for him, reconnect with Jack Daniels, then hit the sack, be up at six thirty, in the office at seven, sort things out, then be back in the mortuary at ten for a full day's entertainment.

He shook Baines's hand and stood up.

'Ahh, darn!' Baines said. 'There is one more thing.' He shuffled through a stack of papers. 'I talked about teeth – remember?'

Only when I dig deep, Henry thought. 'Go on.'

'Dentistry work in the mouths of that dead girl and Jennifer Sunderland – even though the young girl has a few teeth missing from her assault.'

'Yuh?' Henry said.

'Slapped what I had into the database – came up with this.'

He slid a printout to Henry who read it and went coldly excited, at the same time his anus tightening up. 'Shit,' he said. 'Is this for real?'

Baines smiled smugly. 'Love it when a plan comes together.'

Baines had already told Henry about the similarities in the mouths of the dead females, that the work had been carried out by the same dentist. The database search went on to say that at the time the information was entered into the computer, the dentist who had carried out the work had a practice in a place called Coral Bay.

Coral Bay was in Cyprus.

TEN

By leaving it to the last minute, Henry secretly hoped that Steve Flynn would have found somewhere to bed down for the night other than the Tawny Owl. It wasn't to be.

He called Flynn as he left the mortuary.

'Hi, Henry,' Flynn answered quickly.

'Hello, Flynn,' Henry said more formally. 'How are you?'

'For someone who's been half-murdered twice, OK.'

'What's happening with you tonight?'

'In what respect?'

'Sleeping arrangements.'

'Er . . . try to get a room in a Travelodge or something, I guess,' he said delicately.

'You've nothing booked?'

'Not as yet.'

Damn, Henry thought. 'You're welcome to stay at the Owl,' he said, almost choking on the words. 'I mentioned the possibility to Alison and she's fine with it.'

'Brilliant, thanks,' Flynn gushed. 'Slight problem.'

'Oh?'

'Yeah – Diane needed her car back, so I'm without wheels.'

Henry stifled a groan. 'Where are you?'

'At the hospital. I visited Colin and gave Diane the keys . . . just walking to the main exit as we speak.'

'Come down to the mortuary. I'm down here now, just about to set off to Kendleton. I can bring you back across in the morning, but it'll be an early start.' Henry hung up and pulled his face distastefully.

It took five minutes for Flynn to arrive. Henry sat waiting in the Merc, listening to an old Rolling Stones track. He flashed him as he approached. Flynn slumped in, admiring the car for the first time.

'Nice one, Henry. You must be doing well.' He clunked the door shut. 'Super's wages and all that.'

'It's financially crippling to run. I could buy a new Kia every year with what it costs to insure.'

'Mmm . . . Kia . . . Mercedes,' Flynn said as though he was trying to balance something tricky in his hands. 'Not much of a contest.'

'I know,' Henry said, pulling out of the mortuary car park.

Flynn said, 'Genuine thanks, Henry . . . I was probably going to bed down upstairs in the chandlery.'

'Look upon it as victim support.'

'So – not a friend thing.'

Henry almost choked. He drove up to the roundabout at the southern edge of Lancaster and headed north through the city, traffic still quite heavy in the mid-evening.

This was fortunate for the stolen black Range Rover, being driven on false plates, that slotted in three cars behind Henry's Mercedes. That meant it could follow him through the city without drawing attention to itself, something that would be harder, but not necessarily impossible, once out on the country roads.

'Have you made any progress?'

'Depends on what you mean?'

Flynn pouted. 'Investigating the attempt on my life, or this morning's bloodbath, maybe.'

'Forensics and CSI have been sorting the canal boat and I've had a few uniforms going house to house in Glasson – but I haven't had an update so far,' Henry admitted. 'Been slightly busy with today's bloodbath, as you call it.'

'So you're really throwing resources at it,' Flynn said with sullen sarcasm and a shake of the head. 'I doubt you'll get much from the boat or from house to house. The nearest house to the boat is a quarter of a bloody mile away.'

'I know, I know,' Henry said, not taking the criticism too well. 'What are your thoughts?'

'Depends on what you mean,' Flynn mocked Henry, who shot him a cold stare. 'Have you identified this morning's baddie yet?'

'No.'

Henry's mobile phone rang and he answered it on the Bluetooth connection speakerphone.

'Henry? It's me, Jerry Tope. Been trying to contact you all day.'

Henry tutted and rolled his eyes, miffed at himself. Tope was one of the many calls he had decided not to take. 'Yeah, sorry, Jerry, haven't had time, as you'll be aware.'

'Hi, Jerry,' Steve Flynn butted in.

'What . . . who is . . . ?' Tope stuttered.

Henry said, 'Steve Flynn's with me, we're in my car.'

'Oh, can I talk?' Tope asked uncertainly.

Henry hesitated, glanced at Flynn, then said, 'Yeah, go ahead.'

They were out of Lancaster now, heading towards Caton on the A683, passing underneath the motorway bridge at junction 34.

Tope went on, 'I've done some checking with regards to the MO thing, like you asked. You know, the spray in the face?'

'Oh yes?'

'Not as common as it used to be . . . bit of a sixties/seventies London gangster thing. More associated with girlfriend/boyfriend fallouts these days. That said, I expanded my search criteria and bit by bit I found something that might be of interest to you.' Henry waited. 'You still there, Henry?'

'Yeah, go on, Jerry.'

'Two guys operating around the fringes of the Mediterranean. Several gang-related enforcement attacks.'

Henry passed through Caton.

'And when I say gangs, I mean organized gangs as in Russian.'

'Russian?' Henry said.

'Two very bad guys suspected of very nasty attacks in Majorca, Malta and Cyprus. People have been left blind. That said, guess what? They've never yet faced a court for it, because – guess what again? No one wants to give evidence against them. I've got the details of who they are suspected to be by plundering various intelligence databases.'

'Names?' Henry said.

'Yuri Gregorov and Vladimir Kaminski.'

'Photos, prints, antecedents?'

'On file. Just because they haven't been to court doesn't mean they haven't seen the inside of a police cell, rare though that is. They do have a couple of minor convictions, actually . . . and they do have another speciality. They steal cars to order, usually big four-wheel-drive ones.'

'OK, thanks for that. You know what went on up at Joe Speakman's today?' Henry asked. Tope said he did. 'In that case, link up with the scientific people and see if one of these guys is our dead shooter.'

'You serious?' Tope said.

'Deadly.'

'Shit . . . sorry . . . can I add something?'

'Yep.'

'These guys are ex-military and ex-secret police – in the most recent incarnations of these things in the new Russia. Y'know, new versions of the KGB and all that? But now they allegedly work for a big Chechnyan ganglord called Oscar Malinowski, a guy who's grown very fat and rich in the last twenty years as Russia's crumbled internally. And they're both as hard as nails.'

Henry and Flynn glanced at each other.

'Er . . .' Tope hesitated.

'Spit it out,' Henry urged.

'If they're up there, something's going on, Henry – something big and unpleasant. They operate as a team and if you have killed one of them, the other will be mightily pissed off. So just be wary, Henry. They're not above paying cops a visit. In fact they're suspected of maiming and blinding a detective in Cyprus . . . so watch it.'

'That's if they are these guys,' Flynn cut in.

'Yeah, maybe they're not . . .'

'Anyway, Jerry – do some more digging for me, will you – as well as liaising with the scientific people to see if we do have a match.'

'I will.'

'What about that other job?' Henry asked Tope.

'Much as I'd trust Flynn with my life,' Tope lied, 'it's really just for your ears, Henry.'

Even though Tope had said nothing, the implication of his reluctance to speak made Henry suddenly feel slightly queasy – even more ill than hearing he might be prodding a hornets' nest full of Russian nasties.

'No prob . . .' Henry's mind whirred. 'Look, get me what you can on this gangster Malinowski will you and email me with everything else you've got . . . I'll pick it up on my Blackberry . . . and I'll speak to you in the . . . shit!'

During the course of the phone call, Henry had reached the village of Hornby and turned right to head out towards Kendleton in the unlit back of beyond. He had been aware that there was a vehicle behind him, but hadn't paid it much heed as it hadn't been right up his backside and his concentration was on what Tope was saying. Now, almost without realizing it, he was out on the tight, narrow country roads just wide enough for two vehicles to pass with care in opposite directions, a few inches to spare between wing mirrors. So far there had been no oncoming traffic and Henry's car and the one behind had been the only vehicles on the road.

Up to that moment, the car behind had kept to a reasonable distance.

As they hit a stretch of road clinging to a steep hill with one of the tiny tributary streams that fed the River Wenning down an almost perpendicular drop to their left, the main headlight beams of the following car came blazing on like aircraft landing lights and the car itself surged up behind the Mercedes just as he was talking to Tope.

There were four big headlights fitted along a cowcatcher attached the front radiator grille and Henry's car was brightly lit up, casting a long shadow ahead of himself. Then, on this tight, narrow, steep-sided and dangerous road, the vehicle swerved out, the horn sounding angrily, and moved to overtake.

That was the moment he said 'Shit' to Tope.

He had nowhere to go to make space for the idiot who must surely have seen that a manoeuvre like this, on that stretch of road, was not an option.

Flynn twisted round in his seat, looking over his shoulder. He knew from experience that the road was not built for this because he'd once been all but forced off it by – spookily – a black Range Rover, the type of vehicle behind them now.

It wasn't the same car, nor quite the same stretch of the road, but it was the same move, and then it had been daylight and he could see. Henry, despite all the light surrounding him now, didn't have that luxury.

He gripped the steering wheel, hunkered down, decelerated and clung to his position on the road in the hope that the vehicle behind might get past without colliding. He knew that he could not afford to veer to his nearside, he'd be on the grass verge.

But passing clearly wasn't the driver's intention.

The Range Rover blasted its horn again as it came parallel, then deliberately shunted left with a crunch and tearing of metal on metal.

It was no accident. Not a misjudgement. It was a premeditated act.

The steering wheel was almost thrown out of Henry's grasp, but he hung on tenaciously, hardly daring to tear his eyes from the road ahead.

The Range Rover slammed left again.

This time Henry was forced off the road.

The Mercedes crashed through a low hedge, then plunged down the steep hill towards the brook at the bottom of a narrow valley.

Henry grappled with the wheel, fighting it as the front of the car bounced into and out of deep ruts in the banking, throwing him and Flynn around in their seats like they were on a high-adrenaline Disney ride.

Suddenly there was a sheep in the headlights, the beam catching its strange brown eyes. It gave Henry a look of astonishment, then fled into the night a second before the car would have flattened it.

Then the front wheels dropped into a deep rut. The body twisted, then it flipped over and somersaulted, crashed onto its roof, bounced, kept going, landed on all four wheels. But the momentum was too great and it did another three-hundred-and sixty-degree forward roll, moving with agonizing slowness, again thudding down on all four wheels right in the centre of the stream at the bottom of the hill. The engine stalled and died.

Henry was still holding the steering wheel, completely amazed he was still conscious and alive, cowering under the crumpled roof which, though extensively damaged, was magnificently still protecting the occupants. Even then, he thought, 'German engineering.'

He looked sideways at Flynn. He was still conscious, too, but had a deep, jagged gash on his hairline from which blood gushed across his face. He wiped it away from his eyes.

For a few moments, both men were speechless and slightly confused.

Back up on the road, at the top of the steep banking, the Range Rover stopped diagonally across the road, the front wheels just over the edge in the gap that Henry's car had made in the hedge. The powerful headlights shone down on the Mercedes a hundred feet below.

Henry blinked as he looked stupidly upwards at them, his brain in turmoil, trying to work out what had just happened, wondering what the guy in the car was doing now.

In a matter of seconds he'd been forced off the road and was now in a fucking stream!

Then outline of a man shape stepped into the headlights, silhouetted by the beams.

Henry saw it and assumed the driver had stopped to give assistance after his dangerous driving. He had done a ridiculous, fucking stupid, dangerous overtake, lost control on the way past, clipped the car he was passing – and now his conscience had kicked in.

That's what Henry would have liked to think.

The fact that the shadow of the man clearly showed him to have a machine-pistol in his hands made Henry think differently.

Plus it was aimed at the Mercedes, which, though in the stream, was positioned broadside to him, presenting a great and easy target.

He was about to make sure he finished the job he had started.

Henry swore, his dumb brain clicking into gear.

'Get out, get out,' he screamed at Flynn, who was already moving, having seen what Henry had seen, and after releasing his seat belt was cursing as he tried to force open the damaged and stuck passenger door with his shoulder.

The man fired. The muzzle flash exploded spectacularly against his black shape.

Four bullets smacked into the side of the Mercedes.

Flynn banged his shoulder desperately against the twisted door as Henry lurched across his knees to add the force of his hands and body against the door, which opened with a creak.

Flynn tumbled out into the stream.

Henry rolled out on top of him.

The man fired again. Henry heard three cracks as bullets hit his car and felt one whizz just above his head before it thudded into the grass bank opposite.

Flynn scrambled low along the stream, virtually crawling, Henry following in the ice-cold water.

There was a scream of anguish from the man with the gun. Henry glanced back to see him scuttling sideways down the slope, obviously realizing that his intended targets had survived the terrible crash and the hail of bullets.

Henry kept behind Flynn, hoping to put some distance and darkness between themselves and the man.

But Flynn had disappeared.

It was only a slicing cut that Flynn had received to his head as the car tumble-dried itself down the slope. He wasn't even sure what had cut it, but it wasn't caused by a direct blow, for which he was grateful. It meant he kept a clear head.

He'd been kept brilliantly in place by the seat belt and when the car crashed to a stop, like it had just been dropped from a great height flat down into the stream, he knew he'd cut his head, but also that nothing else had been damaged.

He saw the man on the road at the same time as Henry.

Appearing with the headlights behind him, gun in hand, like some kind of murderous demon.

The car door had been twisted, but it opened and Flynn rolled sideways out into the stream, then came up on his hands and

knees in the shallow water. Ignoring its bone-freezing temperature, he scuttled away, knowing Henry was right behind him.

Then, for a few moments, it didn't feel like Henry was there.

Flynn did not look back.

He knew the gunman had run down the slope and if he and
Henry had simply just run away, all the guy would have to do
was stand in the middle of the stream and strafe the darkness
into which they had escaped.

Every chance that at least one of them would be cut to ribbons
like Bonny and Clyde.

Flynn, therefore, knew he had to move.

He scrambled to his right onto the bank, into the cover provided
by a clump of thin bushes which whipped his face, snagged his
new clothing. Thorns cut the palms of his hands as he forced his
way through them and up the banking, keeping as low and silent
as possible, hoping the sounds of his movement were covered
by the burbling of the running water and the noise from the still-
on engine of the Range Rover.

There were more shots.

Flynn powered on upwards, moving like a fast Komodo dragon,
belly just above the grass, driven by instinct, fear, rage and
commando training from many years before.

Twenty metres up, he moved right, still keeping to the ground,
and emerged at a point ten metres below the Range Rover and
fifteen metres to its right, just on the periphery of the sweep of
its headlights.

More importantly he was above and behind the gunman, who
was still in the centre of the stream in front of the Mercedes. He
was crouched low, the machine-pistol in the firing position, not
moving, peering into the darkness.

Flynn's mouth curved into a vicious snarl.

He was about ten metres from the man and the guy clearly
hadn't heard or seen him, or even suspected that one of the men
he'd tried to kill had circled back with murder on his mind.

But ten metres was a big distance in the circumstances.

If Flynn started to move for him, he would surely sense the
approach, pivot and fire.

By which time Flynn might have gone two metres.

Flynn did not move.

He took a moment to control his breathing, try to reduce his heart rate.

Then the man stood upright and like some demented terminator, leaned slightly backwards, screamed something incomprehensible that Flynn could not make out – but could tell from the voice it was yelled in wrath – and fired the machine-pistol, spraying bullets in a wide arc, maybe forty degrees, down the stream and into the darkness where Henry and Flynn had disappeared.

Then the magazine was empty.

It was obvious the man knew the gun would empty, because as it did he flicked the magazine-release catch and let it slide out into the water, then smoothly began to replace it with a magazine from his back jeans pocket.

But it was a senseless move, one brought about by rage, Flynn guessed, who knew that emotion should never play a part in a dangerous game like this. It clouded judgement and let the enemy in. He should have taken cover when he reloaded.

Flynn ran down the slope, estimating he had about three seconds before the gun was loaded and cocked again.

He held back his own urge to scream, moved silently, the only sound the thump of his feet in the grass.

Just before Flynn launched himself, the man must have sensed something. He twisted, still with the empty gun in one hand, the full magazine in the other, almost slotted in place. He tried to use the gun as a club, but Flynn was in the air at a forty-five-degree angle and the gunman could not manage to swing the pistol around with enough force or accuracy to clobber Flynn's head.

Flynn connected and as his hands encircled the man, he realized the guy was all muscle. Hopefully, steroid muscle.

The gun went flying and both men staggered backwards.

With a contemptuous curse, the man broke free from Flynn's grip like Samson bursting from his shackles, and hit Flynn on the side of his face with a huge, hard fist. Fortunately it was a poor, badly aimed, rushed blow, but nevertheless it sent Flynn spinning backwards, far enough away for the man to recover. Flynn saw the glint of a knife blade in the man's right hand.

It wasn't a big knife. A serrated four-inch kitchen knife, possibly.

It didn't have to be long to kill. Big knives were mostly used to intimidate. Smaller, more discreet ones were used to kill efficiently.

The man grinned, the lights from the Range Rover casting an eerie distorted glow across his face. His teeth twinkled.

'We meet again, but this time I kill you proper, fucker.'

Flynn thought there was probably a good chance of that happening, especially when the man moved towards him with incredible speed. In the darkness, mixed with the light from the Range Rover, with long and short shadows intermingling, it was hideously difficult to judge exactly where the man was, at what point the arc of the knife was. Flynn had to fight almost blind, trusting to instinct and his abilities.

He sidestepped, swerving his whole body from the knees upwards like a matador, then went in low and – he hoped – under the trajectory of the knife, so that he came back uptight, face-to-face, body-to-body with the guy and the knife was waving uselessly in mid-air behind him.

Flynn knew that would only be momentary, a fraction of a second before the knife came back around into his back, somewhere under the shoulder blades.

He had that amount of time in which to act.

To win.

Also, he was under no illusions about this man's strength. Even if the muscles were steroid-grown, if Flynn found himself in a bear hug, chances were he would have his ribs crushed slowly, followed by his internal organs, and his spine would be snapped.

It had to be instantaneous. Done with precision.

No hesitation – because what Flynn planned would kill.

His right hand came up between himself and the man, driving upwards in the tight gap between the two bodies. He rammed the heel of the hand under the man's nose, so the septum would be exactly on that hard part between the soft cushions of his thumb and finger pads.

It was like driving a piston into the man's nose.

Under normal circumstances – and this was an old, tried and tested move – this would have worked. The septum would have been hammered up into the frontal lobe of the brain, piercing it like a jagged nail and killing the opponent instantly, or at the very least putting him down, making him into a jellied eel and brain-dead for life.

A good plan.

Unless the opponent had virtually nothing left of that piece of gristle that separated his nostrils. Unless years of snorting cocaine had rotted it away and perforated the cartilage making it nothing more than a paper-thin divider. And all Flynn succeeded in doing was grinding the man's nose to a misshapen pulp.

But there was enough force in the blow to send him teetering backwards with a groan of pain, clutching his mashed face with his left hand, and his right, which was still holding the knife.

Flynn followed up this advantage, lurching after him and bunching his right fist and hitting him as hard as he could in his exposed windpipe, twisting the knuckles on impact, knocking him even further backwards.

The man went backwards, then recovered and dropped into a fighting stance with the knife, despite the blood pouring from the middle of his face and a horrible gagging noise coming from his throat.

And a smile on his face.

He spat out a gob-full of blood and went for Flynn, who jerked side-on, let the knife hand zip past him, then elbowed him right on the nose again, feeling the tip of his elbow sink horribly into a depression in the man's face.

He did it twice in quick succession. Hard, accurate, but then the man's left hand crawled over Flynn's face. His fat fingers dug deep into Flynn's eye sockets and he began to ease Flynn's head backwards whilst at the same time Flynn was wrestling with the knife hand.

And the fight was to the death.

Henry dropped as the bullets zinged around him, full length into the stream, face down for a moment in the shallow water, then rolling out of it onto the muddy bank, no idea where Flynn had gone. He slithered and slurped in the mud and came up into a position that resembled a hunted animal on starting blocks.

He glanced backwards and saw two shapes locked together

– and realized Flynn had doubled back to take on the gunman. Their terrible fight was illuminated by the car headlights. Henry got to his feet and ran back towards them, just as the man pulled Flynn down onto his arse.

Henry splashed through the water and dived at the man, knocking the knife out of his hand and bundling the mass of muscle off Flynn. The man staggered, but with the strength of a bison he shrugged Henry away. Henry found himself sitting back in the stream, landing heavily on a rock, jarring the base of his spine, sending a shot of pain up to his skull.

Flynn seriously thought he had lost. The man was stronger, heavier and clearly used to fighting and taking punishment. The pain was not having any stopping effect. Flynn had lost his edge. He was fit and lean, but there was too much time separating him from the violent life he had once revelled in and his blade was dull.

It was a good job Henry arrived, barging the man off Flynn. It gave him a chance to reassert himself and go for the kill because he knew that this was ultimately the only way to defeat this person.

As the man tossed Henry aside, he was open. Just for a second. Open. Unprotected.

This time Flynn's hard-edge blow to the throat was delivered with accuracy and stunning power, driven all the way from the spin of his hips, up through his torso and along his right arm to the blade that was his hand.

He did it twice.

Flynn felt the cartilage crush and crumble.

The man gurgled and sank to his knees, his hands at his throat, gagging, choking.

Still not enough.

Flynn stepped behind him, a ferocious power now inside him, driving him as he put into effect something he had learned many years before and practised for real on two Argentinian soldiers on the Falklands Islands in 1982 whilst a Royal Marines Commando: how to take a man's head and break his neck with one perfect wrench.

ELEVEN

Eight hours later and exhausted beyond thinking, Henry Christie walked like a zombie through the corridors of Lancaster police station, pushed through the door leading to the rear of the public enquiry counter, lifted the hatch and stepped into the foyer.

Steve Flynn was behind him.

The woman sitting in the foyer with a terrified expression on her face stood up slowly and then rushed to embrace Henry.

'Oh God, Henry,' Alison snuffled into his shoulder. 'You can't believe how worried I was – am.'

Henry held her tightly for a moment, then she stepped back and looked at him. Suddenly he was a much older man after the night's events, drawn, haggard, eyes sunken and red raw. It didn't help that he was now wearing one of those god-awful forensic suits and slippers and looked more like a prisoner than a cop. He realized in that moment how much the age difference between him and Alison mattered. He was almost thirteen years her senior, which seemed a huge gap as he stood there with her.

She glanced at Flynn, reached past Henry and touched his arm tenderly. He too had aged and the scar that stretched from his forehead to temple, still oozing blood through the butterfly stitches, didn't help matters. Nor did the bloodstained zoot suit, the second he'd worn that day. He was going through sets of clothing like nobody's business.

'Steve,' she whispered. She handed him a pile of clothing that she'd brought for him. 'These should fit you,' she said.

He managed a weak smile and a thanks.

Henry fingertipped his face carefully, amazed his broken cheekbone was no worse than before. 'We need to get some sleep, love.'

Alison nodded.

'Apparently my car's a write-off.'

'I passed it on the way. It's a wreck,' she confirmed. 'But you're OK, that's all that matters. Cars can be replaced.'

Henry just shook his head, wanting to cry. 'Take me home, babe,' he said, 'and him too.' He turned to grin at Flynn, who said, 'I am never going to help anyone again. That,' he continued, 'was one hell of a night, Henry. Thanks for sharing it with me.'

Flynn lowered the dead man gently backwards into the stream, the legs still twitching as the last few signals shot down from his brain. Then he stood up, hands on hips, gasping, looking at Henry who, being older and less fit, was bent forward with his hands on his knees and gasping much more desperately than Flynn, sucking in air like it was going out of fashion.

'Is he dead?'

Flynn nodded.

'Good,' Henry said.

'Hell, Henry, you must have cut him up real bad to get a road-rage reaction like that,' Flynn said, wiping the blood from his face.

'Some people have no sense of humour.' Henry turned to look at his car and grimaced. 'And I've just lost mine.' He glanced back at Flynn and the body at his feet and swore.

From that point in the night, after Henry had made 'the' phone call – the treble-nine – and had to deal with a succession of fairly unhelpful people before he ended up losing it and bawling down the line, he and Flynn just allowed things to happen.

The first police to arrive on the scene came in the shape of a double-crewed traffic car, two very experienced cops experienced in dealing with serious situations, protecting scenes (usually just car crashes) and handling victims and witnesses. They soon had the road closed, a big accident investigation van on the way (with mobile scene lighting), diversions in place; next came the paramedics, who tended to Henry and Flynn and realized there was nothing they could do for the other man, who by that time had been dragged out of the stream and laid to rest on the bank, his head grotesquely askew.

More uniforms arrived from Lancaster and scene management was taken over by the local inspector for the time being.

DI Barlow turned up with a DC in tow . . . and then decisions had to be made about what best to do with Henry and Flynn.

Both certainly needed medical treatment – again. Flynn's gashed head bled openly and profusely and needed stitching properly.

Henry took a step back so as not to influence anything. He just helped and waited for the decisions to be made, which came from Barlow as he was the most senior detective on the scene until others arrived and there was a lot of responsibility resting on his shoulders. He took Henry to one side.

Henry was wrapped in a blanket from the back of the traffic car, as was Flynn. He told Barlow what had happened and why it ended up as it did . . . and weight was added to his retelling of events when a PNC check revealed that the Range Rover was in fact stolen and was on false plates.

'Look,' Barlow said, strained, 'I don't disbelieve a single word, Henry, but the fact remains there's a dead man down there.' He pointed to the stream. 'And he's been killed in a fight.'

'Self-defence,' Henry said. 'I was part of it.'

'I know, I know . . .'

'But?'

'What would you do?'

'Go through the motions. Put us through the meat grinder. No choice,' Henry said. 'No matter who is involved.'

Barlow nodded, looked relieved. 'I want to keep you and Mr Flynn separate.'

Henry's mouth twitched sardonically. 'So we can't get our stories straight?'

'Something like that . . . you know the score,' Barlow said. 'That in mind I'm going to get you taken to A&E in a cop car, and Flynn in an ambulance, then keep you apart at the hospital. Once you've been treated, I'll have you brought to Lancaster nick separately.'

'Under arrest?'

'What do you think, Henry? Please don't make this any harder than it has to be.'

'I won't. I'd do the same.'

Barlow looked at Henry closely. 'What's this all about?' he asked.

'Dunno just yet.'

'Yeah, right,' Barlow sneered.

Henry glanced over at Flynn, who was in the back of the ambulance being treated once again by the pretty lady paramedic who had dabbed his wounds following the explosion on the canal boat, looking deep into his eyes as she tended him.

It was a long, tiring night. The two men were kept apart, as Barlow said, and given forensic suits to replace their own clothing. They were booked respectfully into the custody system and placed in cells at opposite ends of the complex so they couldn't shout to each other.

Neither elected to speak to a solicitor.

They were interviewed under caution and on tape, a process that took most of the rest of the night. By dawn it was clear that their recollections tallied, almost word for word.

Following this they were released from custody without bail.

'Yeah, that was great fun,' Henry said to Flynn. Flynn merely arched his eyebrows. They were outside the police station in the chilly dawn with Alison. 'This won't go anywhere,' he assured Flynn. 'The CPS will see what has happened.

'Two deaths in two days,' Flynn stated and pouted. 'Doesn't look good for me.'

'Just a bad run of luck.'

'A run of bad luck is when your car doesn't start then a light bulb goes.'

'Let's just get some sleep,' Henry suggested, 'then reconvene and start digging and find out what this is all about.'

'Yeah, good idea . . . but I won't burden you tonight,' Flynn said.

'What do you mean? You're very welcome to stay at the Owl, you know that,' Alison said sharply.

'I need some TLC,' Flynn grinned and touched his still weeping wound.

'I used to be a nurse.'

'I know – but you've already got a very demanding patient.'

He nodded at the battered little Citroën that was pulling up on the road outside the police station. Henry peered at the driver and saw it was the paramedic who had treated Flynn.

'Ahh,' Henry said knowingly.

'Apparently she has a flat down on St George's Quay.'

'Nice position.'

'Yeah – overlooking the River Lune.'

'Yeah,' Henry said, his memory jarring at the mention of the river.

'So – thanks anyway,' Flynn said to Alison, 'but needs must. I'll get my head down for an hour or two,' his eyebrows rose and fell in a 'wink-wink' way, 'then I really need to go and open the shop in Glasson. I haven't done a great job there, so far . . . and that's where I'll be if the cops want me.'

'Don't frighten the customers.' Henry extended his right hand and the two men shook. Alison kissed Flynn on the cheek and he walked across to the car as the paramedic leaned over and opened the passenger door for him. Flynn dropped into the seat and the car sped off.

Henry and Alison watched it turn right onto the main road, then Henry emitted a long sigh. He turned to Alison, saw the worry on her face and steeled himself for what he was about to say.

'I know there's never a right time and place for this, but if you want out, I won't blame you.'

Astonished, she said, 'Out of what, exactly?'

'Us . . . me, you . . . you know.'

'Why are you saying that?'

'All this shit, all this worry. The job. Coppering, y'know. It rules my life, always has and always will as long as I'm in it. And that's a big mistake, one of many I made with Kate. I don't want to make it again.'

'Well don't then.' Her voice was like granite.

There was silence between them. Both swallowed drily.

'Trouble is, I love you,' Henry admitted.

Alison's face quivered, her bottom lip tightening. 'And I love you – so that's settled then. Being a cop may rule your life, but that's not what living's about. That's about us, you and me, and what we make of what we've got and what we'll have in the future. And I don't know about you, buddy,' she poked him in the chest, 'but I'm bloody well looking forward to it!'

As much as he could, in spite of the swollen face and all the additional cuts and scrapes, Henry's face softened. 'Me too,' he admitted.

Alison shrugged an 'I told you so' shrug.

'And I need my bed.'

St George's Quay was only minutes away from Lancaster nick, at the bottom of the city, by the River Lune.

The lady paramedic, whose name was Liz, drove Flynn down and parked in a reserved bay behind an old warehouse converted into apartments.

'We're here,' she said, switching off the engine.

Flynn looked at her, trying to ignore the pain in his head.

Then there was no problem ignoring it as with passionate groans from each of them, they plunged into each other's arms, kissing madly, lips mashing, until their foreheads clashed and Flynn jerked away.

'Sorry,' she gasped. 'I'll have to be gentle with you.'

'I'm sure you will be . . . that said, I hope you don't think I'm being forward, but I could really do with a shower . . . I need to get out of this.' He pulled distastefully at the paper suit. 'Been a bit of a night.'

Her eyes ran down him, looking at the baggy zoot suit. 'I think I might be able to help you there.'

In turn, Flynn eyed her green overalls under a very unflattering anorak, obviously slung on at the end of her shift. 'Ditto,' he said, feeling a surge of energy.

'Sorry I said that. You know, about you and me splitting. It's the last thing I want . . . I felt it just wasn't fair.'

'I know, Henry. You're a good man.'

Henry's lips warped at that. He hadn't been good to Kate and it constantly seared into his heart. He had allowed a combination of work and his inability to say no where women were concerned to blind him. Yet through it all – 'all' including a divorce and a remarriage – Kate had stayed with him. It was only in the past

couple of years that he had tried to make serious amends, only
to have her taken away from him.

In his heart he knew he had ultimately done his best for Kate,
but he still felt cheated by her death . . . the 'unfinished business'
syndrome.

Then he'd met Alison and started a serious relationship he did
not want to jeopardize, not through work and definitely not
through other women.

They were sitting in Alison's car on a street near the police
station, having been kissing and holding each other.

'Gosh, snogging in a car,' she said. 'Feel like a teenager.'

'Mm,' Henry said. 'That's something else to consider. Age
difference.'

Alison punched him gently on the shoulder. 'I'll just have to
push you in a wheelchair, won't I? Off a cliff if necessary.'

'I'm going to retire,' he said suddenly.

She frowned. 'Where did that come from?'

He shrugged. 'I've got the time in. Been sort of considering
it for a bit and I'd like to be with you all the time.'

Their eyes locked. But then she pulled a face. 'All the time?
Would that be a good idea?' she teased.

'Hey, I'm house-trained. Quite fancy living in a pub with a
busty barmaid . . . I'm sure I could pull a pint.'

'What about your house . . . your girls?'

'Sell it . . . sell them.'

Alison shook her head. 'This needs a long discussion, sweetie,
not a rash decision.

'I know.' He sat back and exhaled shakily. 'Shit, I was scared.'

'I'll bet you were . . . what's it all about, Henry?'

He shook his head. 'Not the foggiest and for a few hours
I'm not going to think about it.' He shook his head, but knew
intuitively that everything he had been investigating for the last
couple of days was interconnected, things had happened so fast
that it had been impossible for him to take stock properly, even
though he'd tried, and work it all out with a proper plan of
investigation. His plan for the time being, though, was to get
some sleep, then look at everything with the help of a team of
people he trusted – unless, of course, he was taken off the
investigation because of the two incidents he was directly

involved with. Those being what had happened at Joe Speakman's house and on the road to Kendleton.

Alison started the engine, Henry settled back into the passenger seat and closed his eyes, only to open them suddenly when there was a tap on the window.

It was DI Barlow, who had been in charge of proceedings throughout the night.

'Quick word before you disappear?' he said through the glass and gestured with his fingers.

'Won't be a moment,' Henry said to Alison and climbed creakily out of the car.

'I've asked an ARV to spend some time in Kendleton,' Barlow said. 'Just in case, just to float around . . . you never know.'

'Thanks, Ralph.'

'But . . . a word to the wise, Henry. I'm thinking caution.'

'In what way?'

'Erm . . .' Barlow looked around furtively and drew Henry aside so he could speak into his ear. 'There's obviously something happening around here that's a bit nooky and dangerous.'

'Tell me about it.'

Barlow looked directly into Henry's eyes. 'Entirely off the record, Henry . . . I think you need to back off. It would be terrible if something did happen to you, you know?' Barlow's eyes went to Alison in the car, the returned to Henry.

'No.' Henry's mouth was suddenly dry. 'I don't know.'

'Look,' Barlow said, searching for the right words as though it was a painful process. 'It's not much more than a feeling, but it might be best, say, if you handed this whole investigation to me . . . let me run with it. I'm sure I can solve it to everyone's satisfaction.'

'What does that mean?'

'Look,' Barlow said for the second time, his voice hardening, 'I'm doing you a favour here, Henry. This is a box of vipers and it needs a lid keeping on it. Just hand it over to me and I'll make certain all the i's are dotted and t's crossed . . . and no one'll get hurt. It's got out of hand for various reasons and I'm pretty sure I can plug it.'

'Plug what?'

'It,' Barlow said. 'Just back off, eh? If you know what's

good for you. Same applies to Mr Flynn.' Barlow's voice was persuasive, not threatening. But Henry didn't like it.

I was right, he thought. 'By the way – what you've just said? Not off my record.'

'Don't be a fool, Henry,' Barlow whispered. 'I'm protecting you here. Let me sort it.'

Henry pulled away. 'You've just made the biggest mistake of your life, Ralph.'

Barlow gave a 'whatever' shrug of indifference and mouthed the words, 'Off the record.'

Henry got back into the car and said, 'Let's go.'

Barlow watched the car pull away.

Alison said, 'What was all that about?'

'I hate to think,' he said through gritted teeth.

Flynn's shower had gone very well. He got cleaned up nicely, as did the lady paramedic – who had 'perspired' a little after a long shift – and once they were well and truly scrubbed, the shower moved on to a whole new different level.

Then, after drying each other, they continued what they had started in the bedroom, going voraciously at each other, but also tenderly and with utmost respect until they finally disengaged and flopped back onto the bed, plum tuckered.

'Jeepers,' Flynn panted. 'Wonderful.'

'Oh, yes,' Liz said dreamily, hardly able to keep her eyes open. She pulled the duvet over and snuggled down against him with a pleasurable murmur.

His eyelids fluttered and they were both on the verge of dream world when Flynn's mobile phone rang.

Normally he would have ignored it in the circumstances, but the events of the last few hours and the possibility of news about Colin, his sick friend, made him reach out for it. The caller display said 'number withheld' and his heart sank. News about Colin, he assumed.

'Steve Flynn,' he answered.

'Mr Flynn,' a voice he did not recognize growled. 'Friendly advice . . . tell Henry Christie to back off . . .' The line clicked dead before Flynn could utter a word.

'Who was that?' Liz mumbled sleepily.

'No idea,' Flynn said and dropped the phone onto the floor – but he knew now there was no chance of sleep. He reached out and picked it up again, dialled a number.

'Henry? It's me, Flynn . . . you hit the sack yet?'

TWELVE

'And that's all he said? But you didn't recognize the voice?'

'Yes – and no.' Flynn had written down verbatim the one-liner phone call from the unknown male.

'You're certain?' Henry persisted, irritatingly.

'I wrote it down with my crayon,' Flynn said, making his point.

Henry said, 'OK, I need to make some calls, see some people across the way.' He jerked his thumb in the direction of the headquarters building of Lancashire Constabulary.

'And then will you tell me what the fuck is going on?'

Henry made a helpless gesture with his arms. 'As if I know,' he said. 'Lots of things have happened and they keep freakin' happening before I can do anything about the last thing.' He stood up.

It was just over two hours since Flynn had called him and Henry had immediately decided he could not afford the luxury of sleep. Although the travelling distance had been a pain, he'd also decided that it would make more sense to convene at HQ, just to the south of Preston, rather than up at Lancaster nick. Apart from anything else, this was his own environment, a place he controlled, amongst people he knew, and where his office was, in what had once been a block of student accommodation at the training centre on the site. The whole building had been commandeered years before to house the SIO team, which subsequently became FMIT. His office was on the middle floor of the three-storey block and had been two bedrooms, now knocked into one decent-sized office. On some training courses way back when, Henry recalled he had slept in one of the bedrooms, although the term 'sleeping' could only be loosely applied. He'd sneaked a nubile and very willing policewoman into the room once – an act, then, against all the rules – and had a glorious but necessarily silent sexual encounter. Unfortunately he'd followed this by honking up in the washbasin, then later peeing in it because he couldn't be bothered to traipse down to the toilet block at the end of a cold corridor.

So his present office had some pleasing personal history for him, which always made him glow fondly as he sat there lording it as a superintendent – a rank he never thought he would achieve in a million years of police service.

'Do you want to grab a brew in the training-school dining room? Give me about half an hour and I'll come and collect you?'

'OK,' Flynn said dourly. He hadn't actually expected to be invited across to the main HQ building but walking over to the training centre was fine.

Henry walked Flynn out of FMIT and they went their separate ways. Henry turned left and headed across the sports field to the front of HQ, sailing in past reception and up to the first floor on which were the offices of power – the chief constable, the deputy and two assistant chiefs. Henry turned right into the carpeted corridor, through a set of double doors and then the door leading to the office that housed the chief constable's admin staff, and staff officer.

They all looked at him, shocked by his battered appearance.

The staff officer was a female chief inspector. She gestured for him to go straight in to see the chief, who was expecting him after an earlier, urgent phone call. He went through the solid mahogany doorway.

He then spent about fifteen minutes briefing the chief, before emerging, giving the still stunned admin staff a jaunty salute and leaving for his next port of call down on the ground floor.

He walked through the less than salubrious corridors to the intelligence unit, tucked away in one corner of the building. He entered by keying in a code and scanning a thumbprint, stepping into a long, narrow office, desks arranged in two rows. The office of the DI in charge was at the far end behind a lot of glass, but just in front of that was Jerry Tope's domain, the man he had come to see.

Henry walked down the centre of the office between the desks, his bashed-up appearance drawing looks of horror. Part of him wanted to drop into the lope of the Hunchback of Notre Dame, cover his ears and proclaim something about 'the bells', but he was a superintendent and had decorum.

Tope did not see him coming. He was in deep concentration at his computer and it was only as Henry dragged a spare chair and positioned it alongside the gable end of Tope's desk and plonked down on it, did Tope glance up.

'Holy cow, Henry!'

Henry gave him a crooked smile – which was the only smile his face was capable of cracking anyway. Anything normal hurt bad.

'Now, then, before our phone call was rudely interrupted last night, you were about to tell me something which wasn't suitable for Steve Flynn's ears – am I right?'

He then spent a further twenty minutes with Tope and emerged from the conflab disquieted but also determined.

He walked slowly back across the sports field, deep in thought, as well as making a phone call on the way. He went straight past the FMIT block and to the training-centre dining room where he found Flynn nursing a half-drunk cup of coffee and an empty plate that had been filled with breakfast.

Henry gave him a 'follow me' gesture. Flynn stood up, swilling back the coffee, and he and Henry then made their way down the outside of the training-centre admin block, past the gym to the new, but not so recently built, firearms range. This time Henry did not have access codes and had to ring the bell before being allowed entry, and had to vouch for Flynn even though he was wearing a visitor's badge.

Once inside they could hear the dull 'bam-bam' of gunfire in the range, making Henry wince at the recent memory. They entered the actual range – at the safe end – to see a demonstration being carried out by an instructor for the benefit of a few would-be firearms officers.

Suitably kitted out in dark blue overalls, a ballistic baseball cap, boots, goggles and ear defenders, and holding a Glock17 pistol in his hands, the instructor made his way down the range, accompanied by another trainer at his shoulder.

It was a simple, no-nonsense walk-through.

At various points targets appeared at the far end of the range, mostly the obligatory charging soldier ones, but occasionally different ones, such as a mother holding a baby, or a mother holding a baby and a gun, just to test the reactions of the shooter.

He had to make several split-second decisions, not knowing in what order the targets would spin into view, nor what was on them. This was done randomly by computer.

It was basic stuff for firearms-officer training, but absolutely vital.

Henry, who had been a firearms officer in his time, remembered shooting dead a vicar on a similar exercise.

The instructor worked his way down the range, watching and responding, double-tapping the appropriate targets brilliantly, and reloading swiftly without the aid of a speed-loader. When he reached the end of the range, he showed his empty gun to his colleague. Then the students, who had watched from the safe area, were beckoned down to witness the results, which were highlighted in chalk on the target. Even from the other end of the range, Henry and Flynn could see it was a 100% shoot. The murmur of approval from the students confirmed this.

'Nice shooting,' Flynn said. Henry nodded.

The students were ushered back down the range by the trainer who had been observing, and once the other instructor had holstered his weapon he wandered back up the range, removing his safety goggles and ear defenders, revealing that he was PC Bill Robbins, long-time firearms instructor and an old friend of Henry's who had fairly recently assisted him on a few investigations.

'Boss,' Robbins smiled, then acknowledged Steve Flynn, who he recognized as an ex-cop, noticing the injuries that both of them sported. 'Flynnie!' he said and shook hands with him. He turned his attention back to Henry. 'You don't half both look a mess . . . is there something I can do for you – like kill the bastards who did this?'

Flynn and Henry exchanged a nervous glance.

Henry coughed. 'Bill, I've just been to see the chief and I've convinced him to let me have your services for a while, if that's OK with you? I'm not sure what it might entail, going to have to suck it and see.'

'Fine by me, but I'll have to run it past my boss . . . I'm just about to start running an initial firearms course – hence the superb demo. Any idea how long you'll want me for?'

'Not long, hopefully . . . I might just need you on tap, that's all. If you have any problems with your boss, tell him to call me.'

'OK . . . then what?'

'My office at FMIT, say half an hour? Refreshments provided.'

'I'll be there.'

Henry and Flynn left the range. Outside, Henry said, 'Something else entirely down to you, Steve, but the offer's there . . . I've arranged for two rooms to be available for us here on the campus, en-suite bedrooms, TVs, desks, all nicely refurbished. I'd really like you to move in for the time being. It'll be safer down here.' Flynn blinked. 'Obviously you'd have to pay for your own food.'

'Substantial threat?' Flynn said, quoting from the witness-protection policy and procedure documents he had once known off by heart.

'Down to you,' Henry said. 'I know you can look after yourself, but until I bottom whatever the hell's going on around here . . . I know you have the shop to look after, but that won't be a problem. I'll stick a uniformed bobby outside when you're there as a deterrent.'

'Deterrent for what?'

Henry shrugged. 'We're into seriously dangerous territory here and I'd rather be safe than sorry.'

'I didn't know you cared.'

Henry weighed this up. 'I care more than I did before, put it that way . . . but on a scale of one to ten, we're still in pretty low numbers.'

'That's reassuring. You say there's a room here for you too?'

'I don't want to drag Alison into this. Haven't told her yet.'

'She'll go ballistic.'

'Understatement,' Henry agreed. 'So what do you want to do? Offer's there.'

'I'm touched and I accept – only problem being transport.'

'My plan is to let you use Alison's car. I'll try and prise one for me out of HQ Transport and Alison will be OK because she can use Ginny's car for the time being.'

'Something else you haven't quite run past her?' Flynn smirked.

Henry shot him a sullen look.

They returned to Henry's office, where Henry set his coffee filter machine going, then brought in some extra chairs. Flynn sat on one, shuffled it to the back corner of the office and crossed his legs.

Henry dragged a flip-chart board in from another office, found a clean sheet and started to brainstorm his thoughts, Flynn observing with interest, saying nothing.

As Henry worked, Jerry Tope arrived carrying a file of papers – almost collapsing from shock when he saw Flynn sitting in the corner. Then Bill Robbins landed followed by Rik Dean, a DI from Blackpool that Henry knew well. In fact Rik was due to marry Henry's flaky sister Lisa next year, so he and Henry would soon be in-laws – for at least as long as the marriage lasted. Henry gave it three months.

Finally the chief constable landed, the very portly Robert Fanshaw-Bayley, a man with whom Henry had had a very mixed relationship over many years. He was known as FB.

Henry finished his jottings and folded the front cover sheet over the flip-chart pad to hide what he had written for the moment. He nodded at his little assembled team – a group of people he trusted implicitly, both with secrets and his life . . . with the slight exception of FB, who he didn't trust with anything except his own agenda.

Rik Dean, who hadn't set eyes on Henry for a few days, was wide-eyed at his appearance. 'Your face is a mess.'

'Really . . . I didn't know . . . in what way?' Henry said.

'And so is yours,' Rik said, turning to Flynn, Henry's sarcasm sailing right over his head.

Flynn grinned. The two men knew each other quite well.

'Right, folks,' Henry began, running a hand across the crown of his head. 'Quite a lot been going on in the past couple of days, as you're probably aware. Myself and Steve have, unintentionally, been at the vortex of things. It's a story that involves violent death, Russian hoodlums . . .' Henry started to enjoy this little opening slot, speaking in a bit of a pantomime voice. 'Unidentified bodies, attempts on the life of a police officer – me – and innocent members of the public – Steve . . .'

They're eating out of the palm of my hand, he thought.

But the moment was broken by a knock on the office door.

'What?' Henry snapped.

The door edged open an inch. It was the FMIT secretary, a lady who had an office on the same floor. She looked apologetic.

'Sorry, sir,' she said meekly. Henry bit his tongue and held back from telling her that he'd said no interruptions, which he had. 'It's just that there's someone at HQ reception who wants to see you. I thought you'd want to know.'

Henry knew the secretary well enough to realize she would not have interrupted unless it was urgent. 'Who?'

'It's the daughter of Joe Speakman.'

He could have done without the intrusion. It seemed that just as he was in a position to get his thoughts back in line, something came along and barged him off track. It was very frustrating, mainly because he knew there was so much going on and he didn't want to forget anything, which was a distinct possibility based on the way his brain was spinning now and how tired he was. He knew he had some very important nuggets and to forget them would be catastrophic.

But the family of a victim could not be ignored.

Henry apologized to the men in front of him, bowing and scraping to the chief constable especially, who breathed out long and hard down his hairy nostrils and said, 'Just give me a call when you're ready to go again.'

Five minutes later Henry led a very clearly distressed lady from reception into a meeting room just inside headquarters, and asked one of the receptionists to go and buy some tea and biscuits with the fiver he handed her.

The woman was red-eyed from crying.

Henry regarded her, wondering if he remembered her at all. He was usually excellent with faces and places – one of his few attributes as a detective – but it was usually where criminals were concerned, not people he might have met socially in the dim, distant past.

'I know you,' she said.

'I think I know you.'

'You came to my twenty-first, just after we'd moved into the barn – you know, Mum and Dad's house in Halton.'

Henry racked his brain cells. That was it! He vaguely knew he'd been to Joe Speakman's house before, but he'd been finding it impossible to say where, when or why. It was for this woman's coming-of-age party, over ten years ago, and he realized why he didn't have a clear memory of it.

'You're Melanie,' he said, 'and I was drunk.'

She nodded. 'And you're Henry Christie and you were drunk to start with, then got very drunk. You did that "Mule Train" thing with a metal tray.'

'Oh God,' Henry said shortly. 'Embarrassing.' In days gone by that had been his little party piece, smashing his head with a tray to represent the whip-crack in the cowboy song 'Mule Train'.

'And you tried to hit on me.'

Oh-oh, he thought.

'I'm really sorry.' Now he remembered going out with the CID from Lancaster and Morecambe for some reason. They'd been for a meal, drinking steadily, then ended up at Joe Speakman's, where they drank even more and . . . from that point Henry wasn't sure. He knew he'd woken up in a friend's front room with his head halfway underneath the sofa, staring at a frightened cat.

She shrugged. The memory went. The present cascaded back and she dropped her head into her hands, started weeping.

Henry let her. By the time she'd got over the bout, the tea had arrived, a cup was poured, a Nice biscuit propped on the saucer. Henry handed it to her.

'What's happened?' she asked. 'To Mum and Dad.'

'Before I get into that, can I just ask how you heard?'

'From my brother.'

'Right, OK.' Henry's brow furrowed. She'd almost spat the word 'brother'.

'And then I saw the news, even though no names were mentioned.' Her voice faded.

Henry watched her. She was a nice-looking woman, early thirties now with nicely trimmed bobbed hair and a fine complexion. She wasn't wearing a wedding ring and Henry assumed she had travelled alone to get here.

'You're the officer in charge, aren't you?'

'I am, and I'm very sorry for your loss.'

'Thank you,' she swallowed meekly. 'Can . . . can you tell me what happened?'

Henry blew out his cheeks. Then he took her through his step-by-step guide to the scene of a double fatal shooting, plus dog. He told her enough to fill in some of the gaps in her knowledge, but not too much. Firstly for reasons of consideration. Relatives rarely appreciated gory details. Secondly because, as always, Henry liked to have the upper hand, just in case. Just in case this woman had something to do with the murders. Maybe she'd planned it. Or maybe not, but any half-decent detective kept something back. That said, unless she was a very fine actor, her horrified reactions to his story were very real indeed.

When he'd finished she stared numbly at him, her mouth open. Eventually she said, 'Unbelievable.'

'We think the person responsible might be involved with Russian gangsters . . . but we have a lot of things to look at before we are certain of that.'

'Russian gangsters?' she said incredulously. Her face was screwed up tightly, but her eyes narrowed fractionally.

Henry picked up on it. 'Do you know anything about that?'

'Oh Christ, oh Christ,' she said rubbing her face intensely. 'No, no not really.'

'I think you do,' Henry said.

Her face then set, as though a decision had been made. Her lips went into a tight line and she breathed through her nose, which dilated.

'C'mon, tell me,' he said.

'Ugh,' she said. 'Look, I haven't had much to do with Mum and Dad for a while now. Not through any fallout, just, y'know – I've been living in London, got a decent job and I don't have a lot of time for travelling up and down the country. So what I'm saying is that I haven't been in their lives much, but we do keep in touch-ish.'

'When did you last speak to them?'

'I spoke to Mum about three days ago.'

'How was she?'

'Uptight . . . fit to burst.'

'About what?'

She snorted contemptuously. 'Fucking Cyprus,' she said with vehemence. 'I'm sorry, didn't mean to swear.'

'That's OK – do it myself occasionally.' Henry poured her a refill of tea and gave her a little time to come down. 'What about Cyprus?' he probed.

She tilted her head from side to side, marshalling her thoughts. 'Mum and Dad have been going out there for years – holidays, y'know? In fact a few people who live in the village go out there a lot and have property there. My brother moved out there and actually set up in the property business. He encouraged Mum and Dad to buy a place and invest in some land. Dad bought a villa – quarter of a million, I think . . . but I also heard it was a good deal. I mean . . . *way* too good. Tom – my brother – introduced them to a well shady developer and I knew it just wasn't right. But Tom said it was and Dad always believed him.

'Fancy investing in a property over two thousand miles from home and in a culture you don't understand, with people you don't know. Trouble at the best of times and I bloody warned them! Tom and I had horrible arguments about it . . . and then I started hearing things about . . . stuff . . .'

'What stuff?'

'It sounds so unreal and dramatic.' She sighed and gave a helpless shrug. 'Russians . . . prostitutes . . .' She closed her eyes. 'Trafficking . . . girls.' Her head was shaking. 'But I truly don't know the details, honestly. I kept my head in the sand. I think they got into a situation they couldn't get out of . . .'

'Or maybe they were trying to get out of?' Henry suggested.

'Possibly.'

'Does the name Malinowski mean anything to you?'

She looked as though she'd been hit by a truck. 'He's the property dealer in Cyprus,' she whispered.

'And did your parents know Harry Sunderland?'

Melanie Speakman's eyes suddenly burned. 'He's the one who got my parents out to Cyprus in the first place. He's got property there, too. He had something to do with setting Tom up in business . . . I wouldn't trust the slimy bastard as far as I could chuck him!'

THIRTEEN

Henry spent an hour talking to Melanie Speakman, after which she said she'd made arrangements to stay over at a friend's house in Bispham, near Blackpool, where Henry could contact her whilst he carried out his investigation.

She got a lot off her chest in that time and although deeply upset and grieving over her parents' deaths – and the dog, of course (who, Henry learned, wasn't Carlo. Carlo had died long ago and been replaced by Milo, same breed) – she seemed more in control when she left than when she'd arrived. Henry Christie the counsellor, acting as a catalyst.

'I don't know if any of this is any use,' she admitted.

'It's hard to say, but when we start digging I'm sure that if what you've told me is a factor, then it'll all become very obvious very quickly.'

To be honest, she hadn't told him much – just names and supposition and grim feelings. But that was the start of the route – information, conjecture, leading to intelligence, then to evidence.

'Thanks.' Her eyes searched his. 'I hope you don't mind me asking,' she said, 'but when you came to my twenty-first, I was sure you were wearing a wedding ring. I know it's a long time ago and it's a bit of a girlie thing to remember . . . but . . .' She glanced down at his left hand.

From the shadow that instantly scudded across his face, she knew she had touched a nerve.

'I'm sorry,' she said hastily. 'Not my business, just being curious. Women, you know . . .'

Henry's expression softened. 'It's OK,' he said with a half-laugh. 'I was married.' Shit, he thought, why is this so hard to say, even to a stranger? 'She passed away last year. Cancer.' He said the word in the same way Melanie had referred to her brother earlier.

'I'm really sorry . . . but I'd like to say that if you hadn't been drunk and wearing a wedding ring, there would have been a good chance of scoring back then.'

'Nice to know,' he chuckled, flushing a little. 'I hope I wasn't too embarrassing.'

'No, you were funny.' She inhaled deeply. 'I'll be off to my friend's, then. Please keep in touch.'

'I will.'

Henry showed her out of the building and watched her walk across the car park to a red Porsche Carrera in one of the bays. She got into it and drove away. He watched the car pass under the raised barrier at the exit, then turn onto the dual carriageway that ran past headquarters.

His mind churned with the new information as he went back inside, intending to take the tea pot and cups back to the kitchen.

He bumped straight away into Jerry Tope, who, he suspected, had been lurking and waiting to pounce.

'Boss, can I have another quick word before we all get back together?'

Henry opened the door to the meeting room he'd been using and graciously wafted Tope in, then closed the door behind them both.

Tope's face was lined with worry. 'I've, uh, been digging again . . . found some more stuff, unpleasant stuff.'

Henry managed to corral his helpers back into his office, with the exception of Steve Flynn, who had felt obliged to get back to Glasson Dock and open up the shop. He wasn't a cop any more and Henry was probably pushing it to have him aboard anyway.

Strangely, Henry was disappointed not to see him, a feeling that made him slightly uneasy. Was he getting to like the guy? Perhaps the life-threatening incidents they'd been involved with in the last couple of days had given Henry a fresh perspective on him.

Henry looked at his assembled crew, although it was not quite true to say that FB was really a crew member. He was just an interested party.

Then he revealed his flip-chart jottings and began to piece

together what he knew for certain and what he surmised, and hoped he hadn't missed anything.

'What's going on, Henry?'

'Ralph, thanks for calling. Just been a bit delayed at head-quarters, all crap stuff mainly,' Henry said. He was talking to DI Barlow, the Lancaster jack, on his mobile phone.

'No probs . . . just need to know what's happening is all. You can't have had much sleep.'

'None, actually.'

'Er, there's couple of guys landed here,' Barlow said. 'I'm not one hundred per cent sure as to why, but they say you told them to get their arses up here.'

'Yeah . . . I'm trying to pull one or two people in to kick-start an investigation.'

'So you're not doing as I suggested?' Barlow said frostily.

'No . . . thanks for the advice, though.'

'Well, so be it,' Barlow sighed, which really sounded to Henry like, 'Be it on your own head, mate.' Barlow was in his office at Lancaster nick and a DI from Blackpool CID was sitting opposite him, lounging indolently in a chair, trying to look bored and pissed off. Barlow made a circle with his thumb and fore-finger and jerked his hand up and down and pointed to the phone at his ear for the benefit of the DI.

The gesture meant *Henry Christie: wanker*.

The other DI nodded agreement.

'Who else has arrived?' Henry asked innocently.

'Some bloody PC from training school. Christ knows what his skills are!'

'That'll be the firearms guy. I wanted him to have a look at the weapon that was used, you know, the machine-pistol. Get his take on it.'

'Oh, right, whatever,' Barlow said rather crossly. 'What's your plan, then?'

'To be honest, Ralph, I haven't completely got my head around things . . . but I think my first port of call is Harry Sunderland.'

'Eh? Why? What's he got to do with you being shot at?' Barlow blustered.

'I know it's a bit lame, but I need to question him about his wife and the circumstances of her disappearance, just to find out how she really did end up in the river. I'm not completely convinced by his story.'

'And what has that to do with last night? Completely unrelated,' Barlow insisted.

'Also I'd like to know why the two heavies wanted to find what was in the wife's property . . . that's really bothering me,' Henry bullshitted. 'So I think I'm going to lock him up for murder and take it from there. A bit thin, maybe, but I want to lean on him.'

Barlow hissed an unimpressed breath.

'Shall I meet you at Lancaster nick in about half an hour?' Henry asked. 'We can go and see him together.'

'Yeah, good idea.'

Barlow ended the call and shook his head despondently at the visiting DI. 'Henry bloody Christie,' he said by way of explanation.

Rik Dean nodded agreement. 'Don't I know it.'

'Look, I hope you don't think I'm being rude here, but I need to make a personal call.' Barlow waggled his phone at Rik, who stood up with a wave of understanding and said, 'Sure, no worries. Brew after?'

'See you up in the canteen.'

Rik left the office, closing the door behind him.

In the corridor outside he leaned on the wall, took his own mobile phone out and made sure it was receiving a signal. It was: full strength.

Bill Robbins poked his head out of the CID office door further down the corridor and arched his eyebrows at Rik.

The wait seemed interminable.

But then Rik's phone vibrated in his hand.

He answered it quickly, listened for a moment, said, 'Right,' tersely, and finished the call.

He glanced at Bill Robbins and nodded.

Henry Christie's mobile phone rang five seconds after Rik Dean had slid his own back into his pocket.

Henry had it ready in his hand and answered it instantly, listened for a few moments, said, 'OK, thanks,' and ended the call.

He glanced sideways at FB and nodded.

As Rik Dean pushed himself upright off the corridor wall and spun towards Ralph Barlow's office door, with Bill Robbins right behind him, the door actually opened before Rik could reach the handle.

Barlow emerged, stunned to almost barge straight into Rik.

'Oh, sorry mate,' Barlow said. 'Need to get going. Something's come up.'

Rik stood immobile in front of him, his eyes stone hard, face deadly serious. 'I don't think so, Ralph.'

'What?' Barlow snorted and tried to ease his way past Rik. 'Excuse me.'

'Can we just go back into your office?' Rik said pleasantly.

'For why?'

'I think you know . . .'

'I know fuck all, except you're in my way.' He tried to move past, but Rik held up a hand – almost the police number one stop signal.

'I'll do it here if you want,' he said, the tone of his voice becoming brittle. 'In the corridor.'

'Do what?'

Two female civilian members of staff walked down the corridor, past the three men at the DI's office door, sensing something very amiss.

Rik sighed. Underneath the surface, he was quite nervous, but did not betray any of this in his outward demeanour. He'd been in tougher situations, but had never had to arrest a fellow officer before. 'I'll do it in front of everyone, if you like,' he said impatiently.

'I don't know what the hell you're on about, but I'd guess you're about to make one big fucking mistake – so let me pass before this gets ugly.'

'It's already ugly . . . back into the office, last time of asking.'

'Go to fuck, Rik,' Barlow snapped and tried to barge past. Rik laid a restraining hand on his chest that stopped him going any further. Barlow froze and looked down at the hand, palm on his sternum, fingers splayed out, then along Rik's arm and into his face. 'You'd better take that away.'

At which point, Rik had had enough pussyfooting about.

'I'm arresting you on suspicion of corruption. You don't have to say anything, but it may harm your defence if—' Rik began to caution him, but wasn't allowed to complete the little speech as Barlow slammed his right fist in a wide-arcing blow into Rik's face, knocking him sideways into Bill Robbins, who had been watching the verbal transaction with trepidation, realizing it was all going very sour.

Barlow was a bigger man than Rik, who was quite small in stature, and he followed up the blow by pushing Rik into Bill then tearing down the corridor.

'Get him,' Rik said.

Bill was no spring chicken. In fact he was stoutly built and getting on a little, but being a firearms trainer meant he was very fit in a lots-of-stamina way, though not especially fleet of foot.

He also heaved Rik out of the way and charged after Barlow, who careened down the corridor, turning sharp left at the end of it.

Bill pounded after him but by the time he reached the turn, Barlow had vanished. But Bill knew he hadn't been *that* far behind, so Barlow must have gone into one of the doors on this stretch.

First was a store room. Locked. Next was a ladies' loo. There was slight hesitation on Bill's part, but he opened the door an inch and called, 'I'm coming in!'

He opened the door fully. Directly opposite the door was a bank of three washbasins and at one of them was one of the lady support-staff members who had just walked down the corridor. She had her back to the basins and a very confused look on her face.

Bill twisted to his left where there were three toilet cubicles, two doors slightly ajar, the third closed.

'Is he in there?' Bill demanded. The woman's mouth popped like a goldfish. But nothing came out of it. Bill cursed.

He couldn't even check by looking under the door because these were fully enclosed cubicles, offering complete privacy, so he had a decision to make he hoped he would not regret.

He stepped across and pounded on the closed door. 'Mr Barlow.'

There was no response.

If there had been an indisposed female in there, Bill would have expected some response – probably a scream.

He pushed the door: locked. So he took a couple of backward paces, picked his spot, prayed there wasn't a lady on the loo, and flat-footed the door by the flimsy lock.

Bill had kicked down many doors in his service. He practised it regularly on team training.

And this one was no problem. It clattered open, slamming back and connecting with Ralph Barlow's back as he knelt in front of the toilet, fumbling with something and reaching for the flush.

Bill grabbed him just as his fingers touched the handle, dragged him by his collar out of the cubicle and deposited him at the feet of the still-shocked woman. The component parts of Barlow's mobile phone came out of his hand and scattered across the tiled floor, front, back and battery.

Rik Dean came in just as Bill was heaving Barlow over onto his front and forcing his arms behind his back.

'Trying to flush the evidence away,' Bill gasped. 'SIM card, I think.'

Rik saw the pieces of the dismembered phone. 'Did he manage?'

'Don't think so. That one,' Bill said, pointing into the cubicle.

Rik tutted, stepped over Barlow's legs into the cubicle. He was holding his face, throbbing from Barlow's punch. He squatted down and peered into the toilet bowl, which was fortunately filled with clean water, but could not see the SIM card.

Only one thing for it.

He unfastened his shirt cuff and pulled up his sleeve, then reached into the water, gently feeling along the porcelain U-bend with his fingertips, hoping he wouldn't find anything other than a SIM card.

He touched something, small, rectangular, placed a fingertip on it and drew it carefully backwards all the way out of the water, then took it between his thumb and forefinger and thought, 'Thank God you were right about this one, Henry Christie.'

*   *   *

Henry had known Robert Fanshaw-Bayley – FB – for almost thirty years now, having first encountered him in the very early 1980s when Henry was a uniformed PC in Rossendale, far to the east of the county of Lancashire. At that time FB was the local DI, ruling the roost like some sort of malicious demigod. Their relationship over the intervening years had been rocky, to say the least, but had survived many ups and downs.

Although he was now chief constable (and had reached the year of his obligatory retirement) FB had the word 'Jack' written through him like a stick of Blackpool rock. He had been a detective for most of his service, a good, if ruthless one – and like most cops of rank, still loved to 'go out playing' on the front line now and again.

Hence his decision to accompany Henry that day.

And now they were parked in the village of Slyne in the constabulary pool vehicle Henry had managed to coerce from the transport department, near the gates of Sunderland Transport. It was a rather beaten-up Vauxhall Vectra and when he picked it up he was warned to check the oil level because it burned the black stuff like an old steam train. FB sat alongside him.

Henry said, 'Right, thanks,' into his mobile phone and ended the call, then glanced at FB as he slid the phone back into his pocket. He pursed his lips and said, 'It's happening, boss, the call's being made now.'

'Let's roll, then.'

A few minutes earlier, Steve Flynn, in Alison's car, had pretended to do a mistaken turn into the car park at Sunderland Transport and had clocked that Sunderland's Aston Martin was parked up in its usual position.

Flynn was here because Henry had decided to tell him what was going on and asked him along – in a purely observational capacity – to witness events unfold if he so wished. Although Flynn had only just opened up the chandlery, he could not resist and joined Henry in Slyne, where they worked out their not very complicated plan, including Flynn's accidental turn around in Sunderland Transport to check out the lay of the land.

After he'd clocked the Aston, Flynn had parked discreetly behind Henry and settled down to see what transpired. He knew he should have been at the shop, but, having been nearly killed on more occasions in the last couple of days than almost all the time he'd been a commando in the Falklands war, he did not want to miss anything. And he promised Henry he would just watch, not get involved, even if Henry was getting his head kicked in.

As Henry pulled away from the kerb with FB, Flynn dearly wished it was himself in the passenger seat. Having left the force under an undeserved cloud he felt he had a lot of unfinished business. He had loved being a cop and still hankered for it and would gladly have forgone his life in Gran Canaria to still be one.

But it was not to be. Life had moved on. He allowed Alison's car to roll forward a few feet and take up the space the Vectra had occupied. He watched Henry turn into the gates.

Henry instantly saw the Aston. He drove into one of the visitors' parking bays and he and FB climbed out. They walked side by side into reception.

Harry Sunderland was behind the desk, tugging his jacket on hurriedly, explaining something to Miranda, the receptionist. He glanced up as Henry entered through the revolving doors, followed by FB. He did a double-take and his expression changed to that of the rabbit in the headlights, about to be mown flat. But it was only momentary – because he bolted out of the headlight beam and sprinted to a fire door behind reception, crashing through it, emerging at the side of the office building, skidding towards the car park.

Henry went after him. He vaulted the reception desk, virtually flying past the bewildered Miranda, who screamed and covered her head. Henry had slightly misjudged the width of the desk and had to scramble untidily off the far side, but he was not far behind Sunderland, who had slammed the fire door shut behind him.

FB did not run. He calmly did an about-turn and stepped into the revolving door.

Sunderland ran hard towards his car, fumbling for the keys and desperately trying to use the remote control to unlock it.

Henry was held back only seconds by the door, then he was through, only feet behind Sunderland, who reached his Aston and wrenched open the driver's door. As he swung himself in,

Henry caught up and manhandled him back out just as FB joined them.

'What the fuck're you playing at?' Sunderland demanded, as Henry, relishing it, spun him and splayed him across the expensive bonnet of the magnificent sports car. He pinned him there, leant over and spoke into the man's ear.

'You're under arrest,' Henry growled as he fought to get the man's arms behind his back to apply the rigid cuffs.

'What for? I've done fuck all.'

'We'll start with murder.'

'Of who, you knob?'

'Your wife, Jennifer.'

Sunderland stopped his ineffective struggling. 'What?' he said incredulously.

'You heard.'

'I didn't kill her.'

'In that case, we can talk about other things . . . like corruption.'

Sunderland started to struggle again, which Henry thought was a good sign. He held him tight and glanced at FB.

'Not sure what your plans are, Henry – but beating a quick retreat might be the order of the day here,' FB said pointing.

Henry's eyes followed the fat finger.

Two large men in oily overalls had emerged from one of the warehouse doors, each with a heavy wrench in hand – and they were jogging towards the scene of the arrest, looking menacing and possibly mistaking an official piece of police business for two men in plain clothes assaulting their boss.

Sunderland twisted his head up and saw them. 'Better let me go, guys, or these two'll enjoy whacking you.'

The men ran on, wrenches raised – just as Flynn sped in through the gates in Alison's car and accelerated across the car park to position himself between the men and the arrest. He swerved the car to a stop on the gravel surface, throwing up stones like pebbledashing, his sudden appearance causing the two men to slow to an unsure jog.

Flynn dropped out of the driver's seat, coming up to his full height and waited for the men to arrive.

He looked pretty awe-inspiring, with his beaten-up, stitched face atop his wide stature, and Henry thought he was definitely a good man to have behind you.

'I'll go for both of you guys,' he said, not boasting, just stating fact. 'Monkey wrenches or otherwise.'

Their run slowed to a stop. They were ten metres away from him.

FB walked up. 'Very commendable, guys,' he said, 'but your boss is under arrest and unless you want to end up in the same cell complex, I suggest you down tools and go back from whence you came. Like now!'

'And who the fuck are you, fatty?' one snarled at him.

FB did something he hadn't done for a very long time: he flashed his warrant card. Relishing the drama, whilst also feeling just slightly silly, he announced, 'I'm the fucking chief constable.'

It would have been unwise to have lodged the two prisoners in Lancaster's cells. Henry needed to get them away from their home turf, particularly Barlow. He was a well-liked detective with a lot of friends at the station, a situation that could conceivably make things difficult for Henry.

To that end, Henry had already warned the custody office at Blackpool to be ready for two prisoners who were to be kept separate and given cells at the opposite ends of the big complex so they could not communicate in any way with each other. Henry did not reveal who the prisoners would be.

Henry had also arranged transport for them, having commandeered the services of two headquarters driving-school instructors, two plain cars and two uniformed constables from the public-order training unit in order to convey the prisoners to Blackpool.

Moments after Henry had made the arrest of Harry Sunderland and the possibility of being battered by Sunderland's wrench-wielding staff had passed, Henry called up the driving-school car that was on standby half a mile away.

When it arrived, Sunderland was pushed into the back of it alongside a burly riot-squad trainer.

Henry gave them certain instructions and assured them he would not be far behind.

Once Sunderland was on his way, Henry called up Rik Dean

to confirm that DI Barlow had also been arrested and was on his
way to Blackpool in the other driving-school car to Blackpool.

So far, so good. Henry liked smooth plans. He and FB looked
at each other and grinned.

Then Henry realized that Flynn was nowhere to be seen. He
looked around to see that he was climbing through a Judas door
set in the larger door of the warehouse unit where the two
employees had scuttled back to. Flynn had obviously followed
them.

Henry tutted.

Flynn's head reappeared through the door and he waved for
Henry to come over. Henry tutted again, but set off with FB in
tow.

'What is it?'

'Feast your eyes,' Flynn said.

He pushed the door open and Henry climbed through into the
warehouse, followed by FB.

'Allo, allo, allo,' Henry said for the first time in his career.

In a row, facing him, stood three almost new top model Range
Rovers, all in black. None bore a registration plate. They stood
side by side, magnificent machines, like knights' chargers.

Henry had a swell of relief.

'Bingo,' FB said.

'Full house,' Henry confirmed.

FOURTEEN

Silence.

Background noise, yes. The sound of a cell door slamming shut. A shout of a prisoner, the response of a gaoler.
The humming of the air conditioning. The hiss of the tape machine
running.

But between the two men, silence.

It always came down to this, Henry thought – and relished
the prospect.

Verbal jousting.

The tapping of a wedge, metaphorically speaking, into a tiny crack, then – tap, tap, tap – opening it up.

Or not.

It didn't matter to Henry. All he knew was that there were not many better feelings than being face-to-face with a prisoner, maybe two feet separating their faces across the interview table, and slicing them to shreds.

But, not far into this encounter, the prisoner had clammed up tight.

Henry wasn't perturbed. Silence didn't faze him. He revelled in it. 'No comment' didn't even touch his radar. You want to say nothing, fine. Your prerogative. Say nowt.

Henry smiled and twitched his eyebrows, held his gaze on the man sitting opposite, a man who had almost as much experience as himself of the interview situation and maybe because of that thought he knew how to deal with it.

But not from that side of the table.

Often silence worked to the disadvantage of the interviewee. Usually they couldn't stand it, somehow felt obliged to speak, to fill the gaps, to drop themselves in it, tie themselves up in knots with convoluted tales that then unravelled like a ball of wool.

This man was different, as no doubt he had used silence as a tool himself – when he was sitting on Henry Christie's side of the table.

'OK,' Henry said, smiling slightly. He nodded at Ralph Barlow, who was the man across from him, his solicitor sitting alongside him. 'You've had the chance, now I'll lay it on the line for you.'

At this stage, Henry didn't have a problem with this tactic. He was fluid in his approach. Go with the flow – but always stay in control.

If Barlow knew he was screwed, that the ball was well and truly spinning in his direction, then it was up to him how he dealt with it.

Henry went on, 'I'll lay out some bare, irrefutable facts for you.' He had a folder in front of him, which he opened, and cleared his throat. 'Your mobile phone is paid for by the police. It's a tool of the trade. All detectives have mobile-phone accounts, paid for by the force, generally without question – unless the

invoices are astronomical.' He extracted a few sheets of paper
from the folder, invoices from a well-known service provider.
'These are your bills for the last two years. On them I have
highlighted numerous calls to a particular phone number. Also'
– Henry slid out another sheet of paper – 'I have this, a bang
up-to-date record of the calls you've made in the last three days,
including several to the particular number I've been talking about
– times, dates, including this morning . . .'

Henry swished the sheet around so Barlow could see it. He
didn't allow his eyes to wander. They were set, but unfocused,
behind Henry's left shoulder.

'Made whilst DI Dean was standing outside your office. You
were making a frantic phone call to this number because I'd just
phoned you to tell you about an intended arrest. I won't even
talk about the comical debacle of you trying to dispose of your
SIM card down a toilet. This is Harry Sunderland's number,'
Henry declared.

Barlow sat there, unimpressed.

Henry shuffled the papers around and pointed to a highlighted
series of calls to Sunderland's phone. 'These calls were made
the morning his wife was found in the river.'

He raised his eyes and looked at Barlow, whose eyes would
not return the look. 'And this call, using 141 to disguise you as
the caller, was made to Steve Flynn's phone this morning, too.'

Henry slid the papers back into the folder. Underneath was a
second one, which he opened, talking as he did. 'I mean, the
thing is you were pretty careless, but in the normal run of events,
none of this stuff would have been spotted. We don't comb
through mobile-phone accounts of our officers, do we, Ralph?
Not unless we suspect something's amiss.'

'It proves nothing,' Barlow said, breaking his silence.

'It proves that when you get cocky, you get caught,' Henry
said. 'Now we come to this,' he said with delight. He laid his
hand on the next folder and said, 'As a divisional DI you wield
a great deal of power, don't you? Not least in terms of the
administration of crime reporting. Absolute power, I'd say.' Henry
looked at him and saw a frown on Barlow's forehead – wondering,
or knowing, what was coming. 'You have the power to write off
crimes, have them deleted from the system – or, *OR*, to invent

crimes in order to facilitate criminal activity. You can cook the books, or burn the books, can't you?'

Barlow shrugged noncommittally.

'See – problem is, once a ball starts rolling, it's usually very hard to stop. Interest is aroused. More digging begins. Unsavoury things are uncovered – and that ball turns into an Indiana Jones boulder which, even though you might not believe it, is what you are now fleeing from.'

'I don't know what the fuck you're talking about, Henry.'

The detective superintendent picked up another sheet of paper.

'Crime forms – for a few very petty offences. Offences which never actually took place but were reported by you as a means to an end.'

Henry read through one carefully. 'This is one from two years ago. Theft from the person. A bag-snatch. Not robbery. That would have caused too much interest. So, just a snatch and a run with the offender seen to jump into a black Range Rover. No arrest made. Nothing much done about it. But, as a result of this so-called crime, you did a PNC check for top-range newish black Range Rovers in the northwest and came up with' – he held up a sheet – 'over twenty.' He smiled. 'Should I go on?'

'You'll have to, because you've lost me here.'

'OK . . . eight of these Range Rovers were subsequently stolen – not all at once – but not one was ever recovered.' His good eye narrowed fractionally. 'What are the odds of that? You'd expect a couple to turn up at least. But not a one?' He fished out another piece of paper. 'This is a recent crime report submitted by you dealing with the theft of property from a building site. Something and nothing, a minor crime. Guess what? The offenders escaped in what was described as a black Range Rover. Then guess what? You did a PNC search for black Range Rovers, which threw up eleven very new ones in the northwest. Then guess what? Four of them got stolen.' Henry's voice became serious. 'And now three of those four are sitting in Harry Sunderland's warehouse. And the fourth is in a police garage – because it was being driven last night by the man who tried to kill me and Steve Flynn.'

Silence – except for a cell door ominously clanging shut, something timed to accidental perfection.

'These reports are all a matter of record, Ralph, as are your phone calls to Sunderland and to Steve Flynn. Now, thing is, his wife is dead and I have yet to be convinced she committed suicide or just had a nasty accident.' He ran his hand over his face, stretching his tired features. 'And because you warned him I was coming to see him – which you did, didn't you – I'm deeply suspicious about her death now – which I wasn't before all this shit started happening.' Henry poked a finger at Barlow. 'You are a bent cop, Ralph, and I'm going to unravel all this and you can either help or hinder, I don't care. But you need to care because, if Jennifer Sunderland was murdered and you knew about it, you've had it. And – big "and" – to add insult to injury, the man who tried to kill me and Steve Flynn was driving a stolen Range Rover that is on your PNC printout, and I don't like people trying to kill me, Ralph. It pisses me off.' Abruptly he said, 'This interview is concluded for the prisoner to consult with his solicitor.' Henry took out the tapes and sealed them and had them signed, then rose to leave.

As he did, Barlow said, 'What was it, Henry?'

'What was what?'

'What was my mistake?'

'Apart from all this, you mean?' Henry indicated the files.

'You know what I mean. What did I do or say to give it away? I'd just like to know what a great detective looks for,' Barlow said sarcastically. 'And you're such a great detective, aren't you? But actually, we all know you're not. You make bad judgement calls and you've been flying by the seat of your pants for years now, all because you're up the chief's arse.'

'Difference is, Ralph. I'm still flying – but you've crashed and burned.' He gave Barlow a subtle wink.

Henry took the coffee that was proffered as he entered the DI's office at Blackpool police station and took a grateful swig. He looked at the people assembled therein – FB, Rik Dean, Steve Flynn and Bill Robbins. They had been watching an audiovisual feed from the interview room on a monitor set up in Rik's office.

'Well?' Henry said.

'Things are moving quickly,' FB commented. 'Though I didn't realize you were so far up my backside.'

Henry laughed. 'If only they knew the truth.' He settled on the corner of the desk feeling excessively weary, his mind fizzing.

The door opened and Jerry Tope came in, a piece of paper in hand.

'Two identifications,' he announced. 'Well, ninety per cent certain . . . the guy at Joe Speakman's house was Yuri Gregorov; the guy who tried to kill you last night – Vladimir Kaminski, the two Russian enforcers, as we suspected. Oscar Malinowski's men.'

Henry ingested the news. 'Russians,' he said quietly. He'd been face to face with bad Russians before and in his experience they were not pleasant.

'What about Sunderland?' FB asked, referring to the other prisoner ensconced in a cell at the far end of the complex.

'We . . . let me think,' Henry began uncertainly. Putting his thoughts in order suddenly became a chore. 'We know what we've got. Dead girl in a mortuary, dead woman in a river, seemingly unconnected, but both having the same dentist in Cyprus. I don't know what the significance is of that, yet, by the way. Dead woman in river is thought to have something in her possession so valuable that Russian hit men come after it – so what is it? I know we've been through this before . . .'

'Document?' Tope suggested.

'Photo?' Bill suggested. 'An incriminating one?'

Henry shook his head. 'The way forward,' he said. 'Husband's in custody, so let's ask him. Get into his ribs about why and how she ended up in the drink and what she might have had that was so important. In the meantime I want search teams at Sunderland's address, Barlow's address and I want a proper job done at Joe Speakman's house, too.'

'Three search teams?' Rik said. 'You'll be lucky.'

'Make me lucky . . . I'll do a preliminary interview with Sunderland, then I'd like to be there when they "spin his drum", as they say. In the meantime, Jerry, will you start trying to make sense of all this . . . you know, timelines, backgrounds, relationships, histories, pull a story together.'

'Love to,' Tope said, relishing the prospect.

'Bill, will you help him?' Bill nodded. Henry then addressed Flynn. 'What do you want to do, Steve?'

'Tag along with you, maybe?'

'OK.' Henry looked at FB. 'Boss?'

'Just get on with it, Henry – do what you have to do and stop brown-nosing, OK?'

Flynn asked Henry, 'So what was it?'

'What was what?'

'The mistake.'

'Yeah, go on, Henry, tell us . . . pretty please,' Rik said.

'Nothing really . . . just that when I went with Ralph to break the news to Sunderland that we'd found his wife, Sunderland said something that he couldn't have known and I picked up on it. The only person who could have told him was someone who knew exactly where the body had been recovered from . . . I just assumed Ralph had told him, but if it hadn't been Ralph, it must have been some other cop, probably. But it was him and I think they're deep into something which probably involves this Chechnyan ganglord, Malinowski. And, unfortunately, Joe Speakman's in that mix, too.'

For the time being Sunderland was content to be represented by a duty solicitor and was sitting alongside him as Henry entered the interview room and plonked himself opposite. After the tape formalities and necessary introductions, Henry explained this was just a preliminary interview to give Sunderland the opportunity to say something, if he so desired. Further interviews would follow later, after securing and preserving evidence.

'What does that mean?' Sunderland asked.

'The search of your business premises, where items of evidence will be seized, such as stolen Range Rovers.' Henry watched Sunderland's reaction to this – just a kink of the mouth. Then Henry said, 'And your house will be searched, too.'

This news jarred Sunderland. His eyes rose and Henry saw apprehension in them and tension in his whole being. 'You can't do that,' he said.

'Just watch me.'

Sunderland turned to his brief. 'He can't do that, can he?'

'I'm afraid he can – with the necessary authorization.'

'Which I've got,' Henry confirmed. He leaned on the table. 'Why? Something to hide?'

Now Sunderland wouldn't lock eyes with Henry.

'What am I going to find, Mr Sunderland? Want to tell me now?'

'You'll find nothing.' Sunderland pinched the bridge of his nose.

'You sure about that? It won't be a cursory search – I'll rip your place to shreds.' No response. Henry paused thoughtfully, sat back and folded his arms. 'Mr Sunderland – what did your wife have in her possession that was so all-fired important? So important that two men committed serious assaults' – here Henry pointed at his own face – 'and almost killed a man to find whatever it was?'

'Don't know what you're talking about.'

'What did you and her argue about the night she fell into the river?'

'Nothing.'

'How did she fall into the river?'

'How would I know? I wasn't there. I've already told the police that.'

'OK – how well do you know Joe Speakman and his wife?'

'Only in passing.'

'How about Yuri Gregorov and Vladimir Kaminski?'

Sunderland shrugged. 'Never heard of them.'

'What about a gangster in Cyprus called Malinowski?'

'A gangster? What planet are you on? I'm a businessman.'

'What's going to happen to those Range Rovers? Where are they destined?'

'Don't know what you mean.'

'How well do you know Ralph Barlow?'

'Who? Does that answer your question?' he sneered.

'OK,' Henry smiled wickedly. 'Just food for thought, things for you to mull on.' He brought the interview to a close, sealed the tapes and stood up. 'Going to search your property now.'

Henry and Rik walked through the narrow corridors and tight stairwells of Blackpool police station. Flynn tagged along behind them like a spare part, along for the ride but with no valuable input to give or job to do. He was feeling frustrated and out of place.

'Search teams are sorted,' Rik was saying, 'and they're all en route, one from Southern Division, one from Eastern and one of ours. I've emailed their sergeants copies of the search authorizations for Sunderland's and Barlow's houses.'

'What about Sunderland Transport?'

Rik winced. 'I've had the stolen-vehicle squad seize the Range Rovers but other than shutting the place down, I think we'll have to come back to that one. It's a busy place, lorries coming and going.'

'Shut it down, then,' Henry said. 'When we have enough people to search it, that is. If the Range Rovers have been seized, that's enough for the time being.'

'Incidentally, Range Rovers are big business with the Russkies, according to the stolen-vehicle guys . . . big trade in them across Eastern Europe . . . could be where they're headed.'

Henry took that on board as they reached the lower floor exit into the police-station car park. 'What have I missed?' he asked.

'I think we're about covered,' Rik said. 'It's just a matter of getting their stories out of them . . . they'll crack,' he said. 'But what do you think it's all about?'

'The usual – money, sex, greed, revenge, blackmail . . . and all the good things that make it worthwhile being a cop.' He looked at Flynn, then glanced at his watch and blanched. He had not realized how quickly time had passed since receiving the phone call from Flynn that morning with the 'tell Christie to back off' warning that had galvanized him into action. Henry Christie didn't back off from anything.

Much had happened since. Something that had not happened – again – was Henry keeping in contact with Alison. He grimaced internally.

'I need to make a call,' he said, suddenly annoyed with himself. Rik nodded, turned and went back down the corridor. Henry stepped out on to the car park, with Flynn behind him.

Flynn watched him with a wry smile as he shuffled off, pulling out his mobile phone and trying to get a signal in the high-walled compound, by holding up his phone high.

Flynn was beginning to feel like the proverbial spare prick at a wedding, but was loath to leave the party because of his deep involvement in everything that had happened since heaving Jennifer Sunderland's body out of the river. He thought that events gave him some sort of right to be here, but in reality he knew Henry was just being generous to him and he also knew FB was uncomfortable with him hanging around. Ex-cops were a pain.

Which brought Flynn to thoughts of Henry and his very much altered perception of the guy.

A thoroughly dedicated detective, Flynn was impressed by Henry's doggedness and attention to detail, even though he could tell that Henry's head was spinning with all the information being chucked at him. But he missed nothing and Flynn was sure that if Henry hadn't clocked Sunderland's river 'mishap', none of the subsequent events would have been linked together so quickly, if at all.

Flynn felt a burgeoning respect for him. And beyond Henry's obvious skills as a jack, the incidents with the two mad Russians had shown Henry to be courageous and brave, and that impressed Flynn, too. As well as Henry's generosity about living accommodation.

'Going soft on the bastard,' he thought. 'Best to keep thinking of him as a bit of a twat, I reckon.'

'All quiet on the Western front?' Flynn asked as Henry returned from making his call to Alison.

'Yeah, thanks.' Henry was relieved – and suddenly extremely hungry.

'What's the plan for me?' Flynn asked.

'Whatever you want. I'm going to oversee these searches, pull in a whole bunch of detectives from across the county who I can brief and then get them interviewing.' He checked his watch again. Time was disappearing fast. 'I'll get the searches started, see if we can find anything of interest, get these two bedded down for the night' – he was referring to the prisoners – 'then really get into their ribs in the morning, after I've had some proper sleep.'

'You think Sunderland killed his wife?'

'Maybe, maybe not . . . but that's not the point. You were once a detective . . . what's the approach for any sudden death, even if it appears straightforward?'

'Think murder.'

'Bread and butter – and another mistake Barlow made, not treating it as murder to start with. Anyone else would have been hauled in if their missus had ended up drowned, but not his mate Sunderland.'

'So, back to me.'

'What do you want to do? You can stick with me if you want.'

'Mm, maybe I'll check out the searches with you . . . but after that, I'll get back to why I'm here in the first place. So far I've not delivered on that. Should have let Mrs Sunderland drift away.'

'You couldn't have, could you?'

'Guess not.'

'The bedroom offer is still open, by the way.'

'Thanks, Henry . . . I almost said you're a pal.'

'Let's not get slushy . . . how about some fast food? My blood sugar has dropped to a dangerous level and only a KFC will remedy it.'

FIFTEEN

It was 8 p.m. Henry and Flynn had been on the go for almost twelve hours that day, plus all the hours from the preceding night and day, so they were perilously close to empty in terms of adrenaline and energy. That despite the KFC meal bucket they'd shared, plus a coffee each. The energy rush was short-lived and though both men had full bellies, all the food did was make them want to crash out like lions after a kill.

Henry led the way out of Blackpool in the HQ pool vehicle, passing close to his house on an estate near to Marton Circle, the roundabout at the end of the M55. He hadn't been there in about a week and he hoped it was still standing. His youngest daughter, Leanne, had access and Henry envisioned her entertaining a series of boyfriends, following her fairly messy break up with her long-term bloke.

He was tempted to call in and drop into his own bed. That would have to wait. The duties and responsibilities of an SIO outweighed this need.

His plan was to check out how the search at Harry Sunderland's house was progressing, then wind them in for the night, securing and guarding the property, and recommencing in the morning. After carrying out this task, he intended to hare back to Blackpool and crash out at home so he wouldn't have a long journey to Blackpool nick when he got up. Both he and Flynn had discounted staying at headquarters.

It was all very well having the landlady of a country pub as a lady friend, but when the pub was so far out in the sticks, it was sometimes inconvenient geographically. The benefits did outweigh this minus point, though . . . and his mind drifted to Alison as he drove.

Behind him, driving Alison's car, was Flynn.

He realized he was supernumerary, just a bit of an annoyance to Henry, and whilst he was keen to stay involved, he knew he had no right to be under Henry's feet.

The decision he took was that when they reached Lancaster, he would flash Henry to stop and tell him he was taking a step out of it. He was going to go to the hospital to visit Colin, catch up with Diane, apologize for all the crap that had dogged him since he'd landed – not least the complete and utter destruction of their beloved narrowboat.

He had an idea that he would actually bed down in the chandlery itself. When he'd had an initial mooch around the place, he had found that upstairs, apart from the room used to store goods that had probably once been a bedroom, there was also a functioning bathroom with an old sink and a loo. It would be good enough for him, should keep him out of mischief and ensure he was right on the shop to look after it.

Damn, he thought . . . he was pining for the simple life he'd carved out for himself in Puerto Rico . . . sun, fishing, uncomplicated sex, more fishing . . . his mind drifted to the Canary Islands as he drove.

Flynn followed Henry up the M6 northbound and they exited at junction 34, north Lancaster, and turned towards the city. It was on this stretch of road that Flynn flashed Henry to pull in and stop. He could have used the mobile, but wanted to speak face to face.

'What is it?' Henry growled irritably by the roadside. It was getting cold and a bit unpleasant and he was shivering.

Flynn grinned and decided not to rile Henry any further.

'Look, Henry, I'm gonna cut and run here. I'm just a pain in the arse to you – no, don't say anything, I know you don't think that. I need to do what I came here to do. I keep saying it and then doing something different. Diane's going to need someone to sort out the salvage of the canal boat and I need to run that shop properly. I'm going to be here for the next week, if you actually need me, then I'm on the big silver bird back to the sunshine – where I belong.'

'So you're going to trust me to do my job?' Henry said sardonically.

'Yup.' Flynn again held back the urge to have a dig.

'Thanks.' Henry tried not to show his relief, because even though Flynn had basically saved his life twice, having him hanging around the investigation was pushing it, ex-cop or not. 'We still need to sit down and get your statements sorted and speak to CPS about stuff.'

'As to whether I'm going to get charged with two murders, you mean?'

'That won't happen.' Henry shook his head. 'Trust me, I'm a superintendent. Are you going back to the Owl?'

'Naah, but thanks. I'll crash down at the chandlery.'

'You know you're welcome . . .'

'I know and thanks. If I could keep hold of Alison's motor for another night that would be good.'

Henry nodded an OK. 'We'll speak tomorrow. I'll let you know what's happening.' They shook hands hesitantly.

Henry got into his car and breathed a sigh of relief. 'Thank G for that.'

Flynn got into Alison's car and again followed Henry as he drove into Lancaster, but as Henry bore right across the River Lune, Flynn carried on up through the one-way system to the hospital.

Sunderland lived in a luxurious seventeenth-century converted barn just outside Halton on the north bank of the Lune. It was about twice the size of Joe Speakman's house and fitted out much more expensively. It was clear that Sunderland had made real money. Henry estimated the house was probably worth in excess of a million, particularly as its location was magnificent, set high on a hill with a great view of a curve in the river.

Henry drew up just inside the gate, stopping at the side of a wide gravelled driveway that swept up to the front of the house. Parking in front of him were several police vehicles and it was apparent that the search teams were already busy.

Henry flashed his warrant card at the constable controlling the comings and goings to the property, then walked on, his eyes taking in the darkening building, including two large detached garages, a stable block and a detached workshop.

'Nice,' he found himself saying.

He found the sergeant in charge of the search, directing operations from the huge kitchen, the house crawling with overall-clad bobbies.

'Boss,' he greeted Henry.

'Hi, Dave,' Henry said, knowing the guy well enough. 'How's it going?'

The sergeant shrugged. 'We've found a lot of documents which relate to various things: the haulage company, property, vehicle hire and purchase and the usual household stuff. Quite a lot of it I don't understand. The financial analysts will love it, I guess.'

Henry nodded.

'Do you actually know what you're looking for?' the sergeant asked.

Henry smiled. 'No, not really – that's why the authorizations are so vague . . . the only thing is that I believe his wife had something on her when she went into the river that is vitally important to someone and when she was fished out, she didn't have it.'

'Where did she go in?'

'That remains a mystery.'

'How about we search the grounds from the house down to the river,' the sergeant suggested.

'For what?'

'For what that thing might be.'

'Nothing lost, though we don't know for sure if she went in

around here, although the garden seems to run right down to the river.'

'We'll have to do it tomorrow, though. Daylight's virtually gone now.'

'Fine,' Henry said. 'How far have you got internally?'

'Just a few rooms on the ground floor. It's a big house, lots of nooks and crannies. I reckon we get back for seven in the morning, then blat the place all day.'

'Sounds like a plan.'

Flynn walked through the hospital corridors, having had a short visit to his friend, Colin. Diane walked along with him, their heads bowed with a cloud of melancholy above them.

Colin had been asleep, under the effects of powerful pain relief and tranquillizers.

When Flynn had walked into the room where Colin's bed had been relocated, Diane was sitting at his bedside, clasping his hand, her forehead resting on it. She raised her head slowly when Flynn coughed quietly, the corners of her mouth turned down, strain beyond belief etched deeply across her features. She placed Colin's hand gently on the bed and stood up, looking weak, then fell into Flynn's embrace and held on tightly for a long time, sobbing, choking into his chest. Flynn stood there numb, holding her and looked at his old friend in the bed.

Eventually Flynn steered her out into the corridor, which was when she looked properly at him for the first time. She gasped, 'Flynnie, what's been happening!'

What he really wanted to know was what was happening to Colin. He presumed it was very bad news. 'Don't worry about me. How's Colin?'

'Really poorly at the moment. I thought he seemed OK at first, but . . .'

'Maybe the side-effects of a big operation?' Flynn said. They were facing each other and he was holding her hands by the fingertips. 'You look tired, sweetie,' he said softly.

She nodded. 'Buy me a coffee? Bring me up to speed with what's going on with you and the boat . . . bet you really regret coming back to England.'

'To help you, I don't regret. Getting involved in the other crap, yes . . . but now I want to concentrate on the shop. Come on, let's find a coffee.'

There was no sign of life in the hospital cafe, so they walked down to the edge of the city to the KFC on the southern perimeter of the centre, which whilst not the most salubrious establishment did do a good roast bean, even though Flynn was a bit caffeined-out and KFC-weary.

Diane said nothing on the short walk, but Flynn noticed her breathing in the air and exhaling slowly, trying to relax. Her blood pressure must have been sky-high.

Flynn brought her up to date with everything that had happened to him, but wasn't too specific with names. He concluded by saying, 'Now it's all down to the cops. I'm going to get a good night's sleep, then open up the shop properly tomorrow morning and do what I promised. Honestly. Chances are I won't find any more floating bodies. I'll sort out the salvage of the canal boat, see what can be saved . . . I'm really, really sorry about the crap.'

'Not your fault. Where are you staying tonight?'

Flynn told her about his idea of laying down his head upstairs in the chandlery.

'That'll be uncomfortable . . . ooh, but we do have some blow-up mattresses for sale in the shop, and sleeping bags. Help yourself to them, they're quite comfy.'

'I think I'm eating up your profits . . . I will pay you back.'

'Steve, we don't make a profit, not yet anyway.'

They strolled back to the hospital, where Diane met up with her sister, at whose house she was going to stay, and Flynn made his way to Alison's car on the car park. His mobile phone rang as he reached it.

'Steve, it's me,' a female voice said. 'The woman who saved your life.'

'My very own paramedic,' he said with a grin.

'One who has a rare night off. Can you come around?'

'It's a really nice offer . . .' he began.

'But? You dumping me already?'

'It's not an offer I want to refuse.'

'But?'

'I'd really like to see you, honestly . . .'

'But!' The 'buts' were getting pithier.

'I'm exhausted,' he revealed. 'Why don't you come down to Glasson and take me for a drink, see what happens from that point onwards.' Even as he said it he knew it sounded awfully egotistical. He wouldn't have blamed her if she told him to go to hell.

She didn't.

Henry's resolve faltered at the first hurdle. His intention had been to spend the night at his own house in Blackpool so he didn't have a long journey to the cells in the morning. He was going to zip down the motorway, but as he reached junction 34, the magical allure of Kendleton and a certain landlady wafted to him and he couldn't resist. So he went straight on instead, driving to Kendleton, passing the point where he'd been forced off the road – and trying not to think about it and his poor car.

Twenty minutes later he was propping up the bar with a couple of the locals, a doctor and a farmer, both solid-gold inebriates, he had come to know and love.

By midnight the place was closed and deserted, just himself and Alison sitting side by side in front of the fire in the main bar. It had been roaring earlier, but was now just red embers, emitting a lovely but dwindling and sleepy warmth. They had a Glenfiddich each, doubles, one ice cube so as not to spoil the flavour. Henry's face began to glow.

He had told Alison as much about his day as he could and also bemoaned the death of his fancy car, but was also philosophical about it. He had managed to have a couple of fleeting conversations with his insurers and knew they were going to write it off.

'In some way it might be a good thing,' he said.

'Why?' Alison said in disbelief.

'I bought it in some kind of response to Kate's death, something to cheer me up.' Henry looked sideways at her. 'That moment has passed, it was just a phase of grieving. When it's all sorted money wise, I think I'll just buy something more sensible. I don't need a fancy motor to make me happy now, just one that gets me from A to B. You're what makes me happy,' he purred.

She pretended to consider his words. 'Don't make it too sensible,' she laughed. 'I quite like fancy cars.' She slid off her chair and knelt down in front of him, laying her forearms along his thighs. 'I never thought I'd be happy again.'

'Me neither.'

He leaned forwards and they kissed lingeringly. She really has the most wonderful lips, he thought. They needed kissing a lot.

Suddenly she broke off the kiss. Her eyes played lustfully over his face.

He picked up the less than subtle meaning. It was a look he had learned to read very well over the past few months. 'No way!' he said, pretending to be shocked. 'No way! Here? Now? What about Ginny . . . she might walk in!'

'In bed, all tucked up, fast asleep. Front door's locked, blinds are drawn . . . no paying guests . . . this rug is nice, soft and fluffy . . .' Her hand moved up his thigh and came to rest on his groin, which had already begun to strain. She gripped him through his trousers, keeping her eyes locked into his.

'Naked?' he asked hopefully.

'Completely,' she said.

The inflatable beds came with inflatable pillows and two pushed together worked very well as a double, as did two sleeping bags, unzipped, then zipped together to form a wide blanket.

The make-do approach certainly sufficed for Flynn and the paramedic, two people who also made love in a fairly unusual location. This time, though, the upstairs storage room above the chandlery.

In fact they had a wonderful time, laughing intensely as they screwed with abandon, taking their joining to new levels of intimacy on the air beds, flipping from one position to the next and back again, not forgetting other forms of stimulation either.

They finished in a blur of orgasmic speed and loud moans before flopping back, exhausted and laughing.

Flynn managed to stay awake for a few minutes of blown-up pillow talk, but then, shattered, he was asleep.

Flynn slept deeply until six-thirty when he rolled off the bed onto the hard, uncarpeted floor of the storage room and banged his forehead. He lay there face down, staring at the grain of the exposed wooden floorboards. Then he eased himself up, blinking the sleep out of his eyes and wondering, for a moment, where he was. Over the years he had woken up in many peculiar places.

He sat up, glanced across and saw that Liz, the paramedic, had gone. He vaguely recalled her saying something and him responding and presumably making some sense. She had probably been saying goodbye, he thought muzzily.

He exhaled, scratched the back of his leg and tried to get his mind to function. His body was stiff and sore and creaky but he forced himself up to his feet and padded naked and shivering into the tiny toilet where he relieved himself, a function that seemed to last a very long time.

Empty of bladder he came back and got back on to the inflatable bed, pulling up the sleeping bag. He lay on his side, blinking, thinking about the day ahead.

The crown of his skull was quite close to the wall and from where he was he could see along the skirting board running along the bottom edge of the wall, where it met the floorboards at ninety degrees. It wasn't a well-fitted skirting board, not helped by the unevenness of the floorboards themselves, several of which were loose, as he had discovered.

He wasn't really looking for anything. He was thinking about running a shop. Quite looking forward to it. Trying to remember how to use the till. Still feeling quite sleepy. But also looking along the bottom edge of the skirting board, which narrowed as it reached the corner of the room because of his perspective.

And then he saw something wedged underneath it in one of the gaps made by a loose, badly fitted floorboard. At first it didn't seem like anything. Something off-white, cube-like. He didn't even care what it was.

Just a bit of rubbish, an offcut from a piece of wood, perhaps. Smaller than a sugar cube. A broken piece of tile?

He could not tell . . . in his mind he was still visualizing how to use that till and asking an imagined customer to enter his PIN number.

Then he remembered . . . Liz wasn't saying goodbye, she was saying, 'See you later. I have to be in work by eight. I finish at four today . . . can I see you tonight?' Flynn remembered saying yes, absolutely. He also remembered the night. And smiled contentedly. And he looked along the skirting board again at that small object wedged under it.

He yawned and flipped on to his back, still smiling. A paramedic. Fancy. He'd always liked paramedics . . . he kept smiling and remembering . . . and then his face creased into a frown as he suddenly realized what the object was underneath the skirting.

In disbelief he scrambled off the bed and scuttled along the floor and tried to prise the object out from where it was by using his thumb and forefinger to grip it. He couldn't quite . . . He cast around and saw Alison's car keys which he grabbed and using the ignition key he started to gently tease the object out. It was tightly stuck in there, but eventually it came out with a pop and rolled a few inches across the floor like a dice. Flynn stared at it, then picked it up, sat back on his naked bottom, and held it up to the light filtering through the curtained window, like it was a precious diamond.

It wasn't a gemstone, though. It was a tooth. A premolar with a gold filling.

SIXTEEN

As Flynn was frowning at the tooth and twirling it around between his fingers, Henry Christie was pulling up on the driveway of Harry Sunderland's house on the banks of the River Lune at Halton.

For five and a half hours, Henry had slept soundly – the culmination of exhaustion and exertion. He had risen as fully rested as possible – he rarely slept more than six hours anyway – and had a shower, kissed a sleepy Alison, and set out on the road in the Vectra for what he knew would be a hell of a day, one way or the other. He was relishing it.

His journey took him, once more, past the point where his Merc had been forced off the road. He stopped for a couple of minutes, got out of the pool car and stood by the roadside, hands on hips, considering just how lucky he had been to survive, first the accident, then what happened after.

He didn't dwell on it, although the horrendous bureaucratic repercussions yet to come did weigh heavily on him.

A man had died, killed in self-defence and quite deservedly so, but one could never predict what a coroner or the CPS might conclude from it. Henry knew that Steve Flynn had done absolutely the right thing, others might be swayed to think differently. Henry knew there was going to be a mighty judicial battle ahead. But he was up for it.

He arrived at Sunderland's house just a short time later.

The room in which Flynn had spent the night was the first-floor store room above the chandlery and he had made room for the makeshift double bed between various stacked boxes and equipment. The bed had gone on the only space on the floor.

Still naked and holding up the tooth, Flynn glanced around the room.

He shivered, placed the tooth down and decided to get dressed, so he pulled on his clothes and started to rearrange the room.

The support unit search team had already arrived, together with a dog handler, Henry was pleased to see. These kinds of cops were a keen bunch, very professional, and Henry had a lot of time for the specialists.

The sergeant from the previous night approached him with two brews in hand from the urn that the support unit always seemed to have with them on their travels, topped up with boiling water from some source or other. It seemed to Henry that the job description for the sergeants must include having the skills, abilities and resourcefulness of a spiv.

'Took a chance, boss,' he said, handing Henry a Styrofoam cup. 'Coffee, milk, no sugar . . . real coffee, by the way.'

'Nail on head, Dave. Cheers.' Henry took a sip of the drink and it tasted wonderful in the circumstances. For some reason he had never had a bad brew whilst out on a police operation.

'We've already started,' the sergeant updated Henry. 'In the house and I got the dog man in just to have a quick skim along the river bank with Fido and also to work out how best we can fingertip-search it later and to see if there's any likely point at which Mrs Sunderland might have gone in. I dunno,' the sergeant said, 'maybe signs of a scuffle of something.'

'Sounds good,' Henry said, pleased they'd got things going so quickly. He sipped the coffee and two things happened simultaneously: his own mobile phone rang and the sergeant was called up on his PR.

Henry flipped open his phone.

The sergeant turned away and said, 'Go ahead,' into his radio.

Before Henry could finish saying his name, the voice at the other end of the phone said immediately, 'Henry, it's Rik – you need to get yourself down here pretty fuckin' quick.' It was Rik Dean calling from Blackpool police station.

'Why, what's going on?'

'High-falutin' briefs putting pressure on the custody sergeant and the divisional chief super is what is going on! Where the hell've you been? I've been calling you for the last hour.'

Henry said calmly, 'Just tell me what's happening, bud.'

'These two – Sunderland and Barlow – are walking unless you can convince the custody officer and chief super otherwise . . . there's talk of unlawful arrests and all sorts of shit, so you need to get here, Henry.'

'I'll be at least half an hour at the soonest,' Henry said, now feeling bile in his throat. Solicitors and a chief superintendent up and about at this time of the day did not bode well. He had one of those horrible in-body feelings, where the sensation was like all the blood was draining out of his legs. He threw his coffee onto the driveway. 'Is the chief super there?'

'No, he's in a conflab with these solicitors and I'll tell you, they're two smooth fucking reptiles.'

'What's their beef?'

'Uh – speculative arrests, neither man should have spent a night in custody. They should have been bailed. You're not working quickly enough – like, y'know, going home for the night.'

'The chief super's falling for that?' Henry said in amazement.

'He's dithering, I know that. They turned him out at five this morning.'

Henry spun as he thought quickly. 'Tell him not to let them go. I'll be there as soon as I can and in the meantime get him to call me and I'll try and speak to him. I've got his number. Oh, why are you there so early?'

'I came in early to clear some of my paperwork,' he said.

'OK.'

The sergeant had had a shorter conversation over his radio and was waiting for Henry to finish.

'Boss?' he said quickly.

'What?'

'Dog man down by the river – his dog has found something.'

Henry waited for the revelation, encouraging the sergeant with his body language.

'A Wellington boot . . . and there's something in it.'

'What?'

'A camera-phone.'

Henry had been on the point of rushing off to deal with the custody office emergency in Blackpool, but he knew five minutes wouldn't change anything. 'Let's go see.'

He traipsed after the sergeant across the wide lawn of Sunderland's garden, onto a path winding through some rhodo-dendron bushes which then sloped down to the river which was running high and fast. Henry could imagine someone falling in and instantly being swept away to the coast and drowned.

The dog man, a support unit constable and the German shep-herd dog, full name LanConBertie, were clustered by a bunch of low-growing bushes, chattering.

'What've you got?' the sergeant asked them.

'It's behind there,' the dog man said and led Henry and the sergeant around the bush where, seemingly tucked out of sight, was a lone pink-and-grey polka-dotted cut-off Wellington boot, for the left foot.

Henry had one of his wonderful, arse-twitching moments, completely the opposite of what he'd just felt on hearing the news from Blackpool. He recognized the boot instantly: the match to the one that Jennifer Sunderland had been wearing when Flynn pulled her out of the river. He swallowed drily.

'It was actually under some leaves,' the dog man said, 'so we moved it a bit and stood it upright.'

Henry nodded. Fair enough.

'And I also looked into it,' he went on. 'There's a mobile phone in there, but I haven't touched it.'

'Brilliant,' Henry enthused. He squatted down by the boot and peered into it, saw a mobile phone of some description inside, laid flat. Temptation nearly overcame him. He wanted to grab it, see if it worked, see what was on it that was so bloody urgent. Clearly this is what the fuss was about, the item that Mrs Sunderland was believed to have had in her possession, and which resulted in the violent incident in the mortuary and the failed attempt to kill Steve Flynn on the canal boat.

'Right,' he said, addressing the sergeant. 'Turn out a CSI now – on my say-so – get photos of it in situ, then I want the boot and the phone bagged separately and securely. I want both items to be put into the safe at Lancaster nick. No one must mess about with the phone – understand?' The sergeant nodded. Both men knew that the curiosity of cops could be the downfall of a case. Hell, even Henry wanted to have a go at switching it on here and now. 'If I find out that anyone has had a go at doing this, I'll have 'em, and I mean it. So – bagged, sealed, tagged and in the safe with specific instructions to the duty inspector that only I am allowed to handle it.'

'Got it, boss.'

'I need to get to Blackpool and head some bastards off at the pass.' He turned to the dog man. 'Well done.' Then he looked at Bertie, who had actually done the finding, and reached out to pat him on the head, but a warning growl made him snap his hand away. Being savaged by a police dog would just be the icing on the cake.

He knew that time was of the essence, so he turned and started to walk briskly back to the pool car.

Fully dressed, Flynn heaved, pushed and re-stacked and rearranged the stock boxes so they were against three of the four walls of the stock room, leaving the fourth wall free, the one against which he had laid the air beds (now deflated), and found the tooth wedged under the skirting. By doing this he also exposed as much of the floor space as possible, which wasn't much. Perhaps seven feet by four of bare floorboards.

It had been a long time since he had been a detective and though obviously rusty and not up to date, some fundamental things never leave. He still had the instinct. Not that he needed much at this juncture. Nor imagination, nor skills, as most people of sound mind and intellect could probably hazard a guess and identify blood stains.

Flynn therefore knew exactly what he was looking at: a crime scene.

'Boss! Boss!' the support unit sergeant called to Henry at the moment he yanked up the car door handle.

Henry turned with irritation as the sergeant almost skidded into him. He tried not to let it show because this man and his team were doing a bloody good job and Henry appreciated it. He forced a smile, well, more a grimace.

'Sorry, I know you're in a rush, but I think we've found something else. In the house and the guys really want you to have a quick look.'

Henry took a deep breath. 'Quick one,' he said.

He trotted behind the sergeant up to Sunderland's lovely house and followed him inside into a huge entrance hallway, then up a wide staircase to the first floor. He was led along the landing, through a door that opened on to another set of stairs which were much tighter and steeper than the main set.

'Up to the converted loft,' the sergeant explained. 'There's a couple of extra bedrooms up here, a shower room and a large sort of lounge, all built under the eaves.'

'Uh-huh,' Henry said.

They emerged on to a long landing corridor, a door either side, one a little further on and a door at the far end.

The sergeant pointed at the end door. 'That one goes into the lounge, these doors are to the bedrooms, and that one is to the shower room, toilet.'

'OK,' Henry said, taking in the geography. He might have been a detective, but he wasn't keen on mini-mysteries and was aching for the sergeant to get on with it and tell him why he had been dragged up here. It had better be good, something to match the Wellington boot and mobile phone. He hoped his face hid how he was feeling. He suspected it did.

Being battered and bruised and swollen hid most things, except pain.

The sergeant opened a door.

Inside was a pair of constables going through items in a chest of drawers. They stopped their work.

Henry glanced quickly around a fairly small, sparsely furnished bedroom, with a three-quarter-sized bed that took up a lot of the floor space, the chest of drawers, a narrow wardrobe and one bedside cabinet. The bed was unmade and several items were strewn on it, including men's clothing.

The sergeant said to one of the PCs, 'John, what have you got?'

John nodded eagerly. He crossed to the bed saying, 'Various things, but these in particular.' He lifted a grubby shirt, underneath which were four passports, which he picked up and came to Henry's side. The PC was wearing latex gloves, so he kept hold of the passports and opened the first one of them for Henry to see, so he didn't have to touch it. It was Russian and on seeing the holder's photograph, Henry went icy cold. He looked at Henry for a reaction.

'Next one,' Henry said.

The PC did the same for that one and the next two. There was another Russian passport, an EU one from Malta and a Turkish one. The photographs were all of the same person, all slightly different, and the names were all completely different.

They belonged to the man who had forced Henry and Flynn off the road and then tried to murder them by spraying them with bullets – but had met his own violent end at the hands of Steve Flynn.

Henry's lips parted with a pop: 'Vladimir Kaminsky.'

'There are two guns underneath the bed with ammunition.'

Henry said, 'The room opposite?'

'Three passports from three different countries, all belonging to the same man – but not this one.'

'Let me see.'

Henry crossed the corridor into the opposite bedroom and inspected the find.

Three passports, two more guns. Each passport with a different name, but all belonging to the man who had killed Joe Speakman, wife and dog, and who had almost blasted Henry to pieces, had it not been for Steve Flynn. Yuri Gregorov.

'Brilliant job, guys,' Henry said. He turned to the sergeant, beaming like the father on the day that his son scored his first hat trick for the school football team. 'Same applies to these passports, as the mobile phone; bagged and sealed in the safe, only me to access. Deal with the weapons as you would normally.'

Henry then rushed out to his car.

The floorboards in the store room were unsealed, planed wood, which is why it had been virtually impossible to clean away the blood that had soaked in. And there had been a lot of it.

Flynn stood and looked at it, his mind working through it and constantly returning to the one fact that made him feel weak: the memory of the snippet of conversation that he'd had with Diane, just a throwaway remark. Two pieces of information that Diane had revealed to him openly and innocently.

One, that Colin had once worked for Harry Sunderland as a driver; two, that this property had been bought from Sunderland.

Flynn's face remained impassive despite the fact that his brain was coming to conclusions that were deeply unsettling him.

'Utter bollocks,' he said out loud. He looked at the tooth again and thought, 'Surely not.'

Grim-faced and angry, Henry screwed the HQ pool car down the M6, leaving plumes of unhealthy looking blue-black smoke behind him, reminding him he needed to check the oil.

He still hadn't heard back from the divisional commander. The man was someone he knew quite well and respected. Henry could not imagine he would buckle under pressure from any solicitor, slick or otherwise. And Henry could not work out why he himself had not been contacted about any of this. That was an extra worry. Was he being cut out of the circle, and why?

The mobile phone was slotted into the crux of his right shoulder and ear as he tried to call Blackpool police station. There was no Bluetooth or hands-free connection in this basically appointed car, so it was back to breaking the law. It rang out for ages before someone in comms answered and Henry asked to be put through to the chief superintendent.

The man's secretary answered and fielded off Henry's insistence to be connected to him. He tried to keep his cool as he spoke to the lady who was a very effective firewall. In the end he gave up and ended the call, then tried to call Rik Dean, holding the phone in his left hand, steering wheel in the right, and thumb-tabbed through his contacts list to find Rik's number and trying to keep the car safe at 80 mph.

He found the number, pressed call and jammed the phone between shoulder and ear again, waiting for the connection. Which never came: number unobtainable.

In frustration, Henry threw the phone onto the passenger seat and almost had a seizure when it bounced sideways off the seat and dropped down into the gap between seat and door with a clunk.

He swore and reached across with his left hand but it was just too far for his fingertips and he had to shoot upright when a car pulled out from the centre lane without warning and Henry had to anchor on, and swerve from the fast lane into the middle to avoid a collision.

The driver of that car was completely clueless that an angry maniac was in the car he'd just cut up.

Henry coaxed more miles per hour out of the vehicle than he thought possible. Hoping there was enough oil in its system to get him to Blackpool without the engine seizing, he overtook the offending car on the inside and gave the other driver a look of incomprehension. The man didn't even glance sideways at Henry, who was fuming enough to give him the international 'dick head' gesture if they'd made eye contact.

Instead he just threw up both hands, grabbed the steering wheel again and shook it, pleading for more speed. None came. Eighty-five was tops.

And then, just to taunt him, his out-of-reach mobile phone started to ring.

Flynn was having breakfast, a bacon sandwich and large mug of coffee from the dockside cafe. He sat on a table outside, even though the morning was chilly, and watched the activity along the quayside at Glasson as the day came to life. A large yacht was working its way through the sea lock, the water draining down to the level of the dock. He watched the boat gradually disappear from view into the lock, until just the tip of the mainmast remained visible from where he sat. The lower lock gates then began to open.

Normally he would have loved watching this magnificent sight.

This morning it meant nothing to him as he munched through his tasty – but to him, tasteless – breakfast butty.

He watched the yacht leave the lock and motor slowly towards the dock gates, pass through them into the Lune estuary, where it went out of sight.

Flynn stood up and walked despondently back to the chandlery, knowing he wasn't going to open up that morning after all. He stood outside the shop and pulled out the clear plastic money bag from his pocket that he'd found by the till, in which was the tooth.

He held it in the palm of his hand, trying to convince himself that there was a simple, rational, non-criminal explanation for the presence of the tooth and the blood stains. Try as he might, he wasn't that persuasive

He made his decision and got into Alison's car, which was parked in front of the shop.

Henry hurtled into the custody office to cast his eyes over the prisoner dry-wipe board affixed to the wall behind the custody officer's desk. As ever, the cells at Blackpool were full to bursting – almost. Henry scanned the names twice and it took a few moments for him to realize that the ones he wanted to see up there – Sunderland and Barlow – were missing.

His knees went to lead and he was rooted to the spot. They had gone. Released. It wasn't just a terrible joke.

He inhaled a steadying breath, walked past the short queue of prisoners waiting to be booked in, went behind the custody desk and caught the eye of the sergeant, whose face fell as he recognized Henry.

He was booking a prisoner in. He nodded worriedly at Henry and said, 'One minute, boss.'

Henry walked into the tiny office behind the desk and stood waiting for him to finish up. The sergeant appeared a few minutes later. The expression on his face told Henry he knew everything.

'What happened?' Henry demanded.

'I couldn't do anything,' the sergeant pleaded.

'Just tell me what happened.'

'I came on at six and the chief super and a solicitor came in and told me to release your two prisoners.'

'On what grounds?'

'Unlawful arrest. Not working expeditiously enough to investigate the case.'

'And you let them go?'

'I'm not going to say no to the chief super, am I? But they're still on police bail – back in a week. I had to argue for that.'

'By which time they'll be long gone.' Tight-lipped, Henry said, 'Not your fault.'

'It's all documented on the custody record,' the sergeant said. 'There was all sorts of talk about civil litigation and I think the chief super was just covering his arse. Sorry, boss.'

'I'll go and see him now.'

'There's something else,' the sergeant hesitated.

'What?' Henry said suspiciously.

'Something I overheard . . . about the house searches . . .' Henry's guts whipped over and a fist seemed to crush them. 'About them being illegal, too, and the chief super saying he would cancel or stop them.'

'Shit . . . thanks, buzz me out, will you?'

Henry barged past him and went out into the police garage where he had half-abandoned the pool car. Here he found a signal on his mobile phone and called the support-unit sergeant in charge of the search at Sunderland's house.

'It's Henry Christie . . . has anyone contacted you about stopping the search, Dave?'

'No, should they have?'

'They might do . . . look, what I want you to do is this . . .' Henry gave him some instructions and at the end of the call he leaned against the pool car. The engine was still creaking as it cooled down from boiling point and a horrible whiff emanated from it. He shook his head, wondering what the hell was happening and who was on whose side.

Steeling himself, he walked back into the station, deciding to take the stairs up to the level on which the chief superintendent's office was located instead of the lift.

*   *   *

Being early in the day, it was easy to find a space in the hospital car park. Flynn walked in and made his way through to the ward, off which Colin was now being cared for. As he turned into the ward, a nurse emerged from an office and asked if she could help.

Flynn's nice smile and general charm worked wonders and although it was well out of normal visiting hours, she said he could have ten minutes – max – with the patient, who was awake and actually eating for the first time since his operation.

Colin looked better than when Flynn had last seen him, but was still exhausted and drawn.

'Flynn!'

'Hi, Col, how you feeling?'

He was sitting, propped up by pillows. Scrambled eggs on toast were on a plate across his knees.

'I'm actually famished and feeling as good as can be expected, as they say. But famished is good. So, what's new? Shouldn't you be minding the shop?'

'Yeah, I should,' Flynn said, knowing that Colin knew nothing about the occurrences of the last few days. Flynn regarded his old mate with a puckered brow.

'Problem?' Colin asked.

The secretary rose defensively as Henry barged through the door of the divisional commander's outer office.

'I want to see Mr Geldhill,' he said, and made to his right to pass her on the wing to get to the divisional commander's office door.

She moved quickly and positioned herself between Henry and the door, shaking her head. 'He's busy. Someone's in with him.'

'Margery,' Henry said, he had known the battle axe for quite a few years, 'I don't give a toss.'

'You can't go in, Henry.'

Henry shot her a pitying look. 'I think you'll find I can,' he said petulantly.

'Henry, please.'

'Just tell him you couldn't stop me. Tell him I was rude and elbowed my way past you – which is what I am and what I'm going to do.'

She saw ire and determination in Henry's whole being, could see he was shaking. She wilted and moved sideways, allowing him to pass, a glint of apprehension in her eyes.

He did not knock, simply opened the door and let himself into the chief super's office.

Tom Gledhill was sitting behind his wide desk, a uniformed inspector sitting opposite him. From their body language they seemed to be having a fairly informal discussion. Gledhill looked up and the instantaneous change in his demeanour was visible, becoming upright in his chair, tense suddenly.

Henry stood there, not saying a word.

Gledhill said, 'Excuse me?' Still Henry did not speak. 'Henry, can't you see I'm busy here?'

Henry knew he was trembling. He pointed a finger at the inspector. 'Get out,' he said.

Dumbfounded, the inspector's mouth actually dropped open in complete horror. He looked for guidance from the commander.

'We'll continue this later, Gerry.'

The inspector stood and sidled warily around Henry, looking at the detective superintendent with a mix of awe and contempt, unable to make up his mind one way or the other.

'And shut the door,' Henry snapped. The poor man reacted as though he'd been slapped by a wet towel in a changing room and jerked out of the office.

Henry's gaze settled on Gledhill, who picked up his desk phone. 'Margery, definitely no interruptions now. Yes, I know.' He glanced at Henry. 'He is, you're right.' He cradled the phone. 'Sit.'

Henry sat on the recently vacated chair. 'What's going on?'

'With regard to your prisoners?'

'Tom, no – with regard to the situation in the Middle East. Please, don't fuck me about.'

Gledhill's face hardened. 'And don't you forget you are talking to someone of senior rank,' he bristled, but not terribly convincingly. Sometimes, even in the modern day and age, rank was pulled.

'Fair enough,' Henry relented. 'Don't fuck me about – sir.'

Henry saw the man was needled. His jaw muscles worked as

though he was chewing something tough and unpleasant. 'Like I said,' Henry repeated, 'what's going on. Sir?'

'I was dragged out of bed at five this morning by an irate solicitor, demanding that he be heard and that his clients were to be released forthwith, following their unlawful arrests.'

'OK – so why wasn't I contacted about this? I would have gladly turned out to defend the position.'

'Henry, I tried to call you several times – no reply.'

Henry held up his phone. 'No missed calls on this,' he said.

Gledhill shrugged. 'I take it you were ensconced with your tame landlady, out in the wilds where the phone signal is non-existent. Not good for an SIO. Hardly professional, eh?' Gledhill was trying to bounce it back to Henry.

'If you knew where I was, why didn't you call the landline?'

'It doesn't really matter now, does it? Fact is I got dragged out of bed, you were uncontactable and someone had to make a decision.'

'So you took the line of least resistance?'

'I did the correct thing under the circumstances, and with regard to the Police and Criminal Evidence Act and the Codes of Practice.' He waited for Henry's challenge.

'Utter cock!'

'The solicitor argued that the arrests were purely speculative, with no evidential foundation or reasonable suspicion. The force was in a very bad position.'

Henry studied the senior officer, senior in terms of rank, not years. He was not impressed. 'Tom – Harry Sunderland probably killed his wife. Ralph Barlow has been feeding him confidential information which was used to commit crime. They could both be linked to the unsolved murder of a teenage girl and the search of Sunderland's house has uncovered some pretty fucking damning evidence about him sheltering two killers.'

'Henry, this is not the good old days, like when you worked down the Valley. You cannot lock people up on a whim and then go looking for evidence, just because you think they might be guilty. That was a seventies trick and you know it. And how come the searches are still going on? I specifically instructed Rik Dean to contact the search teams to call them off.'

Henry held back a smirk. 'Guess the message mustn't have got through – bad reception up there.'

'What have you found?'

'A camera phone which could contain evidence.'

Gledhill rolled his eyes at this. 'Could?'

'Passports relating to the two men who tried to kill me and Steve Flynn, and guns.'

'Shit,' Gledhill breathed.

'Yes, shit.'

The two men regarded each other silently.

'They're still on bail,' Gledhill said. 'They have to come back. You still have a hold on them, time to build up your case.'

'Did you ensure they surrendered their passports?'

'No. I didn't think that was necessary. I was assured . . .' Gledhill's voice trailed off pathetically. 'Sunderland is an upstanding member of the community. He won't be going anywhere. And Ralph Barlow has twenty-odd years of solid coppering behind him. He'll fight any allegation. Neither man will disappear.'

Henry shook his head. 'This is just incredible bollocks and you know it, Tom. I'm going to walk out of here, find those two men and drag their carcasses back in.'

'No you're not.'

Henry pushed himself up, Gledhill watching in disbelief. Henry turned at the door to say something, but Gledhill said, 'Henry?'

'What?'

'Be careful.'

'What does that mean?'

Gledhill's mouth clammed shut and Henry realized he wasn't going to say anything else. He went out.

As the door closed, Gledhill reached for his phone.

SEVENTEEN

'**M**r Christie? This is Melanie Speakman . . . I'm really sorry to bother you.'

'No, that's fine,' Henry said. There was a note of strain in her voice. And in his.

He was sitting in the pool car down in the police garage, brooding and attempting to make some sense of what had happened. The call from Melanie came on his mobile phone as he slumped there in the driver's seat, surrounded by bleak concrete walls, thinking the absolute worst of everyone in the world. He was completely gutted by the chief super's decision, but what was done, was done. Deal with it. Pick up the pieces. The underlying problem was that the force was always running scared of litigation, which always took a huge dent out of its budget.

An hour in unlawful custody easily equated to a thousand pounds for the poor soul, plus substantial legal costs that ensured the lawyers didn't starve. Over eight hours for two people meant a lot of dosh, potentially, so better to take the easy way out, especially when the people in custody had access to slimeball solicitors who enjoyed screwing the cops.

On critical reflection, Henry thought that maybe he had jumped the gun. Arresting people just to see what came out of the woodwork was maybe a little old hat. He should have got warrants first, then there would have been no argument. Or maybe Gledhill was part of the plot. Or am I just being paranoid, he wondered.

It was fortunate that Rik Dean had come in early to clear some of his own backlog, and picked up on what was happening. At least that gave Henry some warning.

His meanderings had been interrupted by Melanie Speakman, daughter of Joe. Dead Joe.

'Can I help you in some way?' he asked.

'I really need to see you . . . I've, I've just remembered something that could be important.' Her voice was shaky.

'Can you tell me over the phone?'

She hesitated. 'No, not really . . . but it's about that man we discussed?'

'Malinowski? Henry said.

'Yes,' she whispered, her voice barely audible.

She gave him the address at which she had been staying, her friend's home in Bispham, just to the north of Blackpool. It was a pleasant semi-detached house, close to a golf course, slightly dated, but not bad for that.

It took Henry about ten minutes to get there, his curiosity fully aroused.

Could this Russian gangster, the one whose name Jerry Tope had unearthed, be the key to all this? If nothing else, he was certainly an important cog in the scenario, but Henry dismissed him as a contender for being arrested. If he was based in Cyprus, then it would be hard to get him back here . . . if indeed he had done anything wrong. Henry was only speculating – a pastime that had just lost him two prisoners.

But maybe Melanie would have something for him.

He pulled up just up the road from the address, which was on a pleasant avenue. Her Porsche was parked a little way down the road.

He had regained control of himself now, got over the emotion, and was working out how to rescue the case. He walked to the front door, knocked and was greeted by Melanie. Instantly he saw terror in her eyes.

'Are you all right?' he asked.

'Mr Christie . . . please come in. Thanks for coming so quickly.'

She stood aside, let him pass and gestured for him to turn right into the lounge. He walked by her, unable to take his eyes off her face, wondering what the hell she had found out that was so important and fearful.

'What is it?' he asked, concerned.

'Please, please, sit,' she gestured with a dithery hand. He perched himself on the edge of a chair, whilst she remained standing awkwardly. 'There's someone I need you to meet,' she said, turned slightly to the still open living-room door.

Henry's mobile began to ring.

'Sorry,' he said, extracting it from his jacket pocket. The caller

was Steve Flynn. He said, 'I probably need to get this.' He put
the phone to his ear and angled away from Melanie.

'I'll have that!'

Henry turned back, the phone coming away from his ear as
he saw the left hand of a man gesturing by wriggling his fingers.
Henry's eyes jerked upwards and took in the whole shape of the
figure who had just entered the room and snaked an arm around
Melanie's shoulders. She seemed to shrink. In the man's right
hand was a snub-nosed revolver, six shot, of the type that used
to be known as a detective's special. It was pointed at Henry's
head. 'No – don't get up, Henry.'

'Ralph,' Henry said. He could hear Steve Flynn's echoing and
tinny voice coming from the mobile phone, saying, *'Hello?
Henry? Hello?'*

Henry folded the phone shut, ending the call.

He reached out with the phone, handing it to Ralph Barlow,
who switched it fully off – all the while keeping the gun pointed
at Henry – and slid it into his pocket. He moved behind Melanie
and slid his left arm around her shoulders, his hand hanging over
her left breast in a curiously intimate gesture – but not a move
that was reciprocated, as Henry could see from her eyes.

'What's going on, Ralph?'

Barlow smirked at Henry, who hadn't moved from his perch,
an eye on the gun, an eye on the people. Barlow curved his
forearm around Melanie's neck and started to apply pressure to
her windpipe. Her fingers circled the arm but could not pull it
away. Barlow then placed the muzzle of the gun against her
temple and a muted scream escaped from her lips. It was easy
for him to hold on to her, his strength and weight outmatching
her small stature. All the while, his eyes were on Henry, his
mouth twisted.

'Great detective, eh? Another judgement call gone to rat shit.'

'I said, what's going on, Ralph?' Henry's eyes moved up and
down, from Melanie to Barlow.

Barlow ignored him, keeping a tight hold of Melanie. 'You
never actually told me what it was, Henry. That thing that put
you on to me.'

He screwed the muzzle deep into Melanie's skin, making her
emit a squeak of pain.

'And that wink – fuck me, that irritated me. Winking at me, you cocksure bastard. Trying to keep the mystique alive. So what was it?'

'Harry Sunderland could not have known that his wife ended up in the River Conder, yet somehow he did, Ralph. And he said it when we went to see him.'

Henry saw the realization flood into Barlow's eyes. 'And from that you decided to access my phone records?'

'And all the other illegal stuff you were up to. It's the kind of thing you do when you're a detective, brilliant or otherwise,' Henry said, hoping the word brilliant would serve to wind up Barlow. 'You dig, you uncover corruption and wrong-doing.'

'Bloody hell, Henry. I bow to you. You really are good, although it pains me to say it. You don't miss anything, do you?'

'I missed Tom Gledhill,' he said.

Barlow gave a short laugh. 'Friends in high places come in useful.'

'So he's part of this whole . . . whatever the hell it is?'

'Duh – yeah.'

Then Henry remembered. 'He was a friend of Joe Speakman's.' Drunk though he was at the time, Henry now recalled seeing Joe Speakman at Melanie's twenty-first-birthday bash. But there were a lot of other cops there too. And he was smashing his head with a tea-tray.

Barlow clicked his tongue and gave Henry a wink. 'Now then, Henry, you've been a bit of a clever boy, haven't you?'

'Probably. But I never know just how clever until the life sentences are dished out.'

Barlow guffawed. 'Nice one, but somehow I don't think this is going to end quite like that. Don't get me wrong, it will end horribly for you.'

Melanie squirmed, then her eyeballs rolled backwards in their sockets and she fainted in Barlow's grip. He simply let her fall into an untidy heap at his feet, stepped back from her. Henry moved to get to her, but Barlow said, 'Leave the bitch.'

Henry ground his teeth.

'I'm reliably informed you found certain items of property at Harry's house.'

Henry tried to disguise the physical lurch in his guts. He said nothing.

'I need to recover them,' Barlow said. 'To, um, liberate them from the safe at Lancaster nick, which is why we've come to this.'

'What's on the phone?' Henry asked.

'Nothing I need to describe to you,' Barlow said. 'My problem is that you, cheekily, left specific instructions that only you can sign out the property, the phone, the passports . . . I'm not fussed about the guns, obviously.'

'I'm not going to sign them out for you, am I, if that's what you're thinking? So it's kind of a fuck up for you, isn't it?'

'Not as much as you might imagine.' He aimed the two-inch barrel of his revolver at Henry, then pointed at the front window – indicating that Henry should turn and look outside.

The life of a landlady/hotel owner is far from glamorous, as Alison Marsh had discovered when she took over the virtually dilapidated business that was the Tawny Owl in Kendleton. The hours are horrendous, the work unremitting, the holidays non-existent, and it isn't a gold mine. In fact, it sucked money. But it was just what she needed when she left the army some seven years earlier following the death of her husband, also a soldier, in a horrific incident in Afghanistan.

She wanted to get out of the forces and do something that would be a long-term challenge and would keep her busy from dawn till dusk and beyond. The Tawny Owl had done that.

She bought it outright using savings and her husband's insurance payouts and dragged the pub right back into the heart of the community.

It had been a hard slog and included bringing up her husband's daughter, Ginny – Virginia – who was only twelve at the time.

But the slog had been worth it. It had been hard and emotional at times. There had been occasions when she would gladly have walked away, but her drive and determination had turned a failed business into a resounding success.

All the while she had kept men at arms' length.

There had been a couple of weak moments, but nothing serious until Henry Christie came along and changed everything. Not that he had been the one to make the running. It had been her doing, but that said, if Henry's wife Kate had still been alive, Alison would not have been with him. She wasn't a marriage-wrecker. But it was her who had made the first, tentative approach a few months after she'd learned of Kate's death. Things took off slowly from there, going from strength to strength.

What she hadn't bargained for were the horrendous hours that Henry worked, nor his passion for the job and his inability *not* to get involved. But she loved those things about him, too. And especially the way he often spoke with such feeling about seeing it as his job to fight for the dead, because they had no one else to do it for them.

She was thinking about Henry that morning after getting up slightly later than him and spending a grim hour in the cellar, playing a form of chess with the beer barrels.

She emerged into the bar area – where she and Henry had made love at midnight – and then went into the kitchen to fire up the cooker and grill for breakfast.

There were only two guests in overnight (she had fibbed to Henry, knowing that he definitely would not have got intimate in front of the fire had he known that people were staying) and she thought they would be last-minuters. She made herself a coffee and some crusty toast which she took out and ate whilst leaning on the bar and surveying her domain, working through the day ahead.

The front door of the premises was unlocked and a man entered.

Alison smiled and greeted him, unperturbed. People came and went at all hours and a visitor at this time of day was not unusual.

'Good morning,' she said and placed down her coffee.

'Good morning,' the man replied and Alison picked up an accent of sorts in the words.

'Can I help you?'

The man was in his mid-forties, slim, extremely handsome in a chiselled, harsh sort of way. He had black hair and a nicely trimmed moustache, a hook nose and dark complexion.

'Yes, I think so.' The accent again. Think said as 'zinc'. 'You are Alison Marsh?'

'Yes,' she said brightly.

'Good.'

He stepped towards her. He was wearing jeans, a black leather jacket, a T-shirt, black trainers and black leather gloves. There was no warning of it. He smiled. His teeth were beautiful and white and even. Obviously he had a good dentist. He pulled up each glove in turn at the wrist, tightening them on his fingers.

Then he hit Alison once. A driving, powerful blow of his right fist, into the centre of her face. She did not see it coming, but it landed with the force of a sledgehammer, crushing her nose and cheekbones, breaking them. It felt as though her whole face had imploded as she staggered back, shocked, disorientated, clutching at her face as blood flooded out of her broken nose.

She swooned.

The man stepped towards her again and delivered a second blow on the exact same spot, equally forceful.

Then her knees buckled and she collapsed on the spot like she was falling into a hole that had suddenly appeared beneath her feet, unconscious before she hit the floor.

Henry lurched to the window, the palms of his hands on the glass panes, unsure initially what he was looking at, then horror-struck by the realization.

A large black Mercedes saloon car had drawn up on the road outside.

For a moment it looked as though a decapitated head was being held up against the window at the back nearside passenger door, a terrible, bloody, and distorted mess, being displayed triumphantly by the man in the back seat whose tightly fisted hand had wrapped the long hair of the head around it and he was holding it pushed against the window, smearing the glass with blood like some sort of medieval war trophy.

Except it wasn't a decapitated head.

Nor was it some gruesome toy bought at the gift shop of a medieval torture museum.

It was a real head, attached to a real body, and it belonged to Alison Marsh, the woman Henry Christie loved.

Her features had been pounded almost beyond recognition. Nose flattened, both eyes black and swollen, lips cut and bleeding, and looking dead. Then just to reinforce the message, the man smashed Alison's head against the window again, making the glass vibrate with the impact.

Henry roared with rage, spun away from the window and

stepped dangerously towards Barlow, fists clenched, his face a vision of fury.

Barlow had been anticipating the reaction. The gun came up and he aimed it directly at Henry's forehead, stopping him dead.

'What the fuck?' Henry growled, his anger rising beyond anything he had ever known, and way beyond the fear he had felt at being confronted by Barlow and a gun. Now he realized he had walked stupidly into a trap manufactured by Barlow and Sunderland, two men desperate to save their own skins by any means possible, having used Melanie Speakman as bait. He took another menacing step, but Barlow flicked the gun, his finger tightening on the trigger.

'I'll tell you what the fuck is, Henry . . . this is deadly serious stuff . . . No, no,' Barlow warned him as Henry's body language telegraphed another move, 'I'll shoot you dead here and now and think of another way through this if you do anything stupid.'

At Barlow's feet, the blood must have worked its way back to Melanie's brain. She stirred and opened her eyes, uncomprehendingly. Then they focused, she realized where she was, and they closed again.

Barlow took a pace back. 'Now then, Henry old son, I want you to drag this nice lady into the kitchen and lay her out there. Don't want any nosy postman peering in, do we.' Barlow waited. Henry did not move. 'Do it, Henry.' He stepped back further and Henry moved behind Melanie, hooked his hands under her armpits and slid her gently backwards out of the living room, into the hallway, then into the kitchen.

Reversing in, Henry didn't at first notice the other body by the back door, but as he laid Melanie out, he turned and saw another woman, shot in the head, her body crumpled up on the floor, lying in a large pool of deep, red, almost black, blood, obviously dead.

'Oh, Jeez! What the hell are you doing, you complete . . .' Henry guessed this was the body of Melanie's friend, the owner of the house.

'Stand back,' Barlow warned and waved the gun, then straddled Melanie and shot her in the head, twice.

Henry staggered back against the sink, dumbstruck by the excessive and casual violence, noticing that the bottom half of his trousers had been splattered by Melanie's blood. It was as if everything had been squeezed out of him.

Barlow stood upright, but still standing over Melanie. 'Now then, Henry, where were we?'

'You murdering bastard. What has she ever done to you? You utter cunt!'

'Words, Henry . . . now then,' he said as though he was simply changing the subject of discussion about world affairs or pop music. 'Ahh, yes, property . . . it was very sneaky of you to make sure only you could access it.' Henry waited, boiling inside, wanting to leap at Barlow and take his chance, but knowing that was a stupid move. He had to stay with this for Alison as he realized that this lack of concern for human life would also apply to her and the image of her dead tore at Henry. He could not shake the sight of her battered head being held against the car window outside. Suddenly hot rage was replaced by ice-cold calculation.

'So what do you want?' Henry asked.

'That's better,' Barlow said triumphantly. 'We need to go for a little ride and retrieve it. All nice and friendly, like, and when you've given it to me, we'll see where we are with things.'

'What does that mean?'

'I get the stuff, your little landlady goes free . . . as for you, dunno yet.' Barlow smirked as Henry looked at Melanie, still in death, but the blood from the terrible wound in her head still collecting and running across the kitchen floor to join up with the coagulating blood of her friend to form a lake.

'Let's get on with it,' Henry said.

EIGHTEEN

They were in the pool car, Henry driving, Barlow sitting alongside, his body turned slightly towards Henry, the revolver pointed at Henry's left hip. Henry's mouth was clamped tightly shut as he steered the vehicle, as per Barlow's directions, towards the M55 motorway.

'Now, you drive sensibly, don't do anything rash, keep to the speed limit, don't draw attention to us, because if you do, she's dead – and then you are, too. Got that?'

Henry nodded, re-gripped the steering wheel with his sweaty hands, controlling the urge to back-hand Barlow.

'Good man. OK – M55, then M6 north, off at junction 33, drive up the A6 into Lancaster, pull in at the nick, then we do the business and after that, who knows? But no shenanigans or I'll . . . well, you know, don't you?'

Henry sped on to the M55, heading east out of Blackpool.

The Mercedes with Alison in it had shot away from the front of the house as Henry and Barlow got into Henry's transport, but as he drove onto the motorway, Henry saw it was behind them.

'And just to confirm matters,' Barlow said, 'just drive along in the inside lane at about fifty for a while.'

Henry did that and the Mercedes pulled out from behind into the middle lane and drew level with them. Henry glanced to his right, saw the profile of the driver, then the Mercedes accelerated slightly so it was a nose ahead of the pool car and for a few seconds the man in the back seat held Alison's face up to the window again, squashing it against the glass.

Then the Mercedes decelerated and dropped back into a following position.

'Now you can achieve the national speed limit, seventy,' Barlow said.

Henry took the car up to this speed, seeing the blue smoke trail behind. Waves pounded through him, his skull doing a dull thu-dud, his vision seeming to have contracted ·into a tunnel. He did not dare to even glance at Barlow, because if he did, he knew he would lose it and probably kill them both in the process. The by-product of this would be to ensure that Alison also died.

He had to keep himself in check. Do as they said. Bottle his rage. Use his brain and figure a way out.

First thing: get a grip.

With this in mind, he told his body to relax, take it down a notch. Stop the beating heart that felt like an alien trying to explode out of his chest, get rid of the awful noises in his head.

There was at least a half-hour journey ahead. Use that to his advantage, and learn what this was all about.

'I wouldn't mind,' he said, 'but I didn't even want to get involved in Jennifer Sunderland's death. As far as I was concerned it was a job for the uniform branch, not FMIT.'

'So why did you?'

'I was asked to attend and then I got interested . . . and even up to the point of getting her to the mortuary, I wasn't *that* interested. It was just a drowning, f'God's sake. If those guys hadn't shown up, you'd still be in charge of it.'

Barlow gave a dismissive, 'Phtt.' Then said, 'Two fuckin' hot heads.'

'So you know them?'

'Course, I do . . . well, knew them until you came along and that Flynn guy. Thing was,' Barlow said, as though it was painful to speak, 'if I'd gone to the mortuary instead of you, none of this would have happened. We'd all be happy pigs in shit – but because you wanted to maintain a chain of evidence, that meant I couldn't go through her belongings. I didn't get a chance at the scene of the drowning – too many people around – and I didn't get a chance at the mortuary and those guys were getting jumpy and I couldn't stop 'em, silly twats! I told 'em not to, but I'm not great at speaking in Russian.'

They had reached the left-hand fork for the M6 North. Henry crossed the lanes, the Mercedes two hundred metres behind. Henry glanced in his rear-view mirror, thought about what suffering Alison must be enduring in that car and again, a surge of anger passed through him.

'And they didn't find anything, of course,' Henry said, 'because there was nothing to be found.'

'Exactly . . . and there was every chance it was lost in the river anyway, but you have to cover all the bases . . .'

'Which is why they visited Flynn.'

'Yup. I learned he had a chequered history – suspected of thieving – so there was every chance he might have helped himself to some of her property, even though he was the hero of the moment. Had to be done.'

'He's anything but a thief,' Henry said, surprising himself.

'Well, we know that now, don't we?'

'What's recorded on the phone?' Henry asked.

Barlow considered this question for a while, then said, 'Ever heard of happy slapping?'

'Uh – yeah. Kids, usually, videoing assaults.'

'Think a step up. Think happy killing.' A look then came over him and he turned square on to Henry and held the gun up to his head. 'And you do not know how happy I'd be to kill you, Henry, you meddling fucker.'

'With the exception of the swear word,' Henry said, 'that could be right out of *Scooby Doo*.'

Barlow clunked the muzzle hard against Henry's temple. The car swerved slightly but Henry kept control, glad he had riled Barlow, but not wanting to push it too far.

'Who did you kill?'

'Someone who didn't matter.' Barlow turned to face the front again.

'Just you?' Henry probed.

Barlow looked at him. 'Time to shut up, I think.'

'Was that someone who didn't matter a prostitute?' Henry ventured.

Barlow's head moved slowly around and he glared at Henry. 'Just drive,' he said, and placed the gun against Henry's thigh, finger wrapped around the trigger.

Steve Flynn looked disgustedly at his mobile phone, annoyed by the fact that Henry had hung up on him and then – apparently – switched his bloody phone off. Possibly they hadn't made as much progress as he thought they had in terms of their 'relationship'. Although he flinched at the word, he supposed it was a relationship, but not the romantic sort. The prospect of kissing Henry made him queasy.

He was sitting in Alison's car on the hospital car park, brooding about his snub, wondering what to do, but knowing that he had to speak to Henry as no one else would really do, or understand the significance of what he had to say.

It was always possible that Henry was just too busy to speak to him, but at least he could have had the manners to say that over the phone before hanging up. Flynn realized Henry would be ultra-busy today and that he would not know that Flynn had anything important to say to him, so with that in mind, Flynn composed a text which he sent to Henry, saying simply, '*Call Me – Urgent.*' He hoped it didn't sound too needy. The last thing anyone needed in a relationship was a needy significant 'other'.

He checked the time, and did a bit of mental maths. He considered taking Alison's car back across to her in Kendleton, then cadging a lift back to Glasson, but maybe that was too big an ask. If she was busy, it would be an imposition too far.

Then his phone rang. It was from a number he didn't recognize. He thought Henry must be returning the call. Flynn answered.

'Steve – it's Rik Dean here . . . Yeah, hi . . . Just wondering if you've heard from Henry, or know where he is?' Rik's voice was hopeful and he sounded unconcerned.

'No. I rang him a minute or two ago, but he hung up. Is there a problem?'

'No . . . I just can't get hold of him, thought you might know where he was. He was at Blackpool nick not long ago and I wanted to catch up with him, but he's gone now. Maybe heading back up to Lancaster after this morning's fiasco.'

'What fiasco would that be?'

'Oh, nothing, nothing,' Rik said quickly. Flynn got the impression Rik thought he'd blabbed too much. 'If you hear from him, tell him to contact me, will you?'

'Vice versa,' Flynn said and hung up. Unable to contact Henry, he thought. Probably not an uncommon occurrence. And what was the fiasco, he wondered. Had Henry cocked up in some way? Again, probably not an uncommon occurrence, he chuckled.

Then he looked up and saw a classic car drive past him – a silver-blue E-type Jaguar. He watched it turn into the car park and drive to the far end, then carry on through the 'Access Only' signs, which he knew led down to the mortuary.

He'd never seen the car before, but knew the driver. He started up Alison's car and sped after the E-type, which had driven on to the mortuary staff only car park and stopped, cheekily straddling two parking bays. Flynn pulled up alongside, but not too close for comfort, and was out before Professor Baines had even climbed out of the E-type.

Flynn met him at the driver's door.

Baines looked at him critically, no recognition in his eyes. 'Can I help you?' he said cautiously.

Flynn knew Baines from the time he'd been a cop. He'd carried out the post-mortems of a couple of drug-dealers Flynn had once been investigating, when they fell foul of a ruthless rival gang from Merseyside and ended up dead on the Lancashire–Liverpool border. Flynn had been involved in the subsequent investigation and one of his tasks had been to attend the PMs. He had immediately recognized Baines when he drove past and knew he was involved with Jennifer Sunderland as Henry had talked about him, and mentioned his teeth fetish.

'You remember me?' Flynn asked.

Baines peered more closely. 'Didn't you leave the police in, um, slightly nooky circumstances?'

'I'll have that.'

'What can I do for you?' Baines reached into his car and heaved out his overweight medical bag.

'You might know I've been involved in, er, some stuff that's been going on recently. Henry Christie might have mentioned my name.'

'He has and I recall you were the person who pulled the drowned lady out of the river. Plus being involved in two more deaths, both of which I will be looking into later today,' Baines said haughtily, referring to the post-mortems he would be carrying out on two dead Russians. 'Neither pleasant . . . I hope you haven't come to kill me,' Baines said. 'Or to try to influence the result of the examinations.'

Flynn could have taken offence at that, but gave a short laugh instead. 'Neither,' he said. 'I'd like you to have a quick look at this, if you have a moment.' He held up the clear plastic money bag containing the tooth he had found earlier.

Baines looked at it laid out on the palm of his right hand. 'Interesting,' he said.

They drove in silence for the next five minutes until the service station at Forton, south of Lancaster, came into view with its huge saucer-shaped building that was a milestone for all travellers heading north or south.

Henry didn't like the silence because he learned nothing from it, other than Barlow emitted body odour that made his nose twitch. A night in the cells.

'What's with the Range Rovers?' he tried, working on the premise that theft of vehicles was a bit easier to chat about than killing.

Barlow looked at him and sighed. 'You want to know everything, don't you?'

'Oh yes.'

'That why you're such a good jack – this need to know?'

'It probably helps . . . but I'm not that good a jack, it's just that the other side are piss-poor and always drop themselves in it or do something silly because they think they can get away with anything. I haven't met a crim yet who thought he wouldn't get away with it – have you?' he asked pointedly.

Barlow sniggered. 'No, guess not.' He had missed Henry's point.

'Not even you,' Henry said, driving it home. He glanced sideways and saw a dark look come over Barlow's face. Riled again, Henry thought, very touchy. 'So yes,' he said quickly, 'I do want to know everything.'

Barlow started to brood, then said, 'You get involved in things, you know . . . things you shouldn't, then you start liking what it brings. You do a favour, it gets returned, then you find yourself in debt and it just spirals and all the time you think, "I can handle this" – and at the time, you can.'

Henry screwed his face up at this. 'Meaning?' he asked.

But Barlow had gone silent again. 'Next turn off,' he said after a pause.

Baines led Flynn through to the mortuary office, where he took off his jacket and put a clean apron on over his shirt and trousers. Flynn had been to this mortuary occasionally, but it was just like all the others he'd had to visit in his time as a cop. Places best avoided.

'Can you handle seeing dead bodies?' Baines asked him. 'If not, stay here. If you think you can – and I don't want to have to deal with any silly fainting, y'know? – come with me.' Flynn just looked at him. 'Here,' Baines said, handing him a surgical mask, 'you have to put this on. But don't touch anything.'

Baines started to fit his own mask and gloves and Flynn pulled on the one he had been given. He followed Baines out of the office and into the mortuary, over to the refrigeration unit. He glanced into the examination room and saw another pathologist at work on a dead body, just extracting a heart between his two hands like taking a delicate present out of a box.

Flynn clasped his hands behind his back and watched as Baines opened one of the chiller doors and drew out the tray on which was the muslin-wrapped body of the young unidentified female, Henry Christie's cold case. Baines stood at one side of the drawer, Flynn the opposite.

As Baines unwrapped the shroud from around the girl's head, Flynn drew a breath as he saw the horrific injuries that the girl had sustained. Henry had described them to him when they were on their way to have a look at the woodland area in which her body had been discovered. Henry's understated description was nowhere near as awful as the reality. And once more Flynn's respect for Henry as a detective notched up a few degrees, realizing that he had to deal with this kind of thing, day in, day out. The result of another person losing it and beating the life out of another for little or no reason, usually.

He wanted to exclaim something, but kept his mouth closed.

Baines tilted the girl's battered head back and opened her mouth, then took the tooth Flynn had found. He spent a couple of minutes with his eyes right up to her mouth cavity, fiddling with the tooth, making odd, thoughtful noises, reminding Flynn of someone building a minute scale model.

Then he raised his eyes to Flynn over his mask and stood up slowly. He pulled down his mask, exposing his mouth. 'This is one of her missing teeth,' he stated. 'Obviously I will have to do more work to confirm it one hundred per cent, but if there's one thing I know, it's teeth.'

Rik Dean cradled his desk phone and sat back. Not knowing where Henry was did not bother him too much; it was just frustrating because he needed to ask him things about the investigation and where it was going from here. Major things had happened with the release of the two prisoners and he had to know what was on Henry's mind and how this was all going to be pulled back.

Rik's PR was standing on his blotter, the volume turned down, a lot of morning chatter going on in Blackpool section, most of it mundane jobs. A minor car accident, a town-centre break in, some criminal damage, nothing really for him as a DI, other than how the crimes would affect the figures overall, which were skyrocketing.

Then the comms operator came on with an urgent tone to her voice asking for patrols to attend an address in Bispham where a neighbour had, apparently, discovered the bodies of two women – one of them the next-door neighbour – in the kitchen and lots of blood.

Two mobile patrols shouted up their attendance immediately. Sounded like a good, juicy job, and there was always competition to get to an incident like this first.

Rik perked up, grabbed his PR and said into it, 'DI Dean here – can you repeat the address. I can attend, also.'

The comms operator thanked him and as she repeated the address for him, he was already on his way out of his office, keen for something to do. It was only as he walked down the steps towards the police garage that the address rang a very loud claxon for him.

'Shit,' he said – and started to run.

They hit traffic on the A6 north into Lancaster, slowing the journey down to a crawl. The Mercedes was two cars behind. Henry glanced in the mirror, keeping tabs on it, but trying not to think about Alison, dragged into this through no fault of her own.

'How's this going to work?' Henry probed.

'What, exactly?'

'Are you going to let me walk into Lancaster nick and just get the property from the safe?'

'No – I'll be right by your side, Henry, then you won't be tempted.'

'OK,' Henry said, trying to visualize the process. 'Is the happy killing video of you?' he threw in.

'Me and others.'

'Others being Harry Sunderland?' Henry guessed. 'I presume Jennifer Sunderland found it . . . a wife going through a husband's phone, sort of thing? Is that why Harry threw her into the river?'

Barlow snorted. 'Actually he didn't throw her into the river, but that's another story. And yeah, she found the phone, had a fuckin' crisis and wanted to tell the cops.'

'And it wasn't as though she could tell you, is it?' Henry said. 'Does it show you and him kicking the girl to death? Stomping on her face? Half-strangling her? Was it your tie?' He was relentless as he put all this together. 'What the hell had she done to deserve that?'

'Nothing really, but I enjoyed it, fuck did I enjoy it.' Barlow's eyes glazed over as he recalled the killing. 'We all did.'

Henry felt sick.

Rik drove the CID car through the streets of Blackpool like a maniac and arrived at the Bispham address in minutes, before even second of the two mobile patrols who had called up. One double-crewed car was there already, pulled up outside the house. A uniformed constable rushed to him, his face ashen.

'What've we got?' Rik asked, climbing quickly out of the car and walking with the officer.

'It's not nice. Two women, one the owner of the house, don't know who the other is yet. Looks like they've both been shot in the head.'

'Let's see,' Rik said. The officer led him to the front door and paused. 'We've been in and out through this door and down the hallway only,' he explained to Rik. 'That's as far as we've gone. Just looked into the kitchen and not in any of the other rooms yet.' He was saying this because he was thinking of scene preservation.

'Good.' Rik followed him inside. At the kitchen door, the PC stood aside and allowed Rik to look in. He caught his breath as he saw the bodies and the blood, lots of blood from terrible head wounds sustained by both women, almost now covering the kitchen floor. His eyes roved expertly around the room, just a normal, well-equipped kitchen. Nice, but nothing special. Except for the death it now hosted.

Then he saw something on the tiled floor by the sink unit. A white laminated card, maybe an inch and a half wide, three inches long. And even from where he stood at the kitchen door, Rik could see the Lancashire Constabulary crest on it.

Although wary of spoiling any evidence, Rik stepped across the first body, tiptoeing on tiled areas free from blood, and picked up the card.

It was Henry Christie's police warrant card.

NINETEEN

They crawled along the A6 into Lancaster, a city where traffic probably moved even more slowly than London.

'I don't want you to park on the police station car park,' Barlow said. 'Pull up on Marton Street, outside the nick, and we'll use the public entrance for a quick in and out. The inspector's office is just on the corridor behind the enquiry desk and that's where the safe is. We walk in, acting all natural, you get the inspector to open up, you sign the property out, then we leave. Seriously, Henry, we're in and out in five minutes and if you do or say anything ridiculous, she will die – that's the pay-off for any stupidity. Do I make myself clear?'

Henry shrugged as the car hit the roundabout at the southern tip of the city – known as Pointer Island – and then headed down South Road into Lancaster proper. He took the offside lane at the traffic lights outside the hospital, then moved across again to bear right into Penny Street then first right on to Marton Street, at the end of which stood the crumbling nick that was Lancaster Police station, not the best-looking building in the world and continually in need of refurbishment.

Access to the public enquiry office was via steps and a ramp off the street and although there were double yellow lines, Henry parked up as instructed. In the rear-view mirror he saw the Mercedes pull in fifty metres behind.

'What if we get a ticket? The traffic wardens are pretty keen around here,' Henry said.

'Getting a parking ticket is the least of your worries, Henry,' Barlow said. 'What we do is go in and tell the public enquiry assistant behind the counter that the car's staying here for five minutes, just so she knows, and then we go in and do the business.'

'OK – get out and let's go do.' He slid the gun into his jacket pocket, keeping hold of it with his right hand.

'Don't blow your foot off,' Henry said. 'No, sorry – please blow your foot off.'

Barlow shook his head at Henry and said, 'Move, funny guy.'

Henry got out and the two men entered the station. There was no one in the foyer, but a PEA was leaning on the desk, filling in some forms. She looked up and smiled at Barlow. 'Hi.'

'Hi, Jane.' He sidled up to her in a curiously intimate way, reminding Henry of himself a little. Jack the lad, streetwise detective. 'Just in a bit of a rush, so we left the car on the double-yellows.' He pointed outside. 'We'll be about five minutes, tops . . . but we need a quick getaway.'

'I'll keep nicks,' she said conspiratorially.

'Buzz us in, will you?' he asked. She reached under the desk and pressed the button that unlocked the entrance door. Barlow pushed it open and allowed Henry through ahead of him.

Mobile phone in hand, Flynn was sitting in the mortuary office with Professor Baines. There was still no reply from Henry and while this wasn't a problem he was beginning to find it increasingly odd due to the nature of the fast-moving investigation Henry was in charge of: surely it was incumbent on the SIO to remain readily available. Going off and being a lone wolf was all well and good – and he had no doubt Henry was capable of doing that – but not at this moment in time.

'Ah well,' he sighed, 'best get going.'

'Henry needs to know about this,' Baines insisted. He pointed to the tooth on his desk. 'Discovering the crime scene will be crucial in this case.'

'I know,' Flynn said. 'I wonder if it might be worth bobbing into Lancaster nick. Maybe they have another number for him, or might know of his whereabouts.'

'Good idea.'

Flynn had walked out to Alison's car and seeing it, he had a minor brainwave. He sat in it and dialled the landline number of the Tawny Owl. Perhaps he'd contacted Alison and spoken to her recently.

The number rang out for a while and he was just about to hang up when a slightly breathless voice answered, 'Tawny Owl, Kendleton.'

It wasn't Alison, but Flynn recognized Ginny's girlie voice. 'Hi, Gin, it's me, Steve Flynn.'

'Oh, Steve, I'm really glad you called.'

'Problem?'

'Have you still got Mum's car?'

'Yes, actually. Does she need it back? Sorry.'

'No, no, it's not that,' she said. Flynn noted a slight tremor in her tone.

'What, then?'

'If she had the car back and it wasn't here, I'd know she was out in it. As it is I don't know where she is.'

Flynn frowned. 'What do you mean?'

'I know she got up this morning soon after Henry left for work and she did some stuff down in the cellar. Then she got the kitchen fired up and made herself a brew . . . and now I don't know where she is. It's like she disappeared, vanished. And the brew is half-drunk on the bar and her toast is still here, cold.'

'Is *your* car still there? She hasn't gone off in that, has she?'

'No – it's still here.'

'Perhaps she went off with Henry.'

'No – he definitely went to work alone.'

Flynn pouted. 'Has she popped into the village for some supplies?'

'I don't think so. We don't need anything – and I do that, anyway.'

'Have you spoken to Henry, just in case?'

'I tried his mobile, but there was no reply.'

'Right – OK,' Flynn said, frown deepening. 'First off, don't worry. There's probably a simple explanation, but if you like I could come across. I'm just in Lancaster now at a bit of a loose end.' *And a shop to open and run*, he thought.

'Please . . . I'm a bit worried. It's not like her just to disappear.'

'It'll be fine,' Flynn assured her. 'I'll be there in twenty minutes or so.' He swung his legs into the car and started the engine, reversing out of the parking slot.

They waited in the inspector's office for the duty inspector to make his way up from the custody suite where he had been tied up doing prisoner reviews. His name was Drummond, a fine name for a fine man who did a good job and had no ambitions beyond that role. Henry had known him for a long time and Drummond nodded pleasantly at him, but came up short when he saw Barlow. His eyes narrowed fractionally. No doubt news of the arrest would have spread quickly, but of the release perhaps not too fast.

'Hi, Jack,' Barlow said affably.

'Ralph,' Drummond nodded unsurely.

'We've come to pick up some property from the safe,' Barlow explained. Henry noticed his right hand was still in his jacket pocket, holding the gun, but trying to appear calm and normal. Henry wanted to believe that this was the weak point, but he felt powerless to act, to rush Barlow and pin the fucker to the wall. He knew he could and if he had been alone in this shitty mess he would have done. *Alison*, he called, *I'll sort this. Be brave.*

Barlow went on, 'It'll be marked for Detective Superintendent Christie only. It's a mobile phone and some passports.'

Drummond nodded. 'Yeah, I know – a support unit sergeant booked it in earlier.' He had a set of heavy looking keys on a detachable fob linked to his leather belt. He unhooked them and selected one, a long, but sturdy one.

The big old safe was in the back corner of the room, not fixed to anything, but unlikely that it would ever move. It was far too heavy and would need specialist lifting equipment to drag it anywhere. It was used mainly to keep any monies that came into police possession and other small valuable items. Most everything else went into the property store.

Drummond bent down and slotted the key in the lock.

Barlow grinned at Henry. 'You OK?' he mouthed.

'Fuck off,' Henry mouthed back.

The safe door opened easily and the inspector pulled out the items, plus a single, cut-off Wellington boot. Henry swallowed at the sight of this and felt his fists bunch up. The phone and the passports were in separate envelopes across which had been written *'To be handed to Det. Supt Christie ONLY'*. Drummond ripped them open.

He handed the property – seven passports, mobile phone and boot – across to Barlow, still eyeing him suspiciously. 'You need to sign for it all.' Drummond gave Barlow the form, which he in turn handed to Henry.

'You'll be wanting to sign this, boss.'

'I don't have a pen,' Henry said awkwardly.

'Here.' Drummond gave him one from his shirt pocket. Henry signed the form.

'Thanks, Jack,' Barlow said. 'We need to get going now. Bodies to deal with.' It was the sort of thing any cop might have said, but to Henry the words sounded ominous: whose bodies?

They walked out of the office and down the corridor. Henry saw Barlow drop the boot into a waste bin, something else so disrespectful to the dead that a shiver of horror went through him. Then they exited through the enquiry office door.

Once in the foyer, Barlow spun to the lady behind the desk who was now dealing with a member of the public.

'All quiet, love?' he asked her.

'No sign of the yellow peril,' she confirmed.

Henry went ahead of Barlow out to the car and walked around to the driver's door, where he paused and leaned on the roof with his forearms.

The Mercedes was still there. Barlow gave the occupants a quick nod and said to Henry, 'Get in.'

Henry stared in the direction of the Mercedes. Someone sounded an angry blast of a horn further down the street and it looked as though a car had pulled up without warning in front of another car, causing a problem.

Henry got in, as did Barlow.

'That was nice 'n' easy, wasn't it, Henry?'

'Jack Drummond wasn't happy. He'll be making phone calls now, you know. He's not stupid.'

'Fuck him. Drive,' Barlow ordered and drew the gun out of his pocket. 'Head north.'

Henry started the car, checked his mirrors and over his shoulder and set off. The Mercedes moved out to follow.

Flynn drove off the mortuary car park and onto the A588, where he turned left up to Pointer Island. The traffic seemed worse than normal, irritating him. He couldn't remember the last time there had been a traffic jam in Puerto Rico, although it did have its moments.

His mobile phone rang and he answered it, securing it between his right shoulder and ear.

'Flynn, it's Rik again. Have you made contact with Henry yet?'

'Tried but failed. I think he's gone AWOL.'

'Shit.'

'Why? Is there a problem?'

Flynn edged forwards in the car and was two cars away from the roundabout. It was then he saw a car he knew pull onto the roundabout from the A6 and sail past him, some fifty metres away and then onto South Road towards the city.

Flynn said quickly, 'Isn't that DI Barlow supposed to be in custody?'

'Ahh . . . why do you ask?'

'Answer the question, Rik.'

'He got released first thing this morning, as did Sunderland. Nothing to do with Henry. A done deal. Again, why?'

The word *Fiasco* rang in Flynn's ears.

'Because Henry's just driven past me towards Lancaster – and Barlow's sat right beside him. What going on, Rik?'

'Double murder in Bispham,' Rik said succinctly. 'Two females, one of which is Joe Speakman's daughter, Melanie. The other is her friend. Both shot in the head – and Henry's warrant card was found at the scene.'

Flynn reached the roundabout, zipped around a more sedate driver and gunned Alison's car down South Road, but was immediately caught up in more snail traffic at the red lights outside the front of the hospital – and he had lost sight of Henry.

He still had the phone to his ear. 'You still there, Rik?'

'Still here.'

'I've lost him.'

'Shit – try the nick.'

'Will do. Oh, by the way, don't know if this is significant, but Alison's gone missing this morning. Henry's Alison, that is. Done a disappearing trick. I'll call you back.' He cut the connection.

The lights seemed to stay on red for ever, but it was far too busy for Flynn to do anything rash, like race down the wrong side of the street against two lanes of oncoming vehicles.

Instead, he had to wait. Then they changed and he tailgated the car in front through the lights, veered into the outside lane on King Street, and then bore right into Penny Street and next sharp right into Marton Street where he almost ran into the back of a black Mercedes parked illegally on the double yellow lines on the left. He swerved, drove on and saw that Henry's classy pool car was parked just as illegally on the double yellow lines outside the police station.

Flynn winced, not quite able to make a decision, but by the time he did he was at the junction at the one-way system again and because of vehicles behind him, he had nowhere to go but forward and edged out into the traffic stream again.

He cursed and picked his mobile phone up from the dashboard, where it was wedged. He didn't have Rik's number, so he had to go through the rigmarole of finding the '*recently received*' calls menu to unearth it, then call him back. By which time he had moved a good twenty metres. Progress was not good.

'Yeah, Flynn,' Rik answered quickly.

'The pool car's parked outside the nick . . . I couldn't find anywhere to park up, so I'm looping back round to see if I can on this run.'

'Right . . . Flynn, what the hell's going on?' Rik asked.

'That question gives me a feeling of déjà vu,' Flynn said. 'I don't know, is the answer . . . but nothing pleasant, I suspect. Why the hell would he be with Barlow?'

He was back at the junction with King Street again, and moving slowly north, into Sun Street, then ninety degrees right into Marton Street again, at which point the motorist in front of him jammed on his brakes and came to a sudden, unexpected stop,

obviously unsure where he was going. Flynn almost upended
Alison's car as he slammed the brakes on.

Up ahead he saw Barlow and Henry emerge from the police-
station door and go to the pool car. Henry walked around it and
leaned on the roof, talking across to Barlow, looking back down
the street in Flynn's direction.

Flynn honked his horn at the guy in front, who still hadn't
made up his mind. The man's arm appeared through his window
and he gave Flynn the middle-finger salute. Flynn pipped again.

The car edged forwards and Flynn could not decide what the
bugger was up to – and then it kangarooed to a stalled stop.

'I don't believe this,' Flynn said and he saw now that Henry
had got into the car with Barlow and was moving off and joining
the traffic Flynn had just left. And behind was the black Mercedes.

Flynn was trapped. He crunched the car into reverse, lurched
backwards, stopping only an inch from the car behind, which honked
with an angry warning. He gave a 'sorry' wave, spun the wheel,
mounted the footpath with two wheels and passed the dithering car
driver.

By the time he reached the junction, Henry was just turning
right, heading north up through the city.

Flynn pushed the nose of the car into the junction, but no one
was willing to give way, so he simply barged out, causing a
concertina of braking cars and a cacophony of horns which made
it sound more like Rome than a Lancashire town.

Even though he had forced his way in, he was still restricted
by the sheer volume of traffic. The only way he could have made
quick progress would have been to get all four wheels on the
footpath this time and mow down a bunch of pesky
pedestrians.

Instead he had to seethe.

There was no way, either, that Henry could rush through the
morning traffic, and its slowness was compounded by a set of
roadworks on the one-way system that for about a hundred metres
reduced two lanes into one and almost brought everything to a
halt.

Not that he was rushing. He was purposely going as slowly as
he could, not taking any advantage of gaps, but crawled

deliberately, feeling a surge of positivity in him because he had seen Flynn in Alison's car and for a moment longer than necessary he had kept his face turned towards him in the hope that Flynn would see him. Surely he had.

He checked his rear-view mirror. The Mercedes was right behind now and he tried to see inside it, but all he could make out were two male figures, a driver and back-seat passenger. Alison, he realized, must be being held down in the space behind the front and rear passenger seat.

'What's the plan?' Henry asked.

'Wait and see.'

'You know that the last person seen with a murder victim is usually the one who did the killing,' Henry said. 'If I turn up dead, which I presume *is* the plan, they'll come a-knocking on your door, pal.'

'That's if there's a body,' Barlow said scarily, sending a tremor of fear through Henry which felt like all his blood had rushed out of his feet.

Henry swallowed. 'You know you have no chance with this, don't you?'

'I'll control it,' Barlow said.

'Like you did Jennifer Sunderland?' Henry sneered. 'That went tits-up straight-off, dinnit?'

Barlow snapped. He slashed the gun in his hand sideways into Henry's face, into his broken cheekbone, then forced the muzzle into Henry's groin, twisting it hard into his flesh.

'A mistake I won't make again.'

Flynn, stationary, was still on the mobile phone to Rik Dean. 'Sorry, pal, this traffic ain't moving.'

'Do your best to try and stay with him.'

'If I can lay eyes on him, I will,' Flynn said. He used the term 'laying eyes' when sighting a marlin out sport-fishing off the Canary Islands. 'Hey, one thing, there's the possibility of another car tagging on with him, a black Mercedes.'

'A big black car was seen outside the murder victims' house by one of the neighbours,' Rik said. 'No make, but it was described as fancy – why?'

'There was one parked on Marton Street and I saw Barlow

give it a thumbs-up when he and Henry came out of the nick, then it set off behind them.'

'Could be . . . Look, I need to speak to some people. I'll call you back.'

'Ditto, when I've got something to tell you.'

Flynn got through the lights and on to King Street at last, but was met by two solid lanes of cars stretching down through the city and in the distance he saw a '*roadworks ahead*' sign and groaned with the injustice of it all. There was literally no way of making progress. He could possibly cut across the traffic at this point and then do a rat run around the western side of the city, but there was no guarantee it would be any quicker.

But Flynn preferred to be on the move and it surely could not be any slower. He signalled left, nudged his way across the traffic and on to Aldcliffe Road that ran down by the Lancaster Canal and, hoping he could remember his way through the back streets and byways of the city, he threw the car quickly along these streets, over the railway line, down by the back of the castle, winding his way down on to St George's Quay where he had spent a short morning of passion with a paramedic in her tiny flat overlooking the river. He knew he would have to rejoin the traffic at the bottom of the city at Cable Street.

He did keep moving and probably it was quicker and as he waited to turn left onto Cable Street, he knew he had jumped the queue a little.

But he could not see Henry's car – and he also knew that he was making an assumption as to where he was headed. It was possible that he could have actually gone in a different direction and cut east across the city centre, but Flynn had the feeling he would still be heading north. Possibly heading towards Sunderland's haulage depot.

But he could have been wrong.

He edged into the traffic which was moving more freely down here after bursting free from the city-centre bottleneck and Flynn motored along slowly, turning on to Greyhound Bridge to drive across the Lune. Traffic here had thinned out considerably and was moving quickly now across the one-way bridge.

As he checked his mirrors and swung across the lanes to keep heading north, he thought he had lost Henry.

But he suddenly found that he had actually beaten him through the traffic because as Flynn drifted across the three lanes, the pool car and the Mercedes came into view behind him.

Even though his left eye was streaming, and the broken cheek-bone was emitting shock waves of pain, Henry saw that somehow Steve Flynn had managed to get ahead of him. The problem was that there were three lanes of traffic over Greyhound Bridge and Flynn moved across to the right-hand lane and Henry was now expected to pass him using the middle lane, then filter across to travel north, as per Barlow's instructions.

This was a problem because they would drive within feet of Alison's car and if Barlow looked across, he might easily recognize Flynn at the wheel, something Henry wanted to avoid, so he leaned forward to restrict Barlow's view and also to distract him with more jolly conversation.

'What do you think of the Millennium Footbridge?' Henry asked and pointed left across at the pedestrian bridge that had been built to span the Lune at the turn of the century.

'What the fuck are you on about?' Barlow snarled.

'Just chatting.'

'Well fucking shut up.'

They were almost level with Flynn now. Henry did not even dare glance sideways.

'It's beautiful, yet modern,' Henry said stupidly, a remark that unfortunately made Barlow look sharply at him – just as the two cars drew level. Henry put his foot down on the accelerator, but the expected increase in speed did not happen. Instead, a huge cloud of smoke billowed out of the exhaust, almost causing a smoke screen around the Mercedes, which was too close behind. A very unpleasant scraping noise came from the engine block followed by a loud 'clank' that sounded as if a very important piece of machinery had come loose in the pistons.

'What the fuck have you done?' Barlow bawled.

'Sorry.' Henry dabbed the accelerator, but there was no response and the car started to slow dramatically with a huge crunching, grating noise coming from the engine like the pistons were pounding pebbles. 'I think the engine's seized.'

'Shit.'

The speed decreased, and suddenly there was no power in the steering.

And without having to use the braking system, the car suddenly came to a bone-jarring stop, throwing Henry against the steering wheel and Barlow against the front windscreen.

And the Mercedes ploughed into the back of them.

Flynn watched the approach of Henry's car through the passenger-side wing mirror, and realized he was going to underpass him, which was a necessity for traffic on the bridge. It was the only way to cross it.

He slid low in his seat as the car came directly alongside, not daring to glance sideways – even though he did, seeing Henry point across towards the river and say something to Barlow in the passenger seat. Henry's attempt at distraction.

Barlow then looked sharply at Henry and as he did Flynn jerked his head to the front, presenting a low profile to Barlow just in case he glanced across from car to car and spotted him.

Flynn braced himself, hoping he hadn't been recognized, and Henry's car edged ahead.

Then came the huge cloud of noxious smoke from the exhaust, enveloping the Mercedes, followed by a huge and horrible metallic crash that Flynn heard clearly and pinpointed it as, basically, the engine in the pool car decided that enough was enough, it needed oil now because there was none left, not a single drop, and engines don't run all that well without it.

What surprised Flynn was exactly how instantly the car stopped. One moment it was going OK, then it seemed to slow just a little – then it stopped as though it had hit an invisible brick wall.

And the Mercedes slammed right into it.

Flynn drove on and veered in front of the car, stopping at a jaunty angle across two lanes, and leapt out of the car.

Then the pile-up started.

Another car hit the Mercedes, and bounced off into the left-hand lane. Another car hit that one. A car stopped in the right-hand lane – why, Flynn didn't quite get – but the one behind it hit that one and then they started to stack up within seconds.

The passenger door of the pool car opened and Barlow rolled out, and staggered, blood on his head.

Flynn saw the gun in his hand.

Then Henry was out. He too loped drunkenly sideways, but gripped the roof of the car and turned to Flynn who was at the bonnet which had smoke and steam hissing out of the gaps and the front radiator grille.

Barlow ran across the left hand lane towards the side of the bridge, holding his side and also limping like an injured wolf.

Henry pointed urgently at him and screamed to Flynn, 'Get him, get him . . .' He yelled something else, but the sound of his voice was drowned out as, way further back, a truck hit a car with an almighty crunch.

As Barlow got to the footpath, he turned and fired the gun twice.

Flynn ducked instinctively, but the shooting seemed more like warning shots than anything. Running and keeping low he knew he would soon catch this man.

Henry hit the steering wheel hard with his chest, the pay-off for not wearing a seat belt. It drove everything out of him, every atom of his breath, and something snapped. Then the Mercedes impacted from behind and jerked him backwards, flicking his head against the head rest.

Barlow's head smacked the windscreen and because he had been sitting sideways-on to Henry, the side of his ribcage connected with the dashboard. He too was then thrown backwards a second later as the Mercedes connected.

Wheezing painfully, Henry exited the car as quickly as he could, noting that Flynn had angled Alison's car across the front of the pool car and was already out on the road.

Barlow got out of the car and started to leg it across the road. Henry shouted for Flynn to go after him, but to be careful, the guy was armed. He didn't know if Flynn heard him.

Ignoring the pain and possible new injuries, Henry ran to the Mercedes, realizing that the poor condition of the pool car had changed matters completely. He tore open the rear passenger door, ignoring the driver, and instantly there was no pain in him, just an all-consuming anger as he saw Alison lying curled up in a foetal ball in the footwell behind the front passenger seat, unmoving.

Henry roared, 'You bastards!'

The youngish, good-looking man in the back seat went for Henry. This was the man who had held Alison's head up to the window, taunting Henry, then smashing her face against the glass, smearing it with her blood. Henry did not know who he was, nor what part he was playing in this whole scenario. He did not care.

Henry sidestepped, grabbed him and hauled him out of the car with a primeval strength he did not know he had. Powered by the red-mist rage, he started to pound his fists into the man's face, punching him so his features were twisted and distorted, again and again, and then he stomped on him, with the man screaming, 'No, no.' Words Henry ignored.

The driver of the Mercedes, stunned for a moment by the accident, got out. Henry turned on him, now a terrible monster. Henry made for him, but he ducked and ran.

Barlow might have been running like an injured wolf, but Flynn simply jogged after him like a hunting dog, keeping a safe distance away, no way he was going to lose the guy, just run him into the ground. Easy.

Barlow reached the Millennium Bridge and started to run across towards St George's Quay on the opposite side of the river. There was a lot of people on the bridge, many of whom had turned and were coming back against him to see what was happening on Greyhound Bridge, where there had obviously been a serious accident involving a number of vehicles, and was still stacking up.

By the time Flynn stepped onto the bridge, Barlow was about halfway across and Flynn thought this was as good a place as any to bring him down because there was nowhere else he could go, other than over the side.

Flynn upped his pace, as, noticeably, Barlow began to slow down and stagger, the effect of the accident now hitting him hard.

Flynn was ten feet behind him when Barlow did a quite spectacular pirouette, probably more by accident than design,

at the same time bringing the gun around. Flynn dropped sideways, the gun discharged somewhere across the river, and Barlow
fell to his knees, clutching his chest, breathing heavily and
obviously painfully. The gun was still in his right hand, swinging
to and fro.

Members of the public began to gather.

Someone shouted, 'He's got a gun.'

Flynn circled him and Barlow's watchful eyes stayed with him
all the way. The gun came up, but dithered, then he dropped it
as he coughed up a mouthful of bright red blood from the internal
wound in his chest.

TWENTY

It was two days before Ralph Barlow was released from
hospital, where he had spent his time under police guard. He
had punctured a lung in the pile-up, but it had been saved by
the quick actions of the doctors in A&E at the Royal Lancaster
Hospital.

It was also two days before the whiplash injury Henry had
sustained when the Mercedes crashed into him kicked in bad.
And although he moved as stiff as a kid's robot, and was in
agony when he moved at all, Henry could not be kept away from
work. With Rik Dean, he waited for Barlow's imminent arrival
at Preston custody office, where it had been decided it would be
best to lodge him under the circumstances, well away from any
friends in high places.

He was back to being represented by a duty solicitor. Henry
almost wished his fancy-pants brief was sitting by his side, but
it was not to be.

Henry and Rik carried out the interview. After he had been
cautioned and the introductions done for the tape, and he had
been informed that the interview was being videotaped, Henry
– sitting bolt upright, hardly able to move his neck without
agonizing pain – said, 'Ralph, one way or the other, I don't
expect this interview is going to be an easy one, but you have

the choice to make it straightforward if you want to. Myself and DI Dean have seen the recording on the mobile phone and if you wish, we will project it up onto a screen and go through it second by second, pausing it and asking you questions about it as we go through it.

'Just for the record, I am referring to a video recording on a mobile phone that was probably the property of Harry Sunderland, the other suspect in this case. It shows a murder being committed by three men clearly identifiable as you, Ralph Barlow, Harry Sunderland and a man we believe to be called Oscar Malinowski. The phone is passed round the three men who film each other as they kick and beat to death a young woman, who has yet to be identified.'

Henry stopped, let the words sink in, then said, 'The choice is yours, Ralph.'

'It's all down to Harry Sunderland. It just got a bit out of hand . . .'

'Bad, bad people,' Henry said. 'You get involved with them and you pay the price.'

He looked at his mini-team – and to do so, he had to move his whole torso in order to keep the pain in his neck manageable. There was Jerry Tope, Bill Robbins, Rik Dean, and, of course, the team leader, Robert Fanshaw-Bayley. Slouched at the back of the office was the unofficial member, Steve Flynn. On the floor next to him was a holdall – hand luggage for his flight back to Gran Canaria later that day.

They were assembled in Henry's office to update progress so far on what was proving to be a challenging investigation.

They all knew various bits of the story – other than Flynn, who knew what he knew, because, over the last six days, he had been doing what he came to the UK to do – help an injured friend and run a shop.

'Where to begin,' Henry said, shuffling various papers. He was sitting at his desk. To his right was a projector screen on the back wall. A laptop had been set up, connected to the data projector that was fitted to the ceiling.

A chorus of muted voices came, 'Why not at the beginning?'

'Ho ho,' he said.

'But keep it brief – I'm at the Police Authority in half an hour,' FB said.

'OK – still have a long way to go with this, but this is where we're at now.' He cleared his throat. 'Background is that Harry Sunderland, leading businessman and Lancaster socialite, gets involved with a Russian crim in Cyprus dealing with cheap property and other criminal activity. Sunderland is a friend of Ralph Barlow, soon to be ex-DI of our parish, through golf and stuff like that. Sunderland was also matey with Joe Speakman, whose own son Tom was/is also friends with Sunderland, so much so that Sunderland set him up in business in Cyprus as an estate agent to sell on the property being built by the Russian crim, name of Oscar Malinowski. Barlow is a boozer and a gambler and a ladies' man, always short of money, and Malinowski, a guy with an eye for the main chance, puts a deal to him: pinpoint new Range Rovers for him using PNC and get paid, in cash and in kind. And he would do the rest – i.e., send his lackeys over to steal the Range Rovers and get Sunderland to ship them across Europe in sealed containers for selling cut price to Range-Rover-mad Russkies. Good money for Barlow – two grand a car – and sex.'

'How sex?' Bill Robbins asked.

'Range Rovers went one way, prostitutes and money came back another – and the girl on the camera phone was one of them. Barlow told us over a dozen girls were sent over, he and Sunderland used them and they were then sent on to brothels in Manchester and London run by Maltese gangsters, affiliates of Malinowski.'

'The ebb and flow of capitalism,' Jerry Tope noted.

'Something like that,' Henry said. 'He and Sunderland got a kick out of beating up the girls, as it were, and videoing themselves doing it. Malinowski liked it too, and during one of his brief visits – accompanied by one of his girls – they start knocking her around but it went too far. They killed her. And this was above a premises that Sunderland owned in Glasson Dock at which the girls were housed for the short time during their transit, when they were used by Barlow and Sunderland, then sent on to the brothels.'

Bill Robbins frowned. 'Didn't they stand out in a place like Glasson? Not exactly Manchester city centre, is it?'

'They were only there for a short time, two days at most, then they were gone – right under the radar. Then Sunderland sold the empty shop to Flynn's friend, an ex-cop, who turned the place into a chandlery. It was only Flynn's sharp eyes that saw the tooth and uncovered the actual crime scene – though what the hell his eyes were doing at skirting-board level, no one will ever know.'

Sniggers went round the room like a little Mexican wave.

Flynn spoke up. 'Colin had loads of boxes stacked up there and just didn't notice anything. It had been cleaned up, scrubbed and that, but if you looked I suppose you could tell. The tooth wedged under the skirting gave it away.'

The sniggers died. Each of them had seen the horrific video of three grown drunken men kicking a young girl to death and stamping on her face. At one point Barlow had even dragged her across the floor with his tie noosed around her neck. Rik and Henry had been forced to watch it over and over for professional reasons. The others had seen it once – and that had been enough.

'It would seem that Jennifer Sunderland found the video for some reason. Maybe she was suspicious of her hubby anyway, and went through his stuff. We'll not know until we find Harry, who has done a very good disappearing trick. She ended up in the river, but we can only surmise how that happened – but finding her Wellington boot in the garden – I don't know,' Henry said. 'She could've been chased, she could've committed suicide – but whatever, she clearly wanted the phone to be found. I guess we'll never know for certain.'

'And Joe Speakman?' Jerry asked. 'What was his involvement?'

'He had to investigate the murder of the girl, her body dumped in woodland near junction 34. My feeling is that he pretty quickly got a line on Harry Sunderland as being one of the suspects . . . his problem was that his son, Tony, was involved with Malinowski via the estate agency in Cyprus, *and* he was an acquaintance of Sunderland, too – and, although we're still looking into it – he may have got a property at a knock-down price in Cyprus. I think he was pressured to drag his feet, ensure the investigation got nowhere. And that's why he retired so suddenly. It wasn't something he could do. He was a detective and finding himself in a position like that was untenable for him – so he went.'

'Why kill him?' Bill asked.

'Because he couldn't keep it bottled up. It was eating away at him. Joe spoke to Ralph – who he didn't suspect of involvement in the murder – and said he was going to give Harry Sunderland an ultimatum – hand yourself in, or else. He was even going to come clean about the property deals in Cyprus. Big mistake. Ralph conveyed this to Sunderland, who spoke to Malinowski, who ordered one of his goons, who was in town to steal the newest batch of Range Rovers, to whack him – which is what me and Steve tripped over, dog and all. Then the deeply upset remaining goon came after me and Steve.'

FB inhaled all this. 'The Speakman family have suffered greatly,' he said.

'Barlow can't stop talking now, but he maintains he doesn't know where Sunderland is, or Malinowski – but we think both might be in northern Cyprus.'

Henry would very much have liked to sit back and relax then, but he had to remain bolt upright like Lurch, the butler from the old US TV series *The Addams Family*.

'And on top of all that, Headquarters Transport are very angry with me for not doing an oil check on that shed of a vehicle they let me have. Fortunately no one was injured in the pile-up caused when the bloody thing ran aground.'

FB rocked forwards on his chair. 'I'm going to be speaking to Tom Gledhill later today,' he announced. 'That could be another retirement sooner rather than later.'

'Mm,' Henry said. He had discovered that Gledhill, the chief superintendent at Blackpool, had recently bought a house in Cyprus at well under market value, via Tom Speakman's estate agency; a house built by a company that was suspected to be a front for Malinowski. 'The two guys helping out Barlow, incidentally, were two more of Malinowski's hoods, one in custody obviously, the other still at large. They were just low-level nothings.' Henry paused and took a breath. 'Have I missed anything?'

Bill Robbins said, 'What about the tooth connection? Anything significant in that . . . you know, Jennifer Sunderland and the girl?'

'Our Cypriot colleagues have been to see the dentist in question, who is legit, by the way. His records show that Jennifer was one of his clients, probably from when she spent time out there with Harry. She had some work done last time she was out there. As regards the girl, who we think was trafficked from somewhere in Russia, she was given treatment under what has turned out to be a false name. This dentist also happens to have Oscar Malinowski as a patient.

'We've a lot of things to do, a long way to go with this,' Henry said, 'and you guys, plus a few more detectives, are going to be "it" for the foreseeable future. Any objections?'

They all shook their heads.

'Good, that's settled, then.'

'Seriously, I would have driven you,' Henry said to Flynn as they stood by the taxi that had arrived to take him to Liverpool Airport.

'I don't think so – you shouldn't be driving yourself. You can hardly move.'

'I know.'

The two men looked at each other.

'Hey,' Henry said and held out his hand. 'Thank you.'

They shook.

'Give my love to Alison,' Flynn said.

'I will. How is Colin, by the way?'

'It's looking pretty good, by all accounts. At least the pressure's off them for the moment, even if I did destroy their boat and help myself to most of their stock – and turn their shop into a crime scene for a day.' Flynn checked his watch. 'Need to dash . . . this time tomorrow I'll be out on that boat, reelin' 'em in.'

'Lucky you . . . maybe one day I'll come out there.'

'You'd be welcome.'

Henry watched the taxi disappear out of headquarters.

'You know, not long before that man turned up I was thinking about you.'

It was hard for her to talk. The punches she had taken to the front of her face had broken every bone the knuckles had touched, the nose, both cheekbones, and had also dislodged four teeth and there was the chance that she would need her face reconstructing, but it would be impossible to tell immediately. There would be a wait until the swelling had subsided completely before any judgements could be made by surgeons.

Painfully, Henry leaned over the hospital bed, listening to Alison's quiet words.

'I was thinking how much I loved you, part of the reason being because you were so passionate about your work.'

She swallowed and her breathing juddered in her chest.

'I'm so sorry,' he said inadequately. 'This should never have happened.' This was the first proper conversation they'd had in the last week, and Henry was dreading it.

'No, it shouldn't,' she whispered and swallowed again. Her eyes were puffed up to the size of Kiwi fruits and much the same colour. Her injuries were terrible and when Henry had scrambled across the back seat of the Mercedes to her, he had thought she was dead at first.

'I'm so sorry,' he said again.

'It's not your fault.' Her lips hardly moved as she spoke, they were so swollen. He touched the back of her left hand, into which a drip had been inserted. It felt frail and cold. She might have said those words, but there was no way on this earth did Henry feel that it wasn't his fault. It was. Intent, effect, all that crap. It had to be his fault and he was creased with guilt and worry.

'Henry,' she said, 'Henry . . . listen to me.' He leaned over even closer so his ear was only inches away from her lips. 'It doesn't matter . . . not to me, not to me . . . know why?'

'No.'

'Because I saw your face at the window when that man was showing me to you, at that house. I saw your face . . . and I knew . . .'

'Knew what?' The memory of that moment would be forever etched into Henry's mind's eye.

'I knew you wouldn't stop. I knew you'd come for me and not let them win. Sounds pretty corny, eh?'

'No, sounds good. So . . . ?'

'Are we still in a relationship? Is that what you want to know?'

'Are we?' he asked, terrified of the answer.

'Bet your arse, copper.'